'*Kyle, wait . . .*'

The whispered words came again, so softly spoken I couldn't even be sure if they came from a woman or a man. Was this someone's idea of a silly joke? Playing silly beggars and messing with my head? I spun round. *Who* was calling me? It was freaking me out.

Ignore it, Kyle. Get to the helicopter, I told myself.

I looked up, but as I watched, the helicopter blades slowed down, their rotation less frantic. Yet the chopper didn't move, didn't descend, didn't even look like it was in any kind of trouble. As the blades slowed, so the very air around me grew thick and still. The slowing down was almost hypnotic. I was having trouble catching my breath.

'*Kyle . . .*' The whisper floated towards me, so faint I could barely hear it. '*Kyle, wait for me.*'

My head jerked round like a puppet's, but I was still the only one standing in the carriage. That voice . . .

MALORIE BLACKMAN

THE STUFF OF NIGHTMARES

CORGI BOOKS

THE STUFF OF NIGHTMARES
A RED FOX BOOK 978 0 552 55463 3

First published in Great Britain by Doubleday,
an imprint of Random House Children's Books
A Random House Group Company

Doubleday edition published 2007
Red Fox edition published 2008

1 3 5 7 9 10 8 6 4 2

'Steve's Nightmare', 'Naima's Nightmare' and 'Roberta's Nightmare' previously
published in different versions as 'Dad, Can I Come Home', 'Skin Tones' and
'Such are the Times' in Not So Stupid, Livewire Books for Teenagers, 1990.

'Joe's Nightmare' previously published in a different version as 'Jon For Short'
in Incredibly Creepy Stories, collected by Tony Bradman, Doubleday, 1996.

'Perry's Nightmare' and 'Elena's Nightmare' previously published in different versions
as 'Behind the Mask' and 'Deeply' in Words Last Forever, Mammoth, 1998.

The Random House Group Limited supports the Forest Stewardship
Council (FSC), the leading international forest certification organization. All our
titles that are printed on Greenpeace-approved FSC-certified paper carry the FSC logo.
Our paper procurement policy can be found at www.rbooks.co.uk/environment.

Corgi Books are published by Random House Children's Books,
61–63 Uxbridge Road, London W5 5SA

www.kidsatrandomhouse.co.uk
www.rbooks.co.uk

Addresses for companies within The Random House Group Limited can be found at:
www.randomhouse.co.uk/offices.htm

THE RANDOM HOUSE GROUP Limited Reg. No. 954009

A CIP catalogue record for this book is available from the British Library.

Printed in the UK by CPI Bookmarque, Croydon, CR0 4TD.

For Neil and Lizzy,
with love

1

There's something about running. Something . . . well, if you don't get it, you won't get it. Every time my foot smacks the pavement, it's like an echo of my heartbeat slamming inside me, telling me that 'I'm here, I'm now, I'm *alive*'. I don't jog – jogging is for posers showing off their latest designer gear. No, I *run*. Tunnels like the one down by the canal and dark places are best. Places where I can't see my shadow chasing me or tantalizing me by running ahead. In tunnels and dark places there are no shadows, no ghosts. There's only me.

This morning was just right, mid spring cool rather than early spring cold, and the air tasted of the new and fresh instead of the usual diesel and dog poo, so I decided to run through the park, which was kind of a mistake, 'cause it wasn't long before I wasn't alone as I ran. *He* crept into my head, where he wasn't welcome. Sometimes, if . . . *when* I inadvertently let my guard down, he does that.

I picked up the pace until I was sprinting just as hard as I could. But I couldn't escape. Instead I found myself running into the past, into a memory of him and Mum – into the very thing that scared me the most.

This morning's memory was the beginning of it all, for me at least. And it started just over a year ago with, of all things, a jar of strawberry jam. A new one. Unopened. I remember everything about that day. It was a sunny, late winter morning and unseasonably warm. Out of our kitchen window I could see a few pale pink blossoms already decorating the tree in the middle of our garden. (Don't bother asking me what kind of tree. I haven't got a clue. I'm not a tree hugger.) Dad and I were sitting at the table eating croissants. Mum was making me a cup of coffee while her croissants sat on the table, getting cold.

'Mum, is there any more jam?' I asked.

Without a word, Mum went over to the cupboard and retrieved a jar of reduced-sugar strawberry jam. Hand wrapped round the lid, she tried and tried to untwist it. After at least ten seconds of Dad and me watching her, she gave up.

'Fitz, could you open this for me please?' she asked.

Dad took the jar, an indulgent smile playing across his face. 'Useless or what?' He shook his head. 'Londie, what would you do without me?'

It was nothing Dad hadn't said before, but I'll never forget the way Mum looked at him, an intense stare that at first rested on him, then lanced into him, then burned straight through him.

'Fitz, if I didn't have you, I'd buy a jar opener.'

'You probably wouldn't be able to work that either,' said Dad.

He turned to wink at me so he missed the *nothing* look Mum gave him. I can't describe it any other way. It was a look full of nothing at all. Just enough nothing to make me frown, but not enough for me to realize what was going to happen. Take it from me, when you have two people living and sharing a life together and one gives the other that nothing look, it means something. It means one hell of a lot.

I ran that far into the memory before I turned round and ran out of it again. I raced for home, concentrating on the precise placement of each foot. No cracks in the pavement, no slab edges, no litter of any kind to be allowed under my feet. *Concentrate, Kyle. Think of nothing. That way you won't think of something you shouldn't.* I sprinted so fast that my breath was too far behind to catch up with me. I reached my front gate with my heart rocketing inside me. And it felt *good!* Bent over, my hands on my knees, I looked up at our house as I gulped down oxygen. Not much of a run today. Only about four kilometres. And my time was crap too. Just under half an hour. I could do much better than that. I *would* have done much better than that if Dad hadn't crept into my head. Again. He's been doing that a lot lately.

I try to run for half an hour each morning, and at least three times that long at weekends. The moment I wake up, I pull on my sweats and my trainers and tiptoe downstairs to head out the door before

Mum can catch me. She doesn't like me running so early in the morning. She doesn't like me running. But what else should I do? Stay home with her and play happy families? Yeah, right. Running before most people even have their breakfast calms me down for the rest of the day. I still make it home in time for a shower and a quick bowl of cereal in my room, so what's the big deal? Running fills me with anticipation, like I'm running *towards* something or *for* something. Like all I have to do is run just that little bit faster, stretch out my hand just that little bit further to grab whatever is just outside my grasp, and then my life will be transformed. That's the word: *transformed*.

The only time my life makes any kind of sense is when I'm running.

Only, this morning, it didn't do its usual trick.

So now here I am on the train platform with my classmates and I swear, if my legs could take off without me, they would. I'm jittery and twitchy, I can't keep still. Six kilometres is usually my minimum distance and I really feel it when I don't do the minimum. I want to crawl out of my skin and *run*. That's what I do best. Running. Alone. No Mum in my thoughts – those days are over. And, more importantly, no Dad. Even now, even after all this time, just thinking about my dad makes me feel hollow inside, like an empty gift-wrapped box.

'You're very quiet,' said my mate Steve, nudging me. Hard.

I rubbed my upper arm to get the blood circulating

again. Steve was only slightly shorter than me and wore his hair just about collar length in thin dreads. He had to be the coolest boy in the class, probably because he wasn't the least bit interested in appearing cool. All I know is he didn't lack for girls buzzing round him – that was for sure.

'Well?' Steve prompted.

'I was thinking about my dad,' I admitted quietly. Steve was the only one in the class who knew what'd really happened to my dad. He was the only one I'd told, after making him swear seven different oaths not to tell anyone and promising to break his legs if he ever did.

'I wouldn't bother thinking about him if I were you,' said Steve. 'He's not worth it.'

I shrugged noncommittally. It was all right for him. Steve's dad doted on him, hanging on his every word and celebrating his every action. How could Steve possibly imagine the gap I felt inside about my dad? Steve and his dad had what I'd always longed for. I would've gladly settled for just half of what they had. The emptiness inside began to feed on me. Time to change the subject.

'What's that train doing?'

I leaned forward over the train platform to peer down the line. The train was like an obscene snake, slinking along the track some way back. Stop. Start. Stop. Start. And the windows at the front were like eyes regarding all of us on the platform.

'Kyle, step back before you get your fool head

knocked off,' Miss Wells, our form teacher, called out.

'Miss, let him stick his head out then!' Naima called out. The girls she was standing with all started laughing. If there was one girl I couldn't stand in our class, then Naima was it.

'Bite me, Naima!' I called out.

'You wish, Kyle! You wish!' Naima winked.

Once again her crew started laughing. Kendra's donkey-bray laugh was unmistakable. One of them, Roberta (or Robby, as she liked to be known), just smiled at me, a smile of almost apologetic sympathy rather than amusement. If I wasn't so sure that Roberta would say no, I'd ask her out 'cause she's a babe. Not Naima though. Naima's totally toxic. She's too busy loving herself to care about anyone or anything else. Her friends only hung around her because they were terrified that if they turned round, Naima would stab them in the back. It was a shame too 'cause Naima was quite pretty on the outside. She had auburn hair cut short and wild and kinda funky, and her big green eyes were framed by some of the longest brown lashes I'd ever seen. She smiled readily, but more often than not it had a sneering edge to it that was all hers. Like I said, on the outside she was a winner. Shame what was inside didn't match. She should've been more like Roberta or another girl in our class, Elena. With them, what you saw was what you got.

After scowling at Naima, I stepped back as Miss Wells had ordered. At the speed the train was going, it couldn't have knocked the head off a pint of lager, but I wasn't in the mood for one of Miss Wells's lectures. A chill Spring wind had picked up since my earlier run. The wind was travelling in the same direction as the train but moving considerably faster, and it kept ripping at my face, which didn't help my mood. I was trying to wrap my head around why I wasn't more excited about our forthcoming trip. After all, for me a trip to the city was about as rare as Action Man poo. Now that we were together again, Mum never, and I mean *never*, left our small town. She shopped locally or used the Internet to order furniture and the like from the websites of bigger department stores nationwide.

'Miss Wells, can we all move up the platform so we can sit in the first carriage?' asked Perry.

Miss Wells looked at the train, which *still* hadn't reached us, before turning back to Perry. She shrugged, and I knew what was coming.

'I don't see why not. Let's—'

'Miss Wells, we should stay here,' I interrupted.

'Why?' she asked.

Think, Kyle. Think. Fast.

'Because everyone always heads for the first carriage and it'll be very crowded and much harder to keep track of all of us if we're in there as well,' I said.

Miss Wells nodded. 'Good point, Kyle. I think we'll stay where we are.'

She moved down the platform to stop Robby and Naima from arguing about who was wearing the best earrings. As if anyone gave a damn.

Perry scowled at me, sucking in his cheeks in his already narrow face. 'Thanks a lot. What did you do that for?'

I shrugged, but didn't reply. How could I? No doubt it looked like I'd scuppered Perry's idea just to be bloody-minded. But it wasn't that. I swear it wasn't. To be honest, I'm not even sure why I'd said what I did. But the thought of going into the first carriage . . . I looked away from Perry, who was still glaring at me. If looks could kill he'd have been banged up for life. Perry was the shortest guy in our class but he never let that hold him back. He was my opposite. Over the last year I'd sprouted up so much that everyone in the class, including Miss Wells, was shorter than me. But although Perry was shorter than the rest of us, he was always the first to volunteer, the first to speak, first to voice his opinion – whether it was wanted or not. No way would he ever let anyone in the class forget he was around. I glanced down the track again, jiggling from foot to foot.

'Come on, train,' I muttered.

Steve nudged my arm with his bony elbow. Although 'nudged' was putting it mildly. 'Damn near broke my forearm' was closer to the mark.

'Are you OK?' he asked me.

I nodded. 'Yeah. Why?'

'You seem a bit . . . restless.'

'No run this morning?' asked Joe, another of my mates.

'No, I ran. But not for long enough,' I replied.

'Ah, that explains a lot.' He smiled. 'I thought you were a bit on edge.'

Joe was a strange one. Dark hair, darker eyes, darkest disposition of all my friends. He was the thinker of our group. Steve was the doer. Perry was the talker. And me? I wasn't quite sure what I was, where I fit in. Perry often said that Joe thought too much, which was true. Joe over-analysed everything to death. He was overweight but not massively so, with mid-brown hair framing a round face and lime-green eyes – lime like the fruit, not the drink. His black jacket flapped in the wind like a bird's wings until he impatiently dug his hands into his pockets to keep the sides down. The train must have been early because it still hadn't reached us, but at least it was moving. I watched it creep along, emptying my mind of all thoughts as I got lost in its slow motion.

Why did you do it, Dad?

I didn't deserve that. Whatever you felt about me, I didn't deserve that. Or was it just that you didn't feel anything for me at all?

Or maybe you had the right idea and none of this is worth a damn . . .

'Watch out! Kyle's lost in one of his daydreams again,' said Joe to the others.

I snapped out of my reverie and back to the train platform. 'What're you on about?'

Joe shrugged. 'You went offline – again.'

'I don't know what you mean,' I said with studied calm. 'I don't daydream.'

'If you say so,' he said, turning to watch the train's progress.

'I do,' I replied, needing to have the last word.

As it was, the train didn't travel much past us. We all bundled into the second carriage. The heat hit me almost at once, blasting out from the vents above my head. The driver must have had the heating on full throttle. I stepped aside to let an elderly couple get off the train and got a dirty look from him and a tut from her for my trouble. Luckily the carriage was almost empty. Only a few heads were visible above the high-backed, blue-patterned seats. Our class were off to the city to see a matinée performance of *Romeo and Juliet*. We'd been studying the play for the last term and a bit, and this theatre trip was our teacher Miss Wells's idea of a treat.

The train doors shut with a hiss and the train started off before we'd all found our seats. Steve sat next to me, Joe and Perry sat directly opposite. Elena and Conor sat across the central aisle from us, opposite each other, holding hands and generally being too wet for words – as usual.

'Conor, what's the matter, babe?' asked Elena softly.

Conor didn't answer.

'You're worrying about your nan, aren't you?' she said.

'It's just . . . she's getting more and more . . . forgetful. A few nights ago she made herself a hot chocolate and left one of the cooker rings on all night. Mum and Dad are starting to talk about putting her in a home for her own good.'

'Well, maybe it would be for the best—' Elena began.

'No way!' The words exploded from Conor. 'Nan would hate it, just hate it.'

'Conor, I only meant . . .' Elena gave a quick glance around, only to see me and my mates watching them and earwigging every word.

'How about I write down our conversation so you nosy toe-rags can have a permanent record?' she bit out.

'No need.' Perry grinned. 'Just speak up a bit!'

Elena and Conor shuffled further away from us and lowered their voices.

'Spoilsports!' said Perry.

Elena gave him a two-fingered salute.

Steve turned away from her. 'Wasn't interested in your conversation anyway,' he muttered.

It was strange about Steve and Elena. She was the only one in our class that he didn't have much time for, though I think I was the only one who knew that. I looked around the carriage, taking it all in. Miss Wells was further along – thank goodness. Some of the girls sat in the next set of seats behind us, already twittering away about not much. As if to make up for its previous tardiness, the train moved out of the station, getting faster and faster until the passing scenery was just a frenetic blur. Hot air blew up from the vents underneath the windows as well as from above the doors and the heat was beginning to make me feel a bit queasy, but apart from that, it was great. Outside the train it became almost impossible to focus on anything at eye-level or below. And in a strange way, I found that restful. It required no thought, no interpretation. The sky was the only thing that was constant. The grey clouds drifted along and wouldn't allow our train to dictate their pace. Below the sky though, the scenery was a smudge of poster-paint colours: mid-green fields merging with the beginnings of darker green crops, merging with brown tree trunks and darker brown branches. Those were the few things I could make out. The rest was pure guesswork.

Even the tropical heat in the carriage couldn't spoil my mood. Less than ten minutes into the journey, I had to take off my jacket and roll up my shirt sleeves, as did my friends, but it didn't matter. I didn't travel by train often enough to make the trip mundane. I loved the speed and the regular rhythmic hum of the train wheels moving along the tracks. We trundled along, pulling in and out of stations for at least forty minutes. I stared out of the window, watching the sky get greyer and darker while my friends chatted around me.

Steve nudged my side, almost breaking my ribs in the process. Man, I wished he'd stop doing that!

'Kyle, d'you wanna have a go?' he asked, indicating the very latest portable games console in his hand.

I glanced down at the screen. Cross-hairs were trained on some creature, its face a mouth filled with razor-sharp pointy teeth and nothing else. I shook my head.

'You sure?'

I nodded. Typical Steve! He didn't own a single

game which didn't involve blowing holes in something. People, aliens, mutants, rabid dogs – Steve didn't care. If the game didn't involve guns, it didn't involve Steve either. Yet in our class, he was the one always prepared to give others the benefit of the doubt. And he'd hand over the shirt off his back without even being asked. Steve told me a while ago that his dad was beginning to question what his son wanted to do with the rest of his life once he left school.

'My dad has become an absolute nightmare,' he admitted. 'All I hear these days is "the army this" and "the army that".'

'Tell him you're not interested,' I advised.

'Don't you think I've already tried that?' Steve shot back. 'Dad loved being in the army and now he's dropping all kinds of unsubtle hints about me following in his footsteps.'

But at least Steve's dad gave a damn. That counted for a great deal.

'I'll have a go.' Perry leaned forward and tried to snatch the game console out of Steve's hand. Steve pulled his hand back indignantly but that didn't stop Perry. Frowning, I turned to look back out of the window as Perry and Steve got into it.

'Just one quick go, you selfish git!' Perry complained.

'Back off! I mean it.' Steve leaped up, his arm up and out of Perry's reach.

Perry jumped up. 'Go on, give us a go,' he insisted, still leaping up and down.

13

I must admit, it did make me laugh. Perry resembled a terrier jumping up for snacks, his blond hair flopping up and down over his face as he leaped.

'Oi!' Miss Wells shouted from further down the carriage. 'Behave, you two. If I have to come over there and sit between both of you, I will.'

Steve and Perry sat down immediately, but that didn't stop the fight for the console. Usually I would've been in there, joining in on one side or the other – it didn't matter which.

But not today.

Ten minutes later the train slowed then stopped, but not at a station. The signal ahead of us must have turned red. Shame, really. We'd really been moving there for a while. The grey clouds had delivered on their earlier promise and now the rain was really teeming down. The wind slammed the rain into the train windows, making it difficult to see much. The minutes ticked by and still we didn't move. How much longer were we going to have to sit here? I looked out of the train window, wondering what was holding us up. A signal failure? Engine trouble? The wrong kind of rain? I'd heard enough people moaning about the train service to know it didn't take much.

It wasn't even as if the view was anything to take a photo of either. This railway bridge we'd taken root upon was way above a busy city street, and all around us there were office blocks – high, ugly buildings with tiny windows. Outside, on Elena and Conor's side of the carriage were any number of train tracks, at least five pairs that I could just about see from my seat. But on my side there was only the edge of the bridge, with a low brick wall separating the train from the road below. I craned my neck to look down. We had to be at least three storeys above the ground. The people rushing around below looked like blurry beetles scurrying to get out of the rain. Where were they all going in such a hurry? And was it worth it?

Maybe Dad got it right, after all . . .

Funny how I was beginning to think that more and more often recently.

Searching for the cause of the faint unease that stirred within me, I looked around. Joe, opposite, pointed to Steve and Perry, who were still bickering. I shrugged, then turned back to the window. Joe didn't say much at all. If he raised his hand in class it was a miracle. But when he did speak, somehow everyone shut up to listen. I wondered where he'd be in ten years' time, twenty years, thirty? I could imagine him running some vast company making multi-trillions, a diamond fist in a velvet glove.

Sometimes, I found myself wondering what we'd all do once we left school. Would we still remain mates or would we go our own separate ways? Where would I be in ten years' time? My trouble was, I had trouble thinking that far ahead. My friends all had plans. Perry wanted to be something artistic, he wasn't quite sure what. Maybe a film director. Steve wanted to travel the world. Joe wanted to study medicine at university. He wanted to specialize but he wasn't sure in what. Maybe psychiatry. My mates had it all sorted. I didn't. What was the point? I mean, look at my dad. He'd had plans, big plans, for the rest of his life with Mum. They were both going to retire in their early fifties and move down south, maybe to Devon or Dorset. Those were Dad's choices.

'Fitz, I think I'd rather move up north than live down south,' said Mum. 'My mum and two brothers are up north.'

'God spare us from your family,' said Dad.

'I could always go and live up there by myself,' said Mum.

'That'll be the day,' laughed Dad. 'What on earth would you do without me?'

Mum didn't answer. Funny how she never bothered to answer that question.

Mum: Fitz, could you take the rubbish out please?

Dad: Of course, love. What would you do without me?

Mum: Fitz, the computer isn't working.

Dad: Hell, Londie! Can't you do a damn thing for yourself? What would you do without me?

Without me . . . Without me . . . Without me . . .

Slowly I became aware that it'd gone quiet. I turned to find my friends watching me.

'What's up?' I asked.

'You were light-years away *again*,' said Joe. 'What gives?'

'Nothing.' I shrugged.

'Liar. Go on, tell us what took you so far away.'

I glanced at Steve. Even though he said nothing, I could see from his expression that he thought he knew exactly what I'd been thinking. And he wasn't far off either.

'If you must know, I was just wondering where we'll all be in twenty years' time.' It was as good a story as any.

'Joe'll be working for his brother,' said Perry cheerfully.

'Perry, don't even start with that crap,' said Joe. 'I'm not in the mood. Not today.'

'That'd be your worst nightmare, wouldn't it? But who knows? It could happen,' Perry insisted.

'Perry, shut up,' Joe said with menace.

'Come on then,' urged Perry. 'If that's not your worst nightmare, what is?'

Joe's lips, like his eyes, were getting narrower and more pinched. I shook my head. Perry never did know when to back up and back off.

'See what you've started,' Steve said to me.

'What're you so afraid of?' Perry asked Joe directly.

'Perry, I'm going to deck you if you don't shut the bloody hell up!' said Joe harshly.

'OK, Joe. Calm down,' said Steve, with mild surprise.

Seems I wasn't the only one who had unpleasant things on my mind.

'Well, he gets on my nerves.' Joe scowled. 'He's worse than Jon – and that's saying something.'

The last thing any of us wanted was to get Joe

started on the subject of his twin brother, Jonathan. I'd met Jon just a few times. There was smug, then there was arrogant, and then there was Jon.

'So how is your twin anyway?' Perry asked on a deliberate wind-up.

'The less said about him the better,' Joe snapped.

'Joe, what's up with you and your brother? In primary school you guys used to be so tight,' said Steve, ever the peacemaker.

'Used to be,' Joe said pointedly.

'Joe, maybe you should let it go,' said Steve as gently as he could.

'Steve, maybe you shouldn't go there,' I warned.

'Let *what* go?' asked Joe, the tone of his voice giving all of us frostbite.

But for once Steve wasn't going to take any kind of hint. 'OK, so Jon passed the entrance exam and got into Peltham College and you didn't,' he said. 'Is our school really that bad? Are we really so terrible?'

'That's not the point,' said Joe.

'Then what is?' asked Steve.

I must admit, I'd been wondering the same thing.

'The point is,' Joe said, exasperated, 'that had our positions been reversed, I wouldn't've gone to Peltham College without Jon.'

'Bullcrap!' Perry barely let Joe close his mouth before launching in. 'If you'd got into Peltham and your twin hadn't, it would've been "*hasta la vista*, brother" – and you know it.'

'I'm telling you, I would've turned the place down,'

Joe insisted. 'I wouldn't've gone to a school that didn't take Jon as well.'

'Well, if you'd turned down a place at one of the best private schools in the country just because they didn't take your twin brother, then you're an arse,' said Perry, tactful as ever. 'Which is probably why you didn't get in. Your brother obviously has all the brains in your family.'

'Uh-oh!' Steve muttered.

Joe was a nanosecond away from going nuclear. The scowl he gave Perry spoke volumes. And anyone but Perry would've shut up.

'What's that look about? Stressy much?' asked Perry. 'Or is it your time of the month?'

Joe launched himself at Perry. It took both Steve and me to pull him off.

'Enough! Joe, you need to take a chill pill, and Perry, you need to change the subject,' said Steve firmly. 'Unless you want Miss Wells to split us up.'

'He said—' Joe began furiously.

'We all heard what Perry said,' said Steve. 'But what he meant was that maybe it's just as well it wasn't your decision to make.'

'Meaning . . . ?' Joe frowned, his attention now directed at Steve.

'Meaning I know you and your brother are in-separable – or rather, you were – but sooner or later you both had to go your separate ways and do your own thing. That's just the way life works. Maybe Jon realized it before you did, that's all.'

Joe sat so far back in his seat, I'm surprised he didn't fall through it. Each of us got a look that was pure daggers before he turned to look out of the train window.

'What did I say?' asked Perry, rubbing his arm where Joe had managed to get a punch in.

'Leave it, Perry,' I said.

'I can't believe all this started just 'cause I asked Joe about his worst nightmare,' said Perry petulantly. 'It didn't even have to be about his brother. My worst nightmare is being buried alive. See? I'm happy to share! So what's the problem? Kyle, what're *you* most afraid of?'

Perry obviously wasn't going to shut up.

'Oh, come on, Kyle,' he wheedled.

'I thought we were dropping this subject,' I tried, knowing it was futile.

'I'm only asking,' Perry persisted. 'So what is it? Or don't you ever have nightmares?'

'Of course I do,' I said impatiently.

Perry looked at me expectantly, waiting for me to carry on. When I didn't, he turned with an exasperated huff to Steve. 'What about you, Steve? What're you afraid of?'

'Disappointing my dad,' Steve replied immediately.

Perry nodded, with no smile or witty, snitty come-back for once. Enough said.

'And you, Joe? What frightens you?'

'Me . . .' said Joe, his eyes burning into Perry's.

'Huh?'

'I frighten myself,' said Joe, the merest hint of a smile twisting his lips. 'So what must I do to the rest of you?'

'Very funny,' said Perry. 'I'm serious. What scares you, Joe?'

Joe shrugged and smiled. Perry gave up on him.

'Your turn, Kyle. What's your weakness?'

'I'm afraid . . .' My mates were watching me. I could feel my face glowing warm. I changed my mind and decided not to confess to the thing that scared me the most. I plumped for one of the things that still made me . . . anxious; had always made me anxious. 'I'm afraid of ghosts.' One look at my friends' faces and I instantly regretted the admission.

'Are you kidding me?' Perry scoffed. 'There's no such thing as ghosts.'

I shrugged. 'As the saying goes, "There are more things in heaven and earth, Perry, than are dreamt of in your philosophy." '

'Where's that from?' asked Perry. '*Star Wars*?'

'Shakespeare's *Hamlet*, you moron,' I replied.

'My name's in *Hamlet*?' said Perry, astounded. 'Cool!'

I opened my mouth, only to snap it shut again. Joe looked at me and smiled ruefully. At least he wasn't angry any more. The train finally began to move. 'Bout time too!

'Go on, Kyle, have a go,' said Steve, trying to thrust his game console at me again.

'No, thanks,' I said, exasperated.

'Why're you being so dry?' he asked.

'I'm not. I just . . .'

Steve regarded me, eyebrows raised.

'Give it here then,' I said with a sigh.

I'd barely got my hand on it when all at once there was a colossal bang like nothing I've ever heard before. So loud, it was like the whole world exploding. And beneath the bang there came the sound of metal twisting and crunching and crushing, like the train carriage ahead was being chewed up and spat out.

Our train had been hit. Hit hard.

Our carriage was slammed backwards, then began to tilt up sharply. I pitched forward, then fell back. Joe and Perry opposite fell towards me as the train was pushed up at a sharp angle.

That's when the train began to turn.

To actually flip over.

2

Without warning, the train smashed back down on its side again. And the noise . . . Glass shattering, crashing and smashing, and metal bolts popping. My body flipped and flopped like some kind of rag doll. I might have been a piece of paper caught up in a tornado for all the control I had over it. My head slammed against something hard; after that I couldn't see anything, hear anything, think anything above and beyond the ringing in my ears and the fireworks exploding behind my eyes. The sky, the train, the carriage disappeared and the world was just a wash of pain and darkness. I groaned; then I disappeared too.

The day of the letter began the same as any other. I went to school, I spent about an hour at Steve's house, playing his latest computer game and listening to some tunes, then I went home. I'd like to say that the moment I set foot in the hall I knew something was wrong. But I can't say that, 'cause it's not true.

'Mum?' I bellowed as soon as the front door was shut. 'Mum?'

No answer. Maybe she was in the shower or the garden or something. I couldn't smell anything cooking either, which was more unusual. I ran upstairs to my room, taking the stairs two and three at a time. I glanced into Mum and Dad's bedroom as I passed. The envelope taped to the dressing-table mirror had me backing up. And even when I saw it, it still didn't click. I walked over to the dressing table. Anthony *was* written on the envelope in Mum's bold, upright writing. And that's when the hollow feeling inside me first appeared, tiny and still, but definitely there. Anthony . . . Mum never called Dad Anthony. Our surname was Fitzwilliam so Mum always called Dad Fitz, or Tony if she was really annoyed with him. I pulled the envelope off the mirror. It was tucked in, not stuck down at the back, so I opened it. There was one sheet of plain, white A4 paper inside. I unfolded it and began to read.

~~Dear~~ Anthony,

This is a hard letter for me to write but it's been a long time coming. I'm going away. Please don't try to find me. You've spent most of our marriage telling me that I'm nothing, I'm useless without you. Maybe you're right. Maybe that's true. But I need to find out for myself before I'm too old or too afraid to leave and have some kind of life of my own. You never listened to me when I tried to tell you now I felt, but hopefully you'll listen to this. Don't try to find me, Anthony. I don't love you any more. I realize now that I stopped loving you a long time ago. It's taken me too long to admit it. Kyle can stay with you until I sort myself out. I'm no good to him or anyone else the way I am now. I hope you can understand that if nothing else.

Yolanda

I read the letter twice and then a third time, my heart trying to punch its way out of my chest. I folded up the letter and put it back in the envelope, exactly the way I'd found it. I opened the fitted wardrobe on Mum's side. The emptiness within was only sporadically broken by a few bare hangers and the odd dress or two that would no longer fit. I opened up the chest of drawers, second drawer down. Empty. Just torn brown paper lining the bottom.

Mum . . .

She didn't love Dad any more.

She'd left Dad.

She'd left me.

I went to my room and pulled on my trainers and my sweats. Grabbing my keys out of my school trouser pocket, I walked out of the door and headed down the road. I had no idea where I was going. It didn't matter. I didn't want to be home when Dad came in from work. I didn't want to be home when Dad found the letter. I started to run.

* * *

. . . is this what it's like? . . . how it feels? . . . stillness and silence after a world of noise and pain and panic? is this what it was like for him? did he gently slide or was it more of a screaming fall? why have I never considered the moments – the moments just before and during and just after? guess I was too busy considering the method to think about the manner. am I dead? this is no way to die, not like this . . . this isn't fair . . . my head hurts . . . pain . . . that's a good sign – right?

The dead don't feel pain . . . Do they?

Open your eyes, Kyle.

I can't. Each eyelid weighs a ton.

Open your eyes, Kyle. Open them now.

Slowly I opened my eyes. Train seats stood to attention on either side of me like oppressive sentinels. My heart was thundering.

Now I was terrified of closing my eyes in case I never opened them again.

You're OK, Kyle, I told myself. *You can still think, so you're all right.*

I had to force my eyes shut so I could focus on bedding down the panic ripping chunks out of me. Surely neither Heaven nor Hell nor any stage in between would be furnished with blue-clothed train seats? Or was it possible to be dead and not even know it? I opened my eyes again and this time it was a little easier. My hand flew to my head. No blood, surprisingly, but it hurt like hell.

'Joe? Steve?' Did I shout that out loud or was it just in my head? I couldn't tell.

Where was Steve? Was he OK? I tried to stand but it was hard to tell which way was up. The train lurched suddenly, to come to a juddering halt on its side. And the silence that followed was like nothing I'd ever heard before. Or wanted to hear again. A silence so deep it was as if all my senses had suddenly shut down and each thought rang clear and loud in my head like some enormous pealing bell.

Someone began to sob. Low, irregular sobs of total terror.

'Are you all right?' I tried to call out, although I didn't know who I was talking to and it was such a ridiculous question. I just wanted to hear something besides that sobbing. But my voice sounded cracked and weak and barely above a whisper.

Someone was groaning now from just behind (above?) me. My eyes were beginning to focus again.

I tried to stand up, but Steve and Perry were sprawled on top of me and Joe was dangling over the side of one of the chairs. I couldn't move. I was on my side, with Perry lying over my feet and Steve over my arm and hip, his head dangling down in front of my chest. I couldn't see Perry's face but Steve's . . . Steve's eyes were closed and his skin looked almost grey. Drying blood decorated his cheek like a Rorschach ink blot. That's when what'd happened to us hit me. Hit me hard. I shoved at Steve, close to panic as I tried to shift him. But he didn't budge.

I had to get out of here.

I took a deep breath to brace myself and then

pushed at Steve again while kicking my legs up with all my might. This time it worked. Both he and Perry fell off me in a heap. I scrambled to my feet, feeling wrung out and queasy, like being seasick. My eyes were sending duff messages to my brain because everything around me was wrongly orientated and I still hadn't wrapped my head around it. The opposite train window was now directly above me and the rain was relentlessly washing in. I stood on what used to be the side of the train, between two smashed windows. The chairs that were still bolted down were now on their sides. I bent to try and pull Joe free but it was no use. One of his feet was wedged in the underside of the chair at an impossible angle. Steve's eyelids were fluttering now, but he didn't open them. I looked around for help. There was no one. I was the only one standing. My head was swimming.

'Focus,' I muttered. 'Just look at something real and focus.'

So I looked up. Above me, I could see nothing but dark grey sky and rain falling like a shredded curtain through the shattered windows. I let the rain wash over my face. I took one deep breath followed by another before I could trust myself to look around again. Squatting down, I forced myself to take Joe's wrist so that I could feel for a pulse. I couldn't detect one but told myself not to panic over that. I was probably checking the wrong part of his wrist. Perry's eyes were closed but he was groaning softly. Occasionally his eyes would flutter open, only to close immediately, as if the light or the sight was too much for him. I stumbled around, trying to find our teacher. Elena grabbed my leg as I passed her.

'Kyle, help . . .' she mumbled.

I squatted down and brushed her hair out of her eyes. 'Ellie, are you OK? Can you stand up?'

She shook her head. 'I can't feel my left leg.'

I glanced down. Her left leg was bent beneath her right one, but it didn't look too bad. Not like Joe's.

'Is it broken?' Elena whispered.

'I don't think so . . .' I said. That had to be better than admitting that I didn't have a clue.

It was back – that feeling of total helplessness. The guilty, useless feeling that lay just a scratch beneath the surface of my skin. What could I do? I could just about apply a plaster on a cut. That was the limit of my medical expertise. 'Help must be on the way by now. We'll all be out of this soon, you'll see.'

But then the carriage gave a terrific lurch and dropped at least a metre, slanting down by about twenty or thirty degrees. Doesn't sound like much, but believe me, it felt like fathoms. Out of control, I skidded away from Elena, trying to stop myself from kicking some poor unconscious woman in the face. I grabbed hold of the luggage rack at my side and swung my legs round just in time. The strange orientation of the carriage was really doing my head in. I stood up slowly, trying not to make any sudden moves that would make the train pitch again. Why had we dropped? It didn't make any sense. And then, all at once, it did.

Horrifying, terrifying sense. The train had flipped over all right, but not onto the adjacent track. It had fallen in the opposite direction. Part of the crunching sound I'd heard before had to be the side of the railway bridge being demolished by the impact of the train carriages. Some of the train had to be hanging over the edge of the bridge. And with no barrier to hold us and the train on its side, what was to stop the whole thing plummeting onto the street below?

That's when the contents of my stomach erupted up through me like a fountain. I vomited violently, half ashamed of myself for letting fear turn my stomach inside out, but the shame wasn't enough to stop me retching wretchedly again. The puddle of sick began to slide downwards, following the slope of the carriage.

And all I could think was, *What if the train falls?*

What will happen to me and my friends if the train falls?

There were a few groans. Someone (Kendra?) was sobbing her way through a bout of the hiccups. A murmur of 'Help, someone, please help me' tried to puncture the shocked silence in the carriage. But those words just made the underlying quiet worse. And it looked like I was still the only one on my feet. I had to get out. I had to get my friends out. I had to get everyone out. But how?

How?

The windows and doors were either directly below us, lying against the tracks, or directly above, pointing at the sky. How was I going to hoist one person, never mind the whole carriage-full, out of a smashed window at least one and a half metres above me? And even if, by some miracle, I did manage to manoeuvre one of my friends out, the movement might send the entire train tipping over the side of the bridge.

What should I do?

I couldn't just stand here like a waxwork and do nothing.

To my left there was a middle-aged black woman, a stranger, wedged between the underside of a seat and the floor, although with the carriage on its side it took a few moments to realize exactly where she was. She had a few drops of blood on her camel-coloured coat and her head was slumped forward. I started towards her, only to stop. All around me were people who needed my help. Steve, Joe, this stranger. I felt totally overwhelmed. I didn't know where to begin, which way to turn. Each view brought new horrors. People moaning. One man was sitting up, rocking, his eyes wide, staring into nothing. Bodies twisted in grotesque, impossible angles. And the smell of rusty nails was getting stronger. Only it wasn't nails – it was blood. I could see little splashes of red up and down the carriage. Just little splashes . . . nothing too bad. Just blood from a nosebleed here or a cut head or arm there. Strangely enough, the sight wasn't so bad, I could just about cope with that. But the smell . . . that smell was making my stomach heave. I wanted, I *needed* to shout with anger, frustration.

Words erupted from me with a force that

immediately made my vocal cords ache. '*Someone, help us . . .*'

The coughing fit that followed at least eased the tension in my throat.

'*Kyle . . .*' My name floated towards me, barely more than a whisper. I spun round but could see no one who looked even remotely able to answer me. It had to be the help I'd cried out for, but who was calling me?

'*Kyle . . .*'

There it was again. So soft and quiet it was almost like a thought in my head. But it wasn't. I knew it wasn't. Unless I was hallucinating. Could I be hallucinating? I made my way back to my friends. What else I could do? Perry must've regained consciousness then passed out again because he was in a different position, sitting up, his head leaned back. Part of me envied my friends their oblivion. Perry's eyelids began to flutter. And his eyes beneath his eyelids were flickering like he was in the middle of REM sleep.

'Perry . . . ?' I whispered, squatting down. 'Perry, can you hear me?'

Perry's eyes flicked open. 'Kyle . . .' he whispered when he saw me. 'Are we going to die?'

'No, we're not,' I said fiercely. 'The emergency services will be hacking through the top of this train any minute and they'll rescue all of us. You wait and see.'

At that very moment, as if to back up my words, I

heard the very welcome sound of a helicopter approaching.

'See.' I grinned at Perry. 'I told you we'd be rescued. I told you . . .'

But his eyes were closed again and his skin was now the sallow colour of cheap, uncoloured candles. I looked from him to Joe, then Steve. I didn't like the look of Steve at all. I took a half-step towards him, ready to shake him awake. I didn't want to be the only one trying to take all this in. I didn't want to be alone. But my hand slowed, then stilled as I reached out towards Steve. I couldn't shake him. I might do more harm than good by trying to wake him up.

Through the window above me I saw an orange and white helicopter overhead, its blades chopping raucously through the air. I'd been right about that at least. Help had arrived at last. I waved my hands above my head, hoping to attract the attention of whoever was in the helicopter. I had to let them know that someone down here was still standing. I needed to know that someone, somewhere, could see me; that I wasn't the only one going through this. Maybe if I climbed up . . .

'*Kyle, wait . . .*'

The whispered words came again, so softly spoken I couldn't even be sure if they came from a woman or a man. Was this someone's idea of a sick joke? Playing silly beggars and messing with my head? I spun round. *Who* was calling me? It was freaking me out.

Ignore it, Kyle. Get to the helicopter, I told myself.

I looked up, but as I watched, the helicopter blades slowed down, their rotation less frantic. Yet the chopper didn't move, didn't descend, didn't even look like it was in any kind of trouble. As the blades slowed, so the very air around me grew thick and still. The slowing down was almost hypnotic. I was having trouble catching my breath.

'*Kyle* . . .' The whisper floated towards me, so faint I could barely hear it. '*Kyle, wait for me.*'

My head jerked round like a puppet's but I was still the only one standing in the carriage. That voice . . . that voice was burrowing inside me. I forced myself to concentrate on the helicopter, only now its blades weren't moving at all. It sat in the air above the train like some kind of natural satellite. Silence devoured me, chewed me up and spat me out, but only for a moment. The longest moment of my life . . .

Then all hell was let loose. Chopper blades and jet planes ripped through the air, machine-gun fire like rapid handclaps surrounded me, as did blast after roaring, deafening blast. I put my hands over my ears to try and drown out the noise but that just made it worse, like the sounds were in my head and my hands gave them no escape.

'*We have to get out of here,*' Steve's voice bellowed from out of nowhere, making me jump. Eyes wide, I looked down at Steve, expecting to see him on his feet, or at least sitting up with his eyes open. But half a glance was enough to see that he was still out for the count.

'Steve . . .' I whispered, just in case it was my eyes, not my ears, playing tricks. But they weren't.

'*Incoming!*' yelled another voice I didn't recognize. Strange how one word could convey so many emotions – so much anger and hatred and, most of all, fear.

'Ohmigod!' I heard Steve's horrified whisper. An impossible whisper and yet I heard it as clearly as I heard my own thoughts. '*It's coming straight for us. Evasive*—'

A high-pitched, deafening whistle came ever closer. So high-pitched it must surely make my ears bleed. A colossal boom had me diving to the floor. Had the train been hit by something else? No, it can't have been. There'd been no movement, no judder, no jolt, no fall. But that noise, like a fireworks factory exploding – what was that? I touched a hand to my ears. No blood.

But in that instant a shock, needle-sharp like static electricity, shot through my body. A rain of images began, images that burned their way through my mind. I squeezed my eyes tight shut but they wouldn't stop. Strange, unsettling images. Of Steve. And explosions. Steve with a gun in his hand. Steve eating. Laughing. At someone. With someone. Shouting. Running. A pack on his back, an assault rifle in his hand. Steve in some kind of plane, spinning round and down, hopelessly out of control, while he desperately pressed buttons and pulled at the stick. I was in the middle of this rain of images, looking past one to the next, trying to see my way past all of them. Trying to focus on what was beyond. Trying, but failing . . . My eyelids felt like lead. The images fell faster and faster. So fast now that I couldn't discern what any of them were. But they were all to do with Steve.

And then, just like that, the rain disappeared. And the train disappeared. And the track. And all my friends. There was just Steve in some kind of booth. And silence. Where was I?

Then Steve began to speak.

But not to me.

3

Steve's Nightmare

'Dad? It's Steve. How are you? How've you been?'

'Steve? Steve! How are you? It's so good to hear your voice. Where are you? Why can't I see you?'

'Only one of the web-cams is working, Dad. Our division has only just returned to the carrier, so the queue to use it stretches right round the ship. It was use this phone or wait another few days before it was my turn to use the web-cam with a working screen.'

'No, it's enough just to hear your voice. God, I've missed you, son. I've been worried sick. Are you all right?'

'I'm fine, Dad.' Steve smiled again, reaching out a tentative arm towards the blank screen before him. 'I've missed you so much. I just can't wait to get home.'

'So it's true? You're really coming home?'

'The war's over for me, Dad. Our unit is off rotation. I should be home within the next fortnight.'

'That's great news. Chris will be thrilled. And wait till I tell Hannah – eh!'

Steve's cheeks burned. 'Dad, stop teasing! Besides, Hannah is probably married with three kids by now. She always said she wanted a big family while she was still young enough to enjoy it.'

'Of course Hannah's not married. She's waiting for you. Mind you, if you told her that, she'd laugh in your face, but everyone here knows it's the truth.'

'Is it, Dad? Is it really?'

'Course it is.'

'Listen, Dad, I can't stay on the phone for much longer. There's a time limit on all comms out of this place until further notice. I . . . I wanted to ask you for a favour though.'

'Go ahead, son.'

Steve swallowed hard. 'You've met Dean, my co-pilot. Did you like him?'

'Yes, of course I did.'

Steve heard the surprise in his father's voice. He ran a dry tongue over his lips. 'It's just that . . . well, we were shot down while on manoeuvres over—'

'*What?* You were shot down? Are you sure you're—?'

'I'm fine,' Steve interrupted. 'But Dean . . . but Dean isn't, Dad. We had top-secret military information to deliver. We were both told that the data came first – nothing else even made it onto the priority list. Dean managed to eject out of our plane with the data, but when it crashed he broke the rules and came back to rescue me. He saved my life.'

'So what's the matter with him?'

'He . . . he was shot while he was dragging me clear.'

'Oh no . . .'

'Exactly. The bullets kept hitting him but he wouldn't leave me. And then they shot him with some kind of chemical agent which burned straight through his flesh. He's lost an arm and both of his legs and his face is severely burned – almost beyond recognition. And he's not eligible for military aid or compensation because our colonel says he broke the rules and risked our unit and possibly the whole war by going back for me. Our colonel says he'll be lucky if he isn't brought up on charges. The army aren't even going to pay for medical care and proper artificial limbs for him. They keep quoting something about contravening regulations. I know those artificial limbs aren't much use but at least they're better than the nothing he's going to get because of me.'

'Oh my God. That poor boy.'

Silence.

'Steve? What's the matter?'

'Sorry, Dad. I was just thinking.' Steve forced himself to continue. 'Dean smiles a lot, but deep down he's terrified and he feels very alone. He has no family, no one to go back to. So I said that he could stay with us.'

'Stay with us? For how long?'

'For good, Dad.'

Steve listened to the silence that filled the air around him. The unspoken plea echoing though his mind was almost deafening.

'Son, maybe Dean can stay for a day or two, or perhaps even a week, but no way can he live with us permanently.'

'Why not?'

'Steve, use your head. I'll always be grateful to Dean for saving your life. Always. But we have to face the facts. Dean is a cripple. He'll need lots of time, care and attention, not to mention money. Our home is too small to have him here permanently and it would cost too much to adapt it.'

'But, Dad, he saved my life. Couldn't we at least try? He wouldn't be too much trouble—'

'Yes, he would, son. Don't you think I'd love to say yes? But I can't. Maybe he could go into a hospital for the war wounded and we could visit him?'

'He'd hate that. Please, Dad—'

'I'm sorry, son, but the answer is no.'

'But I've already told him that he can live with us.'

'Then you'll just have to untell him.'

'Couldn't we at least try, Dad. *Please*. For me?'

'No, Steve. He saved your life and I'll always be grateful for that, but he'd be too much of a burden.'

'A burden?' Steve whispered.

'I'm sorry, Steve.'

'So am I.'

'Come on, son. Let's not argue. I haven't spoken to you in almost six months. Tell me all about—'

'I can't, Dad. My time's up now.'

'Already?'

''Fraid so. I'll see you soon. Bye, Dad.'

'I'm going to give you such a homecoming. And, Steve, I'm sorry about Dean, but you do understand—'

'I understand, Dad. Bye.'

'Bye, son. See you soon.'

Steve switched off the phone. He stared up at the peeling, dingy grey paint on the ceiling, slow tears trickling down his otherwise expressionless face.

'Mr Walker, it's Dean Sondergard here.'

'Dean? Well, hello, Dean. How are you?'

'I'm all right, Mr Walker.' Dean studied the image of Steve's father on the phone. He was just as Dean remembered, his hair grey at the temples but jet everywhere else. A neat, trim moustache and his skin the colour of oak, his body as sturdy as oak. And smiling eyes. A man you instinctively trusted. Solid. Dependable. Only he was frowning now.

'Why, Dean, Steve told me that you'd lost an arm and your legs. Have the charges been dropped? Have you received replacements after all?'

Dean turned away from the screen, his lips a tight, bitter line. He was going home but it didn't matter what the politicians and the diplomats said, the war would never be over . . . not for people like him. Or the man on the screen before him.

'Congratulations! Steve must be so pleased for you,' Mr Walker continued.

Dean turned back to the screen, staring at Mr Walker's broad grin. 'Mr Walker, please . . .' A moment to think, then he took a deep breath. 'Mr

Walker, please prepare yourself. I . . . I have some bad news.'

'Steve . . .' Mr Walker said immediately. 'What's wrong? Has something happened to my son?'

'Mr Walker, I don't know how to say this. Steve . . . Steve committed suicide this morning. I . . . I'm so, so sorry.'

The two men stared at each other.

'Steve . . . ?' Mr Walker whispered. 'He didn't . . . he wouldn't . . . You're wrong.'

'Please, Mr Walker. I'm afraid it's true . . .'

'But why? I don't understand. Why would he do such a thing? Why?' Mr Walker seemed to shrink into himself, to diminish right before Dean's eyes.

'Mr Walker, Steve spoke to you last night. Did you see him?'

'What . . . ?' Mr Walker shook his head, slowly, utterly bewildered now, utterly lost. 'I . . . I couldn't . . . I never saw him yesterday. He said the web-cam wasn't working . . .'

'I see. And what did you talk about?'

Mr Walker's eyes were dazed and glazed with pain. 'Where's Steve?'

'Mr Walker, what did you talk about?'

Mr Walker slowly shook his head. 'You. He talked about you. He wanted you to stay with us.'

'Me?' Dean said, stunned.

'He told me that you'd lost an arm and both legs . . .'

'Oh, I see.'

'I don't understand,' Mr Walker pleaded. 'Where's my son? I want to see my son.'

'Steve left you a letter,' said Dean. 'May I read it to you?'

Mr Walker nodded slowly. Dean removed the letter from his overall pocket. The words, like shards of glass, pierced his tongue and sliced at his vocal cords. He tried to swallow, but it hurt. It hurt so much.

'Sorry, Dad. I love you. You've explained everything to me very carefully and I think this is the best solution for everyone. Steve.'

'What does that mean?' Mr Walker interrupted. 'Steve can't be dead. I don't believe it.'

'Mr Walker, I'm not supposed to do this, but I'll use my security clearance on this computer to show you Steve. He's . . . he's in the morgue. I can transmit the image to you.'

Dean looked away from Mr Walker's eyes. Eyes filled with such sorrow, such pain. It was too much, too searing, like looking at the sun. Dean keyed his password and the necessary commands into the console beside the web-cam and the morgue appeared without warning, filled to overflowing with row upon row of transparent body capsules. Hermetically sealed body containers to stop infection spreading and to preserve the bodies for as long as possible before they were brought home. Dean knew he'd catch hell from his commander for this severe breach of military protocol, but he didn't care. He owed Steve that much. Dean began to key in the commands to home in on one particular capsule.

'Mr Walker, did Steve tell you what happened when we were shot down?'

'Yes, he told me how you saved his life.'

'I didn't save his life, Mr Walker,' said Dean quietly. 'It was the other way round. *He* came back for *me* . . .'

A new image filled the screen now. There, in his capsule, lay Major Steve Walker, with no legs and only one arm and a badly scarred, almost unrecognizable face.

4

'No!'

The cry was wrenched from me at the sight of Steve's mutilated body. A cry that yanked me out of my vision of Steve and back onto the train. Gasps sought to fill my empty lungs. I scrutinized Steve, dissecting him with my eyes. Two legs. Two arms. And his chest was moving up and down, slowly but steadily. What had just happened?

Did I pass out? Was that it? Seeing Steve like that ... watching like some fly on the wall as his life shattered ... What had happened to Steve was unthinkable, unbearable. And yet it had been a respite from my own situation, my own problems. Guilt like acid ate at my insides for even admitting that to myself, but it was true. How had I done it? How had I stopped being me and fallen into Steve's life instead? How was that even possible? I looked down at my hands. They were still shaking.

Look at me! So sure that my dream of Steve was true, was *real*. 'Cause that's what it had to be – a dream. But where had all that come from? I'd had my fair share of nightmares, especially over the past year, but nothing like the one I'd just experienced. Nothing so vivid, seen from the point of view of someone else entirely. Looking around, I found it alarming that I had trouble convincing myself that the train was reality and my hallucination about Steve had been just that – an illusion, nothing of substance.

Think of something else, Kyle. Don't look at Steve, don't think about him. Just think of something else. Turn away and let your thoughts pull you away to somewhere safer . . .

Dad was about to put me in check. I was about to let him. I watched as he scrutinized the board, trying to anticipate my next move. He hadn't looked at or spoken to me in almost an hour. Maybe that's why Dad loved chess so much – you didn't have to converse with your opponent or even look them in the eye.

'Dad, when's Mum coming home?'

Dad's hand slowed on its way to his bishop. 'I don't know, Kyle. But soon.'

'How soon?'

'I don't know.'

'How d'you know she's coming home at all then?' I couldn't help asking.

''Cause it's your mum,' said Dad, as if that explained everything.

'She's been gone two weeks already,' I pointed out.

'She'll be home. You just wait and see.' Dad's attention turned emphatically back to the chessboard. Conversation was over. For Dad, Mum coming home was as obvious, as guaranteed as the sun rising each morning. I watched as he moved his bishop.

'Check!' he said triumphantly.

It was a bad move, but the grin pasted on Dad's face said he needed to win more than I did.

'Dad, why don't you just say you're sorry?' I asked.

'Sorry for what?' Dad's tone veered somewhere between surprise and indignation.

'Maybe if you said sorry, Mum would come home,' I ventured.

'Sorry for what?' Dad repeated.

And the thing is, he really didn't know.

I moved my rook in between Dad's bishop and my king. Dad didn't even think about what he was doing – he pounced on my rook with his knight and swept it off the board with a flourish. Now that his knight was between his bishop and my king, my king was safe. I moved my queen.

'Checkmate, Dad,' I said.

'What?'

I pointed to my queen and my other rook. 'Checkmate.'

Dad's face swooped down hawk-like over the board as he studied it. When he finally sat back, his expression changed like he had an unholy smell beneath his nostrils. I regarded him. Dad turned his thoughts outwards, using them like an iron to smooth *out the creases between his eyebrows and around his mouth. What was it going to be? 'Kyle, I let you win,' or perhaps, 'Kyle, did you cheat?' or maybe even 'You only won that 'cause I was having an off day. All those questions about your mum – they put me off.' But to my surprise, Dad said nothing. We sat watching each other in thorny silence.*

'Well done. That's the first time you've won,' said Dad, finally dredging up a smile from somewhere beneath his toes.

'No, Dad,' I replied quietly. 'It's just the first time you've lost.'

I didn't like those thoughts. They weren't that much safer. Or maybe they were, but that didn't help, because they were just as painful. I looked up again. The chopper blades were rotating as they should. Things were back to normal – if you could call my current situation normal.

'Kyle, I'm coming for you . . .'

There it was again, that faint yet insistent whisper. Where was it coming from? It seemed to be coming from every direction at once. I struggled forward, looking around, but could see no one calling me.

'Kyle . . .' Miss Wells's thin voice had my whole body whipping round.

'Miss Wells.' I was at her side in an instant. 'Miss Wells, d'you want my help?'

Miss Wells shook her head. Her arm was twisted at an obscene angle beneath her back.

If only I wasn't so pathetically feeble. I never knew what to do, what to say. I seemed to spend my life fifteen minutes behind everyone I cared about. It should be engraved on my gravestone – TOO LITTLE, TOO LATE. Story of my life.

'Are you in pain?' I asked. See! How's that for inadequate?

'I'll live,' my teacher replied weakly.

'Miss Wells . . . ?'

'Kyle, the f-first chance you get, you must get off this train . . .'

'I know—' I began.

Miss Wells unexpectedly grabbed my wrist with her good hand, her blue eyes burning into mine. 'Promise me you'll leave us all behind and save yourself if you get the chance.'

I didn't answer. I couldn't answer.

'Promise me,' she insisted, her fingers biting into my arm.

'I promise I'll try,' I said. I covered Miss Wells's hand with mine, partly to stop her from breaking my wrist, partly to reassure her that I was here and would help in any way I could.

'*Kyle, where are you . . . ?*'

That voice again. That terrible, breathy voice that made my blood run so cold. I'd never really experienced what that phrase meant before, but I knew now. I stared down at Miss Wells. She looked straight at me, as if she knew exactly what I was going through. *Exactly*. Without warning, they began – the blurred images of my teacher that warned of what was about to happen. Appalled, I tried to pull away, but Miss Wells held onto me like rigor mortis had already set in. OK, sick joke – but that's what it felt like.

'*Kyle, where are you . . . ?*'

Leave me alone . . . My thoughts were a desperate plea. What were my choices? Face that voice or concentrate on Miss Wells. No choice really. The voice constantly calling me was terrifying. The images of my teacher were getting clearer, like the focus on a camera being adjusted. But could I cope with any more? I could sense what was about to happen. Steve's dream had been bad enough. I didn't want to deal with another one. But although these images of Miss Wells were unwanted and unwelcome, they were better than the alternative.

Miss Wells was in some kind of classroom with a number of other adults. A woman wearing a brown suit and a beige scarf stood at the front of the class pointing out something on an interactive whiteboard. The vision came before the sound, but now I could hear what was being said, as if the volume in the room were slowly being turned up. I yanked my hand out of Miss Wells's grasp, covering my ears. I didn't want to hear it, didn't want to hear any of it. I closed my eyes and shook my head, trying to shake the image of my teacher out of my head.

But it didn't budge.

I opened my eyes. 'Miss Wells, is your first name Rosa?'

Surprise lit her eyes before she nodded. And that's when I knew for sure that it was happening again.

5

Miss Wells's Nightmare

'Rosa, is this course what you expected?'

Rosa turned to Jeanette, the stunning woman seated next to her. 'Pretty much,' she whispered back. 'Why?'

'It's not what *I* expected,' said Jeanette. 'I didn't think it'd be quite so tedious. And reading all that material on Western verses Eastern corporate ethos put me to sleep in under two minutes last night.'

'Look at it this way, Jeanette,' said Rosa. 'Another year and you'll have your MBA. Then the world will be your oyster.'

'What I'm looking for is a rich man. I wasn't born into the "proper" social circle' – Jeanette's tone, though mocking, had an edge to it – 'so this MBA will move me through the proper business circles till I find what I'm looking for.'

Rosa eyebrows almost touched her hairline. It'd never even occurred to her to use her MBA in that fashion. She was doing it to further her education and as a way of introducing the teaching of business administration at her school.

'But with an MBA, you won't need a rich man,' Rosa pointed out. 'You'll be able to—'

'Miss Wells, is there a problem?' asked the lecturer from the front of the class.

'No, Mrs Dyer. I'm sorry,' Rosa said quickly, her cheeks burning. She looked around to find she was the centre of attention, the very last thing she wanted. Even more embarrassing, Tod was looking at her. He smiled sympathetically and winked. Rosa immediately looked away, her cheeks flaming. Groaning, she closed her eyes and mentally berated herself for not smiling back or even acknowledging Tod's gesture of friendship. What was the matter with her?! Why was it that she could make conversation with any man on the planet as long as she wasn't attracted to him? She taught boys in a co-ed secondary school, for goodness' sake! And she'd been known to go toe to toe with some of the toughest pupils in the school. Not for nothing was her nickname 'Miss Well'ard'! But the moment attraction raised its ugly head, look out! She'd struggle hopelessly to find something to say, while her tongue invariably tied itself into the Gordian knot. Rosa sneaked a look at Tod. She could only see his profile as he'd turned back to face the lecturer. She sighed.

It wasn't just the MBA course that had Rosa unsettled. She'd fallen in lust with Tod from the first time she saw him. Desire twisted into longing as the term went on. And longing coiled into burning infatuation. She was beginning to fall in love – for all the good it did her.

During the break Rosa sadly regarded her reflection in the broken mirror in the ladies' room.

'He'd never fall for me,' she told herself, the truth aloe-bitter in her mouth.

Rosa was short, five feet four in her highest heels, with mousy brown hair and mousy brown eyes. Her face, her height, her body, they were all average. She wasn't ugly but she was no oil painting either. Strictly average. And Tod was far from being Mr Average. Rosa had watched him, course day after course day, with enough unconscious yearning to know that for a fact.

'I don't stand a chance.' The phrase became her mantra, but each time it entered her head, it passed by her heart to inflict tiny little cuts all over it. And her regrets were like lemon juice dripping relentlessly onto each and every wound.

'I've got nothing going for me,' Rosa agonized to her reflection in the dress-shop window on her way home that evening. 'I have no conversation. My skirts and shoes are never too high. My language and my tops are never too low. I shop on Saturdays. I go to church every Sunday. I'm not witty or pretty. Even my boobs are only a thirty-two A. I don't stand a chance.' And with that melancholy thought she plodded down the high street, avoiding all further glass-fronted shops.

After a few months something happened to prove to Rosa that infatuation had indeed turned into love. It happened at Tod's birthday party. They all went to a wine bar. Tod sat next to Rosa and actually had a proper conversation with her for the first time. Even more amazing, Rosa managed to talk back. As jazz music swirled deliciously around them, Tod asked her which films she'd seen recently; which plays she'd enjoyed in the past; what kind of music she listened to when she felt lonely or lively. The major plus which sealed Rosa's fate was that he listened to her answers! His responses followed on from her replies. Dialogue twisted and turned into stimulating conversation. Rosa only had eyes for Tod as the rest of the group – the rest of the world – had slowly slunk and shrunk away. The music was no more than a pleasant background hum. The voices of those around were no more than underlying noise, almost welcome, like winter rain heard and spied from the comfort of a warm haven.

Until Jeanette spoiled it all.

Jeanette. Even her name was glamorous. Five feet eight inches in her bare feet, raven-black hair, brown, sultry eyes and boobs that would keep the rain off a small child standing in front of her. She arrived at the wine bar late, then made a beeline for Tod. Tod's attention wandered immediately. Rosa was bitterly disappointed but not at all surprised. Within five minutes she was more miserable than she'd ever thought possible. She had been forgotten. It took only a few more minutes for her to back away and leave. At the wine-bar door she turned to look back at Tod. He hadn't even registered her departure. Jeanette had his full attention.

When Rosa got home she threw herself on her bed.

'I'm just tired!' she tried to tell herself. But as soon as her head hit the pillow, her tears flowed. She beat her fists into her bed linen. She could feel her heart straining and cracking beneath her breast.

'I wish . . . I wish . . . Oh, I would sell my soul to the Devil if Tod would love me. Oh, I would, I would, I w—'

'Would you? Would you really?'

Rosa froze momentarily before she spun round and struggled to sit up. She said furiously, 'Who the hell . . . ?'

'Who the hell indeed!'

Rosa stared, stricken and terrified, at the thing in the room with her. It was a deep boiled red, as if its top layer of skin had been peeled away and salt rubbed into the raw, sensitive flesh underneath. It was a man – of sorts. His voice, like his stance, was arrogant and sneering. The stench of the rotten and the dead and the dying assailed Rosa's nostrils. But what made her shrink back in mindless terror were the thing's eyes. His . . . its . . . his eyes were as red as his skin. The irises and pupils were blood red surrounded by intense white.

The Devil.

Rosa recognized him immediately. She'd read enough of her Bible to know him.

'Go away,' she croaked.

The Devil was annoyed. 'You're the one who called

me – remember? I've got better things to do than pop up here, there and everywhere uninvited.'

'I never invited you – I never.'

'I beg your pardon,' said the Devil, in high dudgeon, 'but you said – and I quote – "I would sell my soul to the Devil if Tod would love me."'

'But I . . . I didn't mean it.' Rosa's whispered protest set the Devil frowning.

'So you don't want Tod to love you?' he asked patiently.

'No, that's not true. I do. I do with all my heart,' Rosa replied. 'But . . .'

'But what?' the Devil prompted when she fell silent. Still she said nothing.

'Rosa, do you want my help or don't you?' The Devil's neck suddenly stretched until it was two metres long, dipping and coiling in Rosa's direction until his face was only inches away from her own. Rosa shrank back, terrified. She felt as if her whole body was being swallowed up by her eyes, which stared at the Devil, too petrified to even blink.

'*Do you want my help or don't you?*' the Devil boomed.

Rosa struggled desperately to think of Tod, her love. Once she had Tod's smiling image in her mind, she clung to it. It felt like clinging to her sanity. Tod . . . She loved him desperately, passionately, hopelessly. Rosa nodded at the Devil. The Devil's neck shrank back down to its normal length with a sudden snap.

'That's all right then,' he replied. 'Sign here please.'

A long scroll suddenly appeared in Rosa's lap. She picked it up and started to read.

'No need to do that,' the Devil cajoled. 'It's my standard boilerplate contract. I give you your heart's desire. You give me your soul. It's all very straightforward.'

'I'd still like to read it,' Rosa replied diffidently.

She didn't want to offend him but she'd read enough stories to know the Devil always tried to include a catch in his contracts. She turned her attention to the contract and read aloud.

' "I, Rosa Maxine Wells, do hereby state that I do of my own free will and without coercion agree to give up my soul upon my death to the Devil in exchange for marriage to Tod Powell. Signed—" Hang on. It doesn't say anything here about him loving me.' Rosa frowned.

'That's your department. I can arrange for him to be with you, but that's all,' the Devil replied.

'But I want him to love me.'

'Perhaps you haven't heard, but I don't deal in love,' the Devil pointed out.

'But it's all pointless if he doesn't love me.'

The Devil scratched his head. 'I'll tell you what – I'll make it so that he'll never want to leave your side. He'll want to be with you for all eternity. How's that?'

Rosa smiled for the first time since the Devil's arrival. 'Sounds like heaven,' she breathed.

The Devil flinched. 'There's no need for bad language.'

'Sorry,' said Rosa quickly. But then a frown visited her face and made itself at home there. 'Hang on. How do I . . . how do I know that you won't try something funny when I sign this?'

'What do you mean?' the Devil asked indignantly.

'How do I know you won't . . . er . . . do something to dispatch me before my time is up?'

'I beg your pardon?'

'I mean, how do I know you won't claim me the moment Tod and I get together for good. I'm not saying you would but—'

Slowly the Devil's head swelled up, expanding widthways until the sides of his face were touching opposite walls. His body remained the same size but his face was now an obscene, grotesque mask. His eyes narrowed, he asked, 'Would you like a guarantee written into your contract?'

'Well, if you wouldn't mind . . .' Rosa answered.

'It is done.'

Rosa glanced down at the contract in her hand. After Tod's name, a new section had been added:

' "The Devil hereby guarantees that he will not claim the aforementioned soul until Rosa Maxine Wells takes her own life," ' Rosa read. 'You mean you won't claim my soul unless I commit suicide?'

Rosa was amazed at the generosity of the new clause. The Devil's head shrank down to its normal size.

'I mean, you won't die unless you commit suicide,' the Devil replied.

'Does that mean that if my head gets run over by a bus, I'll have to live as a vegetable for all eternity?' Rosa asked warily.

The Devil began to tap his foot. 'Those damned fantasy books! They've made everyone so suspicious of the most innocent clauses,' he raged. 'It means that your soul will be mine when you commit suicide. It means no more or less than that.'

'But I won't commit suicide. It's against everything I believe,' Rosa replied.

'Then you have nothing to worry about, do you?'

'And what happens if I'm badly injured. Will I have to live for ever even if I'm brain dead?'

'Would you like a clause in the contract about that as well?' asked the Devil.

'If you'd be so kind.'

'It is done,' said the Devil. 'No matter what life throws at you, you will never suffer anything more serious than a cold. Happy now?'

Rosa examined the new clause very carefully indeed. It seemed to be OK, but the Devil was a trickster – and not a benign one either.

'All right, I'll sign,' she said slowly.

'At last!' The Devil grinned.

'Wait a minute though.' Rosa glowered at the Devil. 'You just said I wouldn't die unless I commit suicide.'

'Oh give me strength!' The Devil lowered his eyes hellwards. 'So?'

'So does that mean that if I don't commit suicide I'll live for ever?'

'Work it out for yourself.'

'Wait a minute . . . I get it now. I'll live for ever and Tod won't. I'll be alone and kill myself. That's your plan, isn't it? I'm not signing this . . .'

The Devil sighed deeply. 'You and Tod will be together for always. He'll exist for as long as you do. And your soul is eternal. Now that's it. I'm not wasting any more time with you. Either you sign the contract or I'll take my business elsewhere.'

'If you put in that bit about Tod living for as long as I do then I'll sign,' Rosa said.

'Done! Now get on with it.'

'I don't have a pen.'

'Hold out your left hand,' the Devil ordered.

Rosa did as instructed. Immediately she felt a sharp stabbing pain at the tip of her ring finger. Drawing back her hand, she was surprised, then not surprised, to see her fingertip covered in blood.

'Now you can sign the contract,' the Devil said.

Though it was awkward to sign with her ring finger, Rosa proceeded to do so, thinking it was lucky she was at least left-handed.

'Why that finger, as a matter of interest?' she asked.

'Heart blood,' the Devil replied, satisfied.

Barely had Rosa added the usual self-conscious flourish under her name than the contract disappeared. With a grin of the purest evil, the Devil sat at the end of Rosa's bed. Inwardly Rosa trembled at the sight of him. She'd been trying not to take too many long, drawn-out looks in his direction. He really was the ugliest, most grotesque entity she'd ever seen. Even now his foetid smell assaulted her nostrils and burned the back of her throat. Rosa's stomach clenched in revulsion.

'You must love' – at this word the Devil spat with distaste on Rosa's short-pile carpet – 'this Tod very much to give up your soul to be with him.'

'I do,' Rosa said simply. She peered over the side of the bed. Where the Devil had spat, the carpet was now singed.

'So what's your plan then?' asked the Devil.

'Plan?'

'For the future?'

'Tod and I will finish our MBAs. And once we've both graduated, I'll give up my teaching job and we'll maybe travel for a year, then get married and have a child right away, followed by another after three years. Tod will get a fantastic job that makes us lots of money before he sets up his own successful financial consultancy. That's where the money is. And we'll buy a house in the suburbs and have two cars and I'll stay home to look after the children until they're old enough to go to school. Then I'll return to teaching part-time and—'

'Dear, oh dear,' laughed the Devil. 'This is going to be even easier than I thought.'

Rosa snapped back to the present with a vengeance. Lost in her own world, she'd almost forgotten about him.

The Devil looked directly into Rosa's eyes.

'You know there's no way out of this contract now?'

'I don't want a way out. I love Tod. I want to be with him always.'

The Devil laughed. 'Corrupting your sort always gives me the most satisfaction. When the sweet, the innocent fall, they're the most fun to torture.'

'You won't get me. I'm not going to commit suicide,' Rosa said confidently.

'We'll see,' the Devil said thoughtfully. 'You know, there's a moment between life and the afterlife when there is nothing. A kind of limbo state where Death lives. Those who believe in something more then Death pass through that state and into something else. Those who believe in nothing after life move into an eternity of nothingness. When it's your turn to die, the door to that state of nothing will not be open to you. You do realize that, don't you?'

'I believe in life after death. I always have,' said Rosa slowly. 'So why would I want to exist in nothingness?'

'I'm just making sure you know that you no longer have the choice of believing in anything else,' said the Devil, his red eyes flashing like celebratory fireworks.

'What does that mean?'

'Nothing,' the Devil dismissed with a smirk. 'Just covering myself, that's all. Why are you in such a hurry to get married anyway? Most of the souls I have in Hell belong to those who committed their crimes as a direct result of being married.'

'You wouldn't understand. It has to do with love

and commitment – words that mean nothing to you.'

The Devil blew his nose into his hand and flicked it off onto Rosa's wall. The paint sizzled and blistered.

'Then why make a deal with me?' the Devil asked with a malicious smile. 'You know, I've done a lot of things during the millennia but I've never got married. I've been thinking for a few centuries now that maybe I need a companion. Someone I can personally torment, instead of the usual souls that I leave to the pleasure of my demon minions. And I need a son, or maybe a daughter would be better . . . If' – here the Devil pointed at the ceiling – 'can do it, then so can I. Maybe a boy *and* a girl would be best. Then, between the three of us, there would be three times the wars, three times the horrors, three times the disease . . .'

Rosa's blood turned to Antarctic whispers in her veins. 'I have Tod,' she whispered. 'You promised me.'

The Devil smiled as he stood up. 'I know . . . but can you trust me?'

And so saying – *peouff!* – he vanished. Rosa crept under her duvet and pulled it up over her head, shivering until she fell asleep, exhausted.

The next day Rosa woke up with a splitting headache and a memory of the most vivid dream she'd ever had. Imagine dreaming about signing a contract with the Devil! But then she saw her wall and her carpet and her heart missed a beat.

'I must have done that – somehow – and then dreamed about the Devil doing it,' Rosa whispered to herself. She could think of no other explanation.

It was the only explanation that fitted the facts.

But when Rosa next got to college, Tod had eyes for no one but her. He was even oblivious to Jeanette's more obvious charms. Almost six months of dinner dates and hand-in-hand walks in the park and deep, meaningful kisses followed. There was only one small fly in Rosa's anti-wrinkle face cream. Why had Tod never, ever tried to make love to her? One late afternoon in St James's Park, while embarrassed almost to the point of self-combustion, Rosa had stuttered her way through the question. Tod turned to her and smiled, saying, 'I can wait.' But Rosa didn't want to wait any longer. She'd never had sex before but she loved Tod so much and knew she always would, so for the first time she wanted to share her body. In fact, she longed to. Rosa decided that on their very next date, she would tell him so. She smiled at how surprised and thrilled Tod would be. But Tod's surprise came first.

That night, in Rosa's local Italian restaurant, Tod said, 'Rosa, will you marry me?'

When Rosa's jaw fell inelegantly open, Tod rushed on, 'Just hear me out. I know we've only been going out for less than a year, but I've never been so sure of anything in my life. We were meant to be together. I can't imagine my life without you. I don't want to imagine my life without you. So please, please say yes.'

Rosa could hardly speak – but somehow she managed. 'Yes, yes, a million, trillion times yes.'

Their kiss after that lasted at least a minute. Tod's lips on hers were so soft and his tongue against hers felt so hot. It was magical. Lost in that kiss, Rosa only slowly became aware of the applause echoing all around her from the other diners. She pulled away, her face hot enough for the chef in the kitchen to cook upon. Tod grinned at her, not the slightest bit bothered by their audience.

'Tod, d'you . . . would you like to spend the night at my flat?' Rosa whispered.

Tod shook his head. 'I want our wedding night to be . . . unforgettable. I can wait.'

'Then I wish we could get married right now,' Rosa admitted.

Tod smiled and took one of Rosa's hands in both of his. Raising it to his lips, he kissed it, never taking his eyes off her. 'I can wait,' he repeated. 'And believe me, it'll be worth it.'

It was only when Rosa got home that night and lay in bed, hugging her arms around her, that she realized that not once, not one single time had Tod told her he loved her.

Men find it hard to say these things, she told herself. *Besides, he must love me, otherwise why would he want to marry me?*

The strange dream about the Devil and his contract was forgotten.

Three months later Tod and Rosa were married. Tod simply didn't want to wait any longer. Tod's parents were both dead and had left him a not inconsiderable amount of money, plus a house which he decided to sell. Not that Rosa cared about that. Tod was enough for her. But the rest was a wonderful bonus. Rosa couldn't imagine how she could possibly be happier.

The wedding was a small affair. Close family and a few friends from school and the MBA course only. There was to be no honeymoon.

'Neither of us can afford the time away from work,' Tod pointed out. 'But soon, I promise.'

Tod had just started a new job, plus he was just beginning to be active in local politics, so he was very busy, and Rosa couldn't go away in the middle of a school term. Besides, Tod was ambitious. He told anyone who cared to listen that he'd be Prime Minister one day. So no honeymoon – but Rosa didn't mind. Tod was hers now. What else did she need? After the wedding Tod took Rosa back to their new home, a large, detached house in suburbia.

'What d'you think?' asked Tod as they got out of his car and stood in front of it.

Rosa didn't know what to say, or think. The house was amazing – incredibly spacious and double-fronted with a separate double garage. It was perfect, as if Tod had reached into her head and plucked out her dream house. A perfect house for the start of her perfect life.

'I know you wanted to see it before I bought it but I wanted it to be a wedding present.' Tod smiled. 'D'you like it?'

'Tod, I . . . I love it.' Rosa sprang at Tod and hugged him, tears in her eyes.

'You're halfway there, but hop into my arms and I'll carry you over the threshold,' he teased.

Rosa happily did as directed, gazing into Tod's eyes, her arm around his shoulders. No one in the world could be happier, or luckier. The front door had barely shut behind them when the smell hit Rosa like a body blow. It made her gag and put her hand to her mouth. She recognized the smell at once.

It was the smell of the Devil.

'Tod . . . Tod, what . . . ?' Rosa looked up at her husband.

His face was the same, in that the features hadn't changed, but his eyes – his pupils and irises – were deep blood red.

'Is something wrong?' Tod asked, still carrying his wife.

'You . . .'

Tod laughed, his face changing with each passing second to reflect the image in Rosa's worst nightmare.

'Welcome to Hell, my darling,' he said. 'Welcome to Hell.'

6

Rosa screamed as Tod roared with laughter, but I could hardly hear them. The volume was being turned down on Miss Wells's life. The film of my teacher's fate burned a furious white in my head, starting with her eyes and eating its way outwards until there was nothing left but an eerie silence. A silence of nothing and nowhere and no one.

'Oh my God!' The words slipped from me in a rush as I stared at her. Even now I could see the skin-crawling, blood-freezing, total terror that had been not just on her face but inhabiting every cell of her body.

'Kyle, what's wrong?' Miss Wells's hand moved forward to take hold of mine.

'For God's sake, don't.' Horrified, I leaped back, away from her.

Miss Wells looked up at me, her eyes glazing over.

'I'm sorry, Miss Wells. It's not you. I'm just a bit . . . a bit edgy.' It was meant to be a real apology but the words came out sharp and jagged as broken glass.

I was still trying to figure out what I'd just seen.

What made it worse was that I knew Miss Wells had just started an MBA course. Was I just hallucinating? Making up bits of my teacher's life from the few fragments I already knew?

'Miss Wells, is there someone on your MBA course called Tod?'

'How on earth did you know that?' Miss Wells's cheeks flamed cherry-red. Her gaze briefly fell away from mine for just long enough to reinforce the truth.

But so what? OK, so there was someone called Tod on Miss Wells's course. That didn't mean anything. I must've heard her talking about this Tod guy and just added him to the hallucination I'd had about my teacher. OK, as a theory, maybe it was just a bit anorexic but it was all I had. And with a giant shove it might've explained about Miss Wells, but certainly not my dream about Steve. No way would Steve join the army. And even if he did, that didn't mean he was going to end up the way I saw him. Where was all this coming from?

Maybe I was letting my thoughts flit like humming-birds so that I wouldn't have to focus on the things that were really upsetting me, like the crash and my friends and the others in this carriage strewn around me like so much litter. But these images, these night-mares couldn't be real. Especially the one about Miss Wells married to . . . to . . . I didn't even want to think the word. I wasn't superstitious, or particularly religious, and yet what I'd seen had scared the bloody hell out of me.

'Miss Wells, I'll go and see if there are any paramedics further down the train,' I said.

I had to get away, escape the images of my friends and my teacher wrecked and racked with pain. Maybe the emergency services were further down the train and working their way towards us.

The rainwater was beginning to pool beneath my feet. The helicopter above sounded slightly louder. I looked up as the chopper started to descend. A man wearing a black helmet and orange overalls was positioned at the side of the air ambulance, ready to be winched down. Frantically I waved my hands above my head. Even through the driving rain, I saw him give me a thumbs-up. It was one of the best sights I'd ever seen in my entire life. In a few minutes we'd all be out of here. We'd all be *saved*.

Grinning like an idiot, I wiped the rain from my eyes and watched euphorically as the paramedic started to descend. The wind was howling outside but it didn't matter. I knew that we were going to make it. We were going to be rescued. He was now dangling slightly below the body of the chopper. But before he could be winched lower, the helicopter became a kite, blown sideways by the gale-force winds. It dipped left, then tipped to the right. The cable holding the paramedic began to twist in the wind. He kicked out desperately, trying to stop himself from becoming tangled in the cable lowering him to the train. Suddenly the helicopter dropped at least a metre, maybe two. The thing was, it fell faster than the man below it. His head slammed into the underside of the chopper.

And he stopped kicking. His head was bent forward like he'd nodded off. Was that a trickle of red I saw run down from one nostril? The rain snatched it away before I could be absolutely sure. I glimpsed another face inside the helicopter before the dangling paramedic was haltingly winched back up. The chopper was still rocking dangerously. Arms shot out from inside to pull the paramedic in and out of sight. Was he badly hurt? He'd certainly been knocked unconscious. What would happen now? They'd have to send someone else down. But as I watched, the chopper began to rise slowly, fighting against the wind all the time. Then it veered to the left before flying away from the train.

'No!' I shouted after them. '*Don't leave us.*'

But I was shouting into the wind and the rain. I doubt if my voice even left the carriage.

'No . . .' I whispered. I watched the chopper until it was no more than a dot in the sky. The stinging rain ran into my eyes, but I didn't close them until it was completely out of sight. I was still on the train and there was no rescue in sight. Was this it then?

No! I couldn't think like that. I was still alive. There was still hope. If the paramedics couldn't use an air ambulance to get to us, then maybe they'd work their way through the train from the back like I'd originally thought. Stepping over some debris, I glanced down to find Joe conscious and looking straight at me.

'*Kyle . . .*' The mysterious voice rang in my head like some form of mental torture.

Leave me alone. Please, just leave me alone! The words were now a shout inside my mind.

'*Kyle . . .*'

'Joe, did you . . . ?' No. It wasn't Joe who'd just spoken. The timbre of his voice was higher, lighter. I was sure of it. 'Joe, are you OK? Let's try and get you free.'

'It hurts.'

'I know.' I nodded. 'Can you lever yourself upwards while I try and work your leg loose?'

Joe raised his upper body by pushing against the side of the chair in which he was tangled. As gently as I could, I tried to disentangle his twisted leg from the metal surrounding it, but the moment I touched it, he howled with agony. I let go like it was red hot. Beads of sweat glistened on Joe's forehead and above his top lip.

'Oh, hell! I'm sorry,' I said at once. 'I'm so sorry.'

'It's OK . . .' Joe said, his voice getting lower and slower.

'Joe? Are you OK?'

'Kyle, promise you'll do . . . something . . .' Joe struggled to get the words out. 'Promise you'll tell Jon—'

'I'm not telling your brother anything,' I interrupted with more force than I'd intended. 'When we get out of here, you can tell him yourself.'

'Tell Jon I'm sorry,' Joe continued, talking over me.

He slowly fell back to his original position, the effort of keeping himself upright clearly too much.

'Sorry for what?' I asked.

'For . . . for hating . . . him . . .' Joe's voice now trailed off altogether.

Hating him? What was Joe on about? OK, so they didn't get on, but surely hate was too strong a word to describe their relationship?

'Kyle, where are you? I need to see you.'

There it was again, that chilling voice, quiet and insistent and ringing straight through me as well as all around me. Each word was like a tiny shard of ice scraping down my spine. The feeling was so real, so tangible, that my hand involuntarily snaked towards my back, rubbing up and down my mid-spine as I twisted my head this way, then that. How I longed to get out of there, to be anywhere but where I was.

'Kyle . . .' Joe breathed.

'Kyle, where are you . . . ?'

I squatted down beside Joe. 'Don't worry, Joe. I'll tell Jon if I need to, if I have to. I promise. But we'll get out of this.'

Joe didn't reply but he didn't look terribly convinced. When I remembered how the chopper had deserted us, I couldn't blame him. Was it going to come back? Now that it had gone, the rain had lessened and the wind was dying down. Joe carried on looking at me, not saying another word, not even blinking. But that was OK because I was blinking enough for both of us, my eyelids moving in time to my rapidly increasing heartbeat. And each time I blinked, Joe's face changed. Subtle changes. More stubble above his top lip. Slightly longer hair. His face was filling out so slowly that it was only because I had his true image behind it that I could tell. It was disconcerting. Different, almost transparent, images of Joe were superimposed on the real one. And then the images stopped. Joe's image was solid, more instantly recognizable than Steve's had been. Joe was older but not by much – a couple of years at most. One blink later, and all at once Joe wasn't in the train any more. And neither was I.

7

Joe's Nightmare

Muffled footsteps sounded in the darkened bedroom. Dim torchlight danced eerily across the walls. The footsteps slowed as they approached the bed. Carefully, silently, the torch was placed on the bedside table. A brilliant flash of metal glinted in the torchlight. The glare of a knife blade ... And as the blade flashed downwards, it seemed in the dim light to be winking. Winking. Winking ...

'Of course not! To tell the truth, I feel kind of sorry for him. It would've been better for him if he'd died . . .'

At first I thought I was still dreaming, but then I realized that the voice was outside my head – for once – not inside. So I had to be awake. I turned my head in the direction of the woman's voice and opened my eyes. It was Nurse Holmes. She jumped back and stared at me. She'd obviously thought I was fast asleep. She was ancient – forty-something at least – with brown hair highlighted with streaks of brassy blonde and swept back into such a severe ponytail that it pulled her eyelids out towards her ears.

'I just came in to make sure you were all right.' Nurse Holmes's voice was steady but her lips were a thin slash across her face. 'Can I get you anything?'

I shook my head. She left the room without a backward glance. I closed my eyes wearily and was instantly asleep again. My nightmare washed me away like a tidal wave.

A brilliant flash of metal glinted in the torchlight. The glare of a knife blade . . . And as the blade flashed downwards, it seemed in the dim light to be winking. Winking. Winking . . . Arms came up to ward off the flashes of light, but it did no good. The flashes just grew harder and faster. HARDER AND FASTER . . . HARDER AND FASTER . . .

When I woke up this morning, my left arm had been taken. I knew it was no longer there because it hurt so much. My left shoulder roared with pain. I'd only experienced pain like it once before – when they took my right arm. That was just under (just over?) a day ago. (A week ago?) In this place I've lost all track of time. But this place is all I have.

Because I can't remember . . .

What's wrong with me? Why did they take both my arms? I don't know. My mind's an empty box. I want to remember. I really do. I get the feeling the doctors don't believe me when I say that, but it's the truth. It's just that, every time I try to force myself to remember what happened, what brought me here, the memory dances away from me like a shadow in a darkened room. Every morning I wake up and the memories are *almost* there. But when I reach out for them, they slip away, elusive, like water running through the cracks in my mind.

My name is Jonathan, Jon for short, and I'm sixteen, almost seventeen. Just remembering that much leaves me exhausted. I turn my head from left to right, looking around. I'm in hospital. I've been in hospital for a long time – only I can't remember why. I can't remember seeing this room before either. Have I been moved? If so, from where?

It's a small room, with light-coloured walls and a door to my left, but apart from the bed I lie on (I assume it's a bed), there is nothing else in it. The only light comes in through the small, frosted pane in the door.

Remember, Jon. Remember.

The door to my room slid open. I waited a few moments before turning my head. In spite of the pain, I had to be careful. I couldn't show anyone just how terrified I was. And how lonely. I looked at the nurse who stood by the door. His eyes were chips of blue ice. He didn't like me, that was obvious. But why?

'I'm Nurse Jennings,' the man said, looking away.

I wanted to ask about my arms, but my voice refused to work. And the nurse still refused to look at me.

'I've come to give you your medication,' he continued. 'I'm going to roll you over onto your side so that I can give you an injection in your thigh. Doctor Jacobs will be coming to see you soon. She's a psychiatrist. Just a moment.'

Nurse Jennings went out of the room, only to return moments later with the elderly nurse who'd checked on me during the night. Her expression was hostile, which she was trying and failing to hide behind a mask of professional detachment.

'Joseph Forman, number J42935,' the elderly nurse said.

'Joseph Forman, J42935,' Nurse Jennings repeated.

I shook my head. That wasn't right. My name was Jonathan, not Joseph. They'd got the wrong name.

The elderly nurse scooted out of the room without another word. Nurse Jennings rolled me over and jabbed me in the thigh. It should've hurt, but it didn't. I couldn't feel a thing. Nurse Jennings turned me onto my back. I smiled at him. I wanted so much for him and all the other nurses to like me. Being so alone was hell.

'Keep smiling,' Nurse Jennings said, straightening up. 'It won't do you any good. You won't pull the wool over Doctor Jacobs's eyes. And I'll tell you something else—'

'Thank you, Nurse Jennings. That will be all.'

'Oh, Doctor Jacobs, I was . . . I was just . . .' Nurse Jennings trailed off.

Nurse Jennings and Dr Jacobs stood watching each other for countless silent seconds. I gave up trying to smile. It didn't feel right anyway. Nurse Jennings left the room without another word. Dr Jacobs slid the door shut and walked over to me. My head began to feel fuzzy, muffled, like it was being stuffed with cotton wool. And heavy. So very heavy.

'That's it, Joe. You go to sleep. It's the best thing for you.' Dr Jacobs's voice came from long ago and far away.

It's Jon, not Joe. I wanted to tell her that, but I couldn't open my mouth. I fought against falling asleep. I *couldn't* fall asleep. That was when the nightmares came . . . But it was no good. I couldn't keep my eyes open. Moments later I was washed away again.

HARDER AND FASTER . . . His legs kicked off the bedcovers, kicked up towards the glinting and winking. The flashes of light moved up and down, up and down – striking at his arms, his legs. He twisted and writhed . . .

I opened my eyes slowly. The room was dim with evening light. And then the pain started. My knees were on fire. I knew what that meant. They'd taken more of me. My legs below the knee were gone. I bit down on my bottom lip until my mouth filled with blood. My whole body shook with pain and dread. Whimpering noises burst through my lips even though they were still clamped shut. I couldn't help it. Scalding tears burned my eyes. If only the pain would stop. If only . . .

The door to my room slid open. Dr Jacobs entered.

'Good! You're awake.' She smiled. Then she saw the tears on my face.

'D-Doctor Jacobs, please, *please* don't take any more of me,' I pleaded. 'I didn't say anything when my arms were taken but you shouldn't have cut off my legs as well. I didn't deserve that.'

Dr Jacobs frowned deeply. 'There's nothing wrong with your arms or your legs. Look for yourself. You still have limbs. We haven't done anything to them.'

'*Don't take any more of me!*' I shouted at her. 'You all skirt around me and whisper about me. You want to drive me crazy. But I won't let you do it. D'you hear? You're the ones who are crazy. This isn't a proper hospital. It can't be. You just wait till my mum comes to see me. I want to leave this place. I need to leave—'

'Joe—'

'*I want to leave. Now!*' I yelled. '*Now! Now! Now!*'

A nurse ran into the room.

'Get me fifty milligrams of pethidine,' Dr Jacobs commanded.

The nurse dashed out again.

'Now then, Joseph—' the doctor began.

'Stop calling me that. My name is Jonathan. *Jonathan.* I know what you're doing. You drug me until I'm senseless and then you cut off my limbs one by one . . .' Unbidden, unwelcome tears streamed from my eyes. Snot ran from my nose, but I couldn't wipe it away. The pain in my knees was easing slightly now, but what did that matter? I'd lost more of myself. I'd cried in private for my arms. But to take my legs as well . . .

Dr Jacobs walked over to me and threw back the bedcovers. 'Look! There are your arms, your legs . . .'

I glanced down in spite of the fact that I knew she was lying. My legs below my knees and both my arms weren't there – I knew they wouldn't be.

The nurse came back carrying a small tray. Dr Jacobs picked up the hypodermic syringe from the tray and immediately injected it into the top of my thigh. Within seconds my head was fuzzy again. The doctor handed over the needle to the nurse, who left the room at once. Nobody lingered around me. Except maybe Dr Jacobs. She laid a cool hand on one of my thighs.

'Joe, can you feel that?' she asked. Her frown was so deep it cut parallel grooves like train-track lines between her eyebrows.

'My thighs are still there,' I sniffed, impatient with this game the doctor was playing. 'It's the rest of me I'm talking about.'

I swallowed hard. *Come on, Jonathan, control yourself. Don't let them mess with your head. Don't let them make you cry. Don't let them.*

Dr Jacobs just shook her head slowly.

'Can I have some water, please?' I whispered. It was a question I'd given up asking any of the others. They either looked at me with a loathing that dazzled so much, I had to look away, or else they told me to get it for myself – or both.

The doctor picked up the plastic tumbler beside the

bed, filled it and held it out to me. I just looked at her. She pulled a tissue out of the box on my bedside table and wiped my eyes and nose. Frowning, she bent over me and placed the tumbler to my mouth. I drank thirstily, while sniffing inaudibly at the scent of Dr Jacobs's flowery perfume. I would've drunk the whole glass of water but Dr Jacobs removed the tumbler before I'd finished. I licked my lips slowly. My tears slowed. The pain in my knees was reduced to a dull throb.

'Doctor Jacobs, please don't let them take any more of me,' I begged softly. 'Please . . .'

I wanted to grab her arm, hold it and not let go until she promised. I tried to raise my arm, until I remembered that there was nothing there any more. The doctor regarded me, shaking her head again. I wondered at her strange expression. It was a mixture of pity and something else that I couldn't quite make out. There was a knock at the door.

'Joe, you have to go for an X-ray now. I'll see you when you get back,' Dr Jacobs said.

'I'm not going anywhere,' I said, turning away.

But they knew how to get round that. Two nurses I'd never seen before lifted me up against my will and put me in a wheelchair. Then a porter appeared and wheeled the chair along the hospital corridor.

'Why did you do it?' the porter asked suddenly.

'Do what?' I asked slowly.

'Do what? Are you serious? You . . . you . . .' The porter spluttered and coughed as his words crashed into each other in their haste to be heard. I tilted my head back to look at him. The porter clamped his mouth shut when he realized how ridiculous he sounded. I too kept quiet. I hadn't been trying to wind him up or goad him. I genuinely didn't know. *I couldn't remember.* As he pushed me along, I struggled to keep my eyes open as the painkiller took over. I failed.

The flashes of light moved up and down, up and down – striking at his arms, his legs. He twisted and writhed. His legs kicked out, kicked hard – but it didn't do any good . . .

When I awoke, I was back in my bed, lying propped up on three or four pillows – and the rest of my legs had been taken. My whole body was numb. I lay perfectly still, staring up at the ceiling until Nurse Holmes walked into my room, a food tray in her hand. Nurse Holmes didn't like me. But then, no one really liked me. It'd always been that way. If I could only remember why . . .

'I suppose there's no point in asking you to feed yourself.' Nurse Holmes's lips curled with contempt.

I didn't bother to answer. We both knew I had no chance of feeding myself. My arms had been taken. Why did she have to be so cruel?

'What is it?' I asked, turning my head slightly to look at the tray in her hands.

'Mushroom soup and lamb casserole,' she replied, putting my tray down on the wheelie table at the foot of my bed. She pushed the table further up over my bed until it was nearly at my chest.

I didn't like meat but I was starving. And I had to eat. I had to rebuild my strength. The sooner I was strong again, the sooner Mum would take me home. I'd be back with Mum and my brother, Joseph, and everything would be—

I had a brother called Joseph.

At last I'd remembered something else about myself. And that explained why they kept getting my name wrong. They were confusing me with my brother. I closed my eyes, trying to conjure up his face. I couldn't remember anything about him. Was he older or younger? Did I have any other brothers or sisters? Lots of questions. No answers.

Nurse Holmes took the plastic cover off the soup and removed the plate-warmer from over the casserole. She turned to me.

'You might have some people fooled with this act of yours, but I'm not one of them,' she hissed. 'You can feed yourself or starve.'

And with that she strode out of the room. I lay there, smelling the lamb and the soup. I had no legs to push myself up with. No arms to feed myself. I was so hungry, the smell was making me feel sick. I closed my eyes and willed myself not to mind about the hunger so much. I had to think of something else. To take my mind off my stomach, I concentrated on my heartbeat. It beat more slowly than before they'd taken away my limbs.

What did I look like?

No . . . I didn't want to see myself as I was now. I wouldn't be able to bear it. I'd survive as long as I couldn't see myself.

Think of something else, Jon.

Although I concentrated on the slow beat of my heart, the rumble of my stomach was louder. I decided to go to sleep. To sleep for as long as possible. After all, what else was there for me to do? If only I could get through this dread of closing my eyes. To stay awake meant agonizing over my lost limbs and the gnawing pains in my empty stomach.

But to sleep . . .

I closed my eyes. So tired. I'd sleep. I should be safe now. What else could they take? And maybe this time the nightmare wouldn't come.

His legs kicked out, kicked hard – but it didn't do any good. He turned towards the light. And I saw his face for the first time. Only it wasn't his face. It was my face. His body – my face . . .

'Joe? Joe, can you hear me?'

I opened my eyes slowly. It was Dr Jacobs. She sat on the bed and smiled and asked me all kinds of inane questions about how I was feeling and did I hurt anywhere. I gave her what answers I could but all the time I was trying to drive my nightmare out of my head. It wouldn't budge.

Dr Jacobs asked, 'Joe, d'you remember what happened two weeks ago? D'you remember the reason you were brought to this hospital?'

I shook my head. 'My name is Jonathan, Jon for short. And no, I don't remember. Why won't anyone tell me?'

'Do you really want to know?' the doctor asked softly.

'Yes, I do. I want to know why everyone here hates me so much. I want to know why you've stolen my legs and my arms. I need to know . . .'

There was a long pause. The vertical frown lines between Dr Jacobs's eyebrows deepened as she battled to make up her mind about something. At last her expression cleared. This was it. Now I would find out why I was here. I needed to remember. The truth was only moments away.

'I'm going to take a chance,' Dr Jacobs said at last. 'I think you should know what happened – what you did. I think you're ready. And it will help you.'

And very slowly, very carefully, she told me. 'Joe, you had a brother called Jonathan. He was your identical twin brother. But you weren't close. In fact, according to your mum, that's an understatement . . .'

And she carried on. I heard her words but they bounced off me until there were too many of them to bounce off, and then they sank into my flesh like razor-sharp barbs – and still she spoke. My body shook with horror, and the more I shook, the more my body hurt.

And still Dr Jacobs spoke. I wanted to yell, to howl and not stop. It was all lies. It had to be lies. I would never, *could* never, do that – the mindless, horrific thing she spoke of. I wouldn't do that to anyone, let alone my own twin brother . . .

'No . . .' I whispered. 'No, it's not true.'

I had to do something to drown out her words. My shoulders started to hurt. My hips started to hurt. I covered my ears with my hands and sat up, drawing up my legs.

'No! No! No!' I battered at the doctor with my fists. 'Liar . . . Liar . . .'

All at once, the room filled with people. I was pushed back onto the bed. I battered at them all. Battered at them with my fists and kicked at them with my feet until the room swallowed me up like a whirlpool. Dr Jacobs and the others faded to nothing. There was just me and my brother left in the whole, wide world. Jon lay there, looking up at me, his eyes burning into mine. His blood drenched the bed sheets. It dripped down from the knife in my hand – dripdripdrip . . . He whispered my name over and over before he died. *Joe . . . Joe . . .*

When I awoke this morning, they'd taken my whole body. There's nothing left of me now except my brain in my head, sitting here in the centre of this pillow. I don't know how they're keeping me alive – I don't care. I just wish someone would tell me what I did to deserve this. I really do want to know. What did I do?

I wish . . . how I wish I could remember. All I know for certain is that I'm sixteen, almost seventeen, and my name is Jonathan, Jon for short.

8

A yell tore me away from Joe's mind and back to the train. I couldn't catch my breath. As bad as the nightmares of Miss Wells and Steve had been, this one was worse. Joe's nightmare had been so much more . . . up close and personal.

Someone help me . . . Please, someone help me, I whispered.

What did all this mean? Was I in Hell? Maybe Hell for me would be living through the worst nightmares of all my friends, losing more and more of myself in them until I didn't know where my friends ended and I began any more. And the worst thing of all? I still had my own nightmare to deal with, which was far worse – because mine was true. Joe's wasn't. His nightmare couldn't be real because he was in front of me, his eyes now closed.

'Kyle . . .'

There it was again, that awful, faint voice. Like a cliché from a horror film. The only difference was, it was real – and terrifying, like the growl of some prowling, predatory animal. It was exactly like being hunted. I could no longer dismiss the voice as just imagination.

Why didn't someone do something to get us out of here?

I checked out the upturned carriage seats. Maybe I could use the one which had popped its bolts as a boost to work my way up to the broken window above. If I could hoist myself up and out, I'd *escape*. I'd be off this train. The thought was so tantalizing, my foot was already on the upturned seat. The train juddered and slipped a few centimetres, the sound of crunching metal stinging my ears. I removed my foot immediately.

'I wasn't going to – not really,' I whispered in supplication. 'Not really. I wouldn't leave my friends. Please don't fall.'

Was I praying to God or the train? I didn't even know any more.

Footsteps crunched on broken glass behind me. I spun round. It was a girl, not much older than me. Her pale face was lean, with almond-shaped brown eyes and a wide, generous mouth. Her hair hung loose around her shoulders and was the colour of conkers, streaked with red lines so bright and vivid they looked like thin rivulets of blood. She wore black jeans and, underneath her long, black, leather coat, a white T-shirt which read in dark letters:

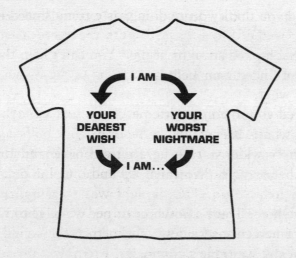

I AM

YOUR DEAREST WISH

YOUR WORST NIGHTMARE

I AM...

She was the best thing I'd ever seen.

'Oh, thank goodness.' The girl's voice trembled as she ran up to me, dodging around debris and people.

'You've come from the first carriage?' I grinned inanely. 'Am I glad to see you!'

In spite of the collision, there were people still alive ahead of us. *I wasn't alone.*

'I'm Rachel,' said the girl. 'Hurry! We have to get out of here.' She grabbed my hand and pulled me back towards the front carriage.

'Hang on . . .' I tried to slow down but Rachel kept tugging me after her. She stepped over Elena, who was lying on her side, as if she were no more significant than a blade of grass. It was when she tried to do the same to Roberta that I decided that crap wasn't cute.

I pulled away, determined not to take another step.

'What d'you think you're doing? My friends need our help.'

Rachel looked straight at me. 'You can't help them now. But I need your help.'

'For what?'

'I need you to come with me.'

'For what?' I repeated.

Rachel's wide, staring gaze darted back and forth along the carriage. 'We can't stay here. Come on. We have to go.'

'Go where? There's nowhere to go. We have to wait for the emergency services.'

'We can't wait. He's coming.'

'Who's coming?'

'We have to hide.' Rachel's eyes were screaming at me.

A strange scraping sound drew my attention to the end of the carriage. But just as I turned my head, Rachel hissed, 'Down!'

She crouched, yanking me down after her.

'This is ridiculous,' I said, trying to pull away and stand up. 'I don't even know you. What's going on?'

Rachel pulled me back down, almost dislocating my shoulder in the process. 'I'm the only one who can help you. If *he* finds you, all you'll get is pain – pain like you've never even imagined before.'

'If *who* finds me?' I asked.

'Is this girl a friend of yours?' hissed Rachel, indicating Robby at her feet.

I nodded, wishing she'd give me a straight answer to at least one of my questions.

'What's her name?' she whispered.

'Roberta, but we all call her Robby,' I replied, also whispering though I had no idea why.

'Good. She'll do. This'll be much easier if it's someone you know,' said Rachel. 'We can hide inside her mind. He won't find us there.'

'We can do *what*?' I wasn't sure I'd heard right.

'You've already done it,' Rachel told me stonily. 'I know you've done it at least once. I can see it in your eyes. And each time you leap you get better at it. You get in closer and stay for longer, but this time I want you to take me with you.'

I stared at her. How on earth did she know what had been happening to me? None of it made sense. I wanted to deny it, to shout at her, 'I don't know what you're talking about?'

But it would've been a lie and we both knew it.

'Hurry up,' said Rachel.

What was I supposed to do? I looked from Rachel to Roberta. A glance was all it took. I sensed the tide of fear sweeping through Roberta's unconscious mind, fear which had nothing to do with the train, and let myself get washed away by it. Only this time I didn't make the journey alone. I sensed rather than saw that Rachel was somewhere near by. I felt her presence. I didn't want to think too much about what was happening – or, maybe more to the point, how and why. I was afraid if I analysed what I was doing too closely, I'd fall away from Roberta's world but be unable to find my way back to my own.

And even if I could do this, even if all this was real – what gave me the right to invade my friends' heads like this? Like a dimmer switch being turned up, I could feel as Roberta felt, see as she saw. And it was appalling. I instantly tried to think of the train, to pull back, but I couldn't. Robby wasn't on the train. She wasn't anywhere near it. She was somewhere far, far worse.

9

Roberta's Nightmare

I tried not to panic, I really did. But the rain was only minutes away, I could smell it. I walked faster, then my walk broke into a run. The dying sunlight glittered through the trees like a tinkling laugh, a laugh directed at me and the futility of trying to escape the rain. The sky was more blue than white but experience had taught me that that meant nothing. Here I was in a nameless forest with no cover in sight, and if I didn't find shelter soon, I would die.

And I didn't want to die.

I didn't have much – like thousands (or were there still millions?) of other people left in this godforsaken country, I was used to living hand to mouth, day to day. Everything I had in the world I carried in the bag on my back and it contained nothing I wasn't prepared to lose in a hurry. If I were to get caught in the rain, there would be no one to remember me, let alone mourn my passing. But I wasn't ready to give up yet.

So I ran, round gnarled trunks, over the concrete-hard ground, my head darting first here, then there, searching for some kind – *any* kind – of shelter. Ten minutes in the rain were enough. The rain was still full of the acids and pollutants created by the last civil war, a war with a new chemical weapon.

When my parents separated, my mum packed up and moved back here, to her home country. I wasn't sorry about the separation. Dad punctuated his sentences with his fists more often than not when talking to Mum. Over the years I grew to despise him and everything he stood for. I hated his belief that might was right. I hated the way he couldn't bear to see Mum happy, as if her happiness was something he couldn't control so it had to be knocked out of her. I'd lost count of the number of times over the years that I'd told Mum to leave him.

'But he's my husband . . . But how would we live . . . ? But you need a father . . .'

Not a father like that, I didn't. I swore when I was old enough to mean it for life that I'd never let any man treat me the way Dad treated Mum. I'd rather die first. Every time Dad hit her, I'd scream at him to stop. I'd cry just as hard as Mum. I'd feel every blow as if it was aimed at me. When I was old enough it would be me and Mum on one side, crying and hugging each other as he looked down at us. After that, Dad rarely hit Mum when I was around. But the moment I set foot through the door, I could always tell if something had happened. Dad thought Mum was telling tales, as he put it. He didn't understand that she didn't need to open her mouth.

I could always tell.

But then, when I was fourteen, he made the mistake of hitting Mum in front of me. And why did he hit her? Because she gave me a birthday card and the most beautiful necklace I'd ever seen. It was a single, exquisite pearl at the end of a delicate gold chain. And the card was signed, '*With all my love, Mum*'. Dad dug into his pocket and handed me a few notes. No card, no happy birthday. He'd obviously forgotten all about my birthday. And I made the mistake of ignoring him and hugging Mum and telling her how much I loved her present. Later that evening, over dinner, I wore my necklace and felt like a princess; the day was perfect. I kept smiling at Mum. I couldn't help it. I was so happy. Mum smiled back, just as happy as me.

'What the hell is this swill?' Dad shouted. 'I'm so sick of this . . . this dog food you keep giving me.' He picked up his dinner plate and threw it across the table.

And in that instant the mood around the table changed. I knew what was going to happen next. Dad jumped to his feet and moved round the table, hauling Mum out of her chair. Before I was even aware of what I was doing, I was there and in Dad's face.

'You lay one hand on her and I'm calling the police,' I warned him.

And I meant every word. And Dad knew I meant every word. I glared at him, making no attempt to hide the loathing I felt. He let go of Mum, who fell, half on, half off her chair. I was vaguely aware of her crying and trying to pull me away from Dad but I wasn't about to move. Dad stared at me, breathing just as hard as I was. And then, without warning, he hit me. Hard and fast and sharp as razors – he hit me.

I was down on the ground and my head was ringing and I had no idea how I'd got there. Mum was at my side in an instant, screaming words I couldn't hear at Dad. The ringing in my ears began to subside, but I still couldn't make out a word she was saying. Then I realized Mum was screaming at Dad in her home language, the language I understood and could even speak a little, though Mum and Dad wouldn't allow me to use it in the house. And all the time Mum screamed at Dad, Dad didn't say a word. The pitch of Mum's voice grew lower as she spoke, making her easier to understand, but she wasn't letting Dad off. In a voice brittle with sadness, she asked him what had happened to the man she fell in love with; where had he gone? Dad looked at her for countless seconds before he slammed out of the room, then out of the house.

He didn't come back for three days, and when he did, he tried to smile and joke with me as if nothing had happened. I swore then and there that no man would ever hurt me again and get away with it. Never ever. But that was enough for Mum. She waited until the school year ended and Dad was away at some conference or other for the week. She emptied their joint savings account, then we packed up and headed for Mum's home country. I was sorry I didn't get to say a proper goodbye to all my friends, but to be honest, it was worth it to get away from *him*.

We'd been in this country for a little over eighteen months when the civil war started. A war between those who wanted their own separatist state against those who insisted that the country shouldn't be divided. And the country was already so small, little bigger than a question mark on any world map. The war was brutal and bloody and the rest of the world just wasn't interested. But then the separatists got hold of chemical weapons and some lunatic actually used them. That's when the rest of the world started paying attention, but by then it was too late. Our rain had become lethal, and unlike people, the rain didn't discriminate. My mother had called it the Sad War; I thought the name apt. Some of the people I met on my travels were sad – remembering how things had once been. More people were unfriendly, belligerent even. I could understand that. In these times it was the only way to survive.

I felt a drop of rain on my cheek. A second or two and then the pain began, like a red-hot needle thrust into my skin.

Find shelter, Robby. Find something fast.

Another drop on the sleeve of my leather jacket. A tiny, perfectly round hole appeared in the material. My heart was screaming at me to get undercover. That's when I saw it – a light up ahead. I pelted for it, ignoring my aching legs, the pain in my ankles. I turned my face to the sky and sniffed. The rain was closer; the sky beyond the trees was rapidly turning to darker shades of grey. At last the light I'd seen revealed its source. It was a house, more like a cottage really, with a light on in one of the ground-floor windows. I didn't care about that. It was shelter. I would take my chances with the occupants. In the rain I had *no* chance.

I banged on the door, again and again. I felt a raindrop wet on my cheek. The pain arrived only a fraction of a second later. Another red-hot needle. I panicked, felt for the door handle and turned it. Thank God it was open. Another scalding raindrop fell on my forehead before I stumbled across the threshold. Kicking the door shut, I leaned against it, forcing myself to calm down. I was inside now. Safe?

'Hello? Is anyone home?' There was no answer.

'Hello?' I shouted again, looking around with tired curiosity. It wasn't particularly clean. It smelled musty, uncared for . . . but it was dry and that was all I cared about. I entered the closest room, the room with the light.

'Hello,' I tried again feebly. Maybe the house was empty. I hoped so. I wanted to be alone, to relax for the first time in weeks. The occupants were probably sheltering from the rain somewhere. I couldn't help but wish they got caught in it; then they would die and the house would be mine. The thought made me squirm inwardly with guilt but it didn't stop me from thinking it.

The room was quite large, its walls a dingy

yellow-brown. What light there was came from a fireplace and two candles on a battered, three-legged stool. Opposite the fireplace was a light-coloured settee, possibly once beige or maybe even yellow but now grubby and worn, with the stuffing appearing in odd places through the cushions. Still, it had to be more comfortable than the hardwood floor, so after taking off my backpack I sat down and continued to look around. The only other furniture was a tiny table beneath the one small window to my right. I leaned my head back and sighed softly. I was right. The settee was soft, the fire was warm and I was out of the rain. I closed my eyes gratefully.

Suddenly my head was yanked back and something sharp and cold pressed against my throat. Instantly I knew and felt that it was a knife – with a *very* sharp blade.

'Who the hell are you?'

I couldn't see the man behind me. I was too frightened to turn my head. Besides, the tiniest movement on my part and he would cut my throat, that much I did know. Hell! He might cut my throat anyway.

'Answer me,' the man demanded again. 'Who are you and what are you doing in my house?'

'I . . . my name's Rob . . . Robby. I'm fourteen . . . It started to rain. I came in for shelter. I'm . . . tired. I didn't mean to trespass . . .' The knife moved fractionally away from my neck.

'I want you out of my house . . . *now*,' the man said harshly.

'But . . . but it's raining,' I protested. 'I'll die if you send me out there. Can't I just stay until it's over?'

'The rain is your problem, not mine. And besides, it might last for a week or more. You're certainly not going to stay here that long.'

'It won't be for that long,' I argued eagerly. 'It's only going to last two days, then I'll be on my way.'

'I don't want you in my house for two minutes! And how d'you know it's only going to last for a couple of days?'

'My nose told me,' I replied reluctantly, feeling foolish. 'I can always tell when rain is coming and how long it's going to last.'

'Yeah, right.'

'It's true.'

'You can't stay here—'

'Please . . . please . . .' I begged, wishing I could turn my head to look at him. 'I won't be any trouble. I can cook, clean, chop wood . . .'

'In the rain?' he said scathingly.

'I won't be any trouble,' I argued. 'Please . . .'

Inside the room, the silence echoed around us. Outside I could hear the rain sheeting down now.

'Please,' I tried again.

'I'm going to move the knife away from your neck now, but one false move and you'll be dead before you can blink.' The tip of the knife was reapplied with force to my neck. 'D'you understand?'

'I get the point,' I replied.

The knife left my throat and I heard him move out

from behind the settee. Slowly, carefully, I raised one tentative finger to my throat. When I examined it I was chastened but not terribly surprised to see blood. I had a slight cut, and it hurt. Still, that was better than not feeling anything at all . . . ever again. I remained seated as the man moved to stand before me. I recoiled deeper into the settee at the sight of him. The candles cast strange, dark shadows over his face, but even in the strong sunlight I would have given this man a wide berth. He was tall, at least six feet, with dark hair flopping across his forehead, and he had hard, icy eyes. I guessed he was over thirty and under forty. His face was the meanest I'd seen in a long time, and it had nothing to do with the deep scar running from just below the corner of one eye and across his cheekbone. I glanced down at the knife, which he still held in his hand.

'What did you mean when you said your nose told you it was going to rain?' he demanded.

'I can smell it,' I said. I decided that with this man it would be prudent to keep my answers direct and to the point.

'How old did you say you were?'

'Fourteen,' I replied – too quickly.

His eyes narrowed. 'How old?'

'Seventeen,' I said reluctantly.

'I thought you didn't look fourteen. But isn't your voice a bit high for a seventeen-year-old?'

'I know.' I frowned. 'That's why I tell everyone I'm fourteen. I'm lucky though. My voice may not have broken yet but that's the only side-effect I've suffered from the chemical fallout. I've seen people who're a lot worse off than me.'

Shut up, Robby. You're rambling! Short, concise answers.

The man continued to scrutinize me. I shifted on the settee, suddenly aware of every lump and bump in the cushion under me. Wasn't he going to say anything? Why didn't he say anything?

'I've travelled a lot since my mother died,' I continued, more for the sake of saying something than for any other reason. 'I don't like to stay too long in one place—'

'You talk too much.'

He wasn't the first person to tell me that. But something in the way he said it sent ice crystals dancing through my veins and made me shut up immediately. That's my trouble, you see. I don't like silences and I always try to fill them. The man walked to the window, his eyes rarely leaving my face. I watched as he closed the inside wooden shutters.

'Now I won't get any more uninvited guests,' he said stonily, glaring at me.

'Er . . . what's your name?' I asked. 'I've told you mine.'

'What's it to you?' he snapped. 'Anyway, you won't be staying here long enough to make use of it.'

'I've got to call you something while I'm here,' I pointed out.

Besides, I knew the rain would last for five days, not

two, but I had sense enough to realize that if I told him the truth he'd want me to leave immediately. Two days under his roof he might tolerate; five was asking a bit too much. But once I'd been here two days, I could stretch it to another three.

'Carter,' he said suddenly.

'What? Your name is Carter?' I queried. 'Is that your first or last name?'

Carter strode across to where I was sitting, grabbed the top of my jacket and pulled me out of the settee towards him. 'Listen, Rob or Robby or whatever the hell your name is. Let's get a few things straight. If you want to stay here, you'll keep out of my way and you won't talk so much. I don't like a lot of questions. Get it?'

I nodded vigorously.

He released me and I slumped back onto the settee.

'Does that mean I can stay?' I asked immediately, straightening my clothes.

Carter's glare became even more penetrating. 'Only until the storm passes,' he said at last. 'But first let me see what's inside your backpack.'

'Why?'

'Damn it! Stop answering everything I say with a question.'

Without another word I reluctantly emptied my backpack out on the seat beside me. Some bunches of herbs and a pouch filled with nuts and berries fell out first, followed by a dented flask of fresh, uncontaminated water and lastly two books given to me by my mother: the Bible and a science-fiction novel.

'What are you looking for?' I frowned as Carter rifled through my belongings. 'If it's jewellery or weapons or alcohol, you're going to be disappointed.'

'I'm glad you don't carry weapons,' Carter said brusquely. 'Because I don't want to have to fight off some maniac in the middle of the night with a knife in his hand.'

'You're the one who tried to slice my neck – remember?' I said indignantly.

'I may still do it,' Carter said belligerently.

I shut up. What was the man's problem? I ran a nervous hand over my head, my hair so short as to be practically non-existent. After searching my bag a second time, Carter walked over to the table and sat down. He removed a small pot from the shelf behind him and, using a wooden spoon, began to eat.

'Aren't you going to offer me any?' I wheedled.

I couldn't believe he was going to sit there with me watching and not offer me a mouthful. He glared at me before silently turning back to his food, shoving another spoonful into his mouth. Casting a filthy look in his direction, I repacked my belongings, everything except the herbs, which I munched on slowly. I watched the steam rise from Carter's bowl. I hadn't eaten hot food in a long time.

'Oh, for goodness' sake!' he snarled, retrieving another small wooden bowl from the shelf. 'You can have some, but only because I'm tired of you staring at me.'

I almost ran to the table. This man was so tetchy, he'd probably change his mind before I'd tasted a morsel. Carter poured about four spoonfuls from his bowl into mine. I scrutinized the orange-greeny-brown puddle before me.

'Has this been regurgitated?'

'If you don't bloody want it, just pass it back.' Carter snatched at my bowl, only I got to it first.

'I didn't say I didn't want it,' I said. 'And I trust that this is just a taster. I mean, if this soup – is it soup? – is OK, will you give me some more?'

Carter stared at me, his expression hovering somewhere between thunderous and incredulous. Then, unexpectedly, he started laughing – a low, reluctant, rumbling sound.

'You have more goddamn nerve than any ten people I know,' he muttered. 'No, you can't have any more.'

'Can I have a spoon then?' I asked, after searching my side of the table for one. Carter took a spoon from the shelf behind him and slammed it down in front of me. 'Boy, you are turning out to be more trouble than you're worth.'

'My name is Robby, not Boy,' I said, picking up the spoon and tasting the puddle in my bowl. Instantly I began to retch. It was disgusting. 'What the hell is this?' I asked angrily.

'If you don't like it, just give it back,' Carter ordered.

'With pleasure!' I pushed the bowl away from me.

'I could make it better than that with one hand tied behind my back and one eye closed.'

'Well, tomorrow you'll get a chance to prove it,' Carter said silkily. 'If you stay here, you'll have to earn your keep. Tomorrow you'll get your chance to cook and clean.'

I looked around the dingy room. 'I couldn't do any worse than you.'

'Robby, you are *this* close' – Carter held his thumb and index finger tight together under my nose – 'to getting your arse kicked out into the rain.'

We watched each other for a few moments.

'Sorry,' I said. 'Sometimes I go a bit too far.'

'I'm surprised you've managed to live this long.' Carter shook his head, returning to the muck in front of him.

'So am I,' I admitted. I turned to stare at the wooden shutters covering the window, listening to the sound of the rain beyond.

'Why did you say that?'

I turned to find Carter watching me curiously. I shrugged. 'I travel a lot. I told you. I've almost been caught in the rain on more than one occasion.' Again we watched each other. 'I watched someone die in the rain once,' I continued quietly, looking away again. 'I was in a house full of people when it started – the only house for miles with a decent roof. A woman arrived . . . she'd been caught in it. She pleaded with us to let her in, but the man who owned the house bolted the door and stood guard over it with a knife in either hand. He wouldn't let anyone near it. She'd been out in the rain too long. I watched with five others through a side window. She kept banging on the door, screaming. The skin blistered on her face, her arms . . . Then it began to peel right off, dropping with the rain. I watched the rain burn, then wash the flesh off her. It rained for a whole day. When it stopped raining all that was left of her was sludge . . .'

'She shouldn't have been stupid enough to let herself get caught in it,' Carter said harshly, picking up my bowl to finish what I hadn't started.

I watched him, careful to keep any derogatory expression off my face. I remembered the woman's husband, safe inside with us, begging for her to be let in. When the woman's screams faded, so did the man's pleas. Finally he fell to his knees and sobbed. I had watched his wife die . . . I watched him survive. That's the way it worked.

I walked back to the worn-out settee and sat down. Picking up my herbs again, I started to munch. 'Is this where I sleep tonight?'

Carter glanced at me. 'You can sleep where you please. But I warn you, I'm a very light sleeper and I *always* sleep with a knife close by.'

'Is that how you got the scar on your face?'

Ignoring my flippant question, he continued, 'If you try anything, anything at all, I'll slit your throat first and ask questions later.'

'Were you born anti-social, or did the war do this to you?'

'If you had any sense,' Carter said curtly, 'you would cultivate the same attitude. Your age might've brought you some sympathy before, but now you're getting old, just like the rest of us. If you don't toughen up, kid, you're going to get trampled underfoot.'

'I can take care of myself,' I told him sternly. 'The last person who thought otherwise is now dead.'

'You don't look as though you could kill a fly – not that there are that many left in this country,' Carter said disdainfully.

One good thing to come out of the war? I wondered. Though the fish and frogs who had to live on flies might not agree with me. The animals alive nowadays had cultivated the same sixth sense as me when it came to the rain, and they always headed for shelter hours before it started. The chemicals in the atmosphere weren't supposed to kill any living creatures except humans, but maybe the animals knew more than the scientists. I watched Carter stand up and walk to the door.

'I can look after myself,' I repeated. 'I'm vindictive and vengeful. It helps me survive.'

Carter laughed in my face. 'And very, very young.' His expression hardened. 'So stay down here if you plan to get older.'

He left the room. I placed my backpack on the stained, grubby floor and stretched out on the settee, switching the knife I kept in my right boot to my left boot as I decided to lie on my right side. I liked to keep my knife close to hand. Carter was a morose pig, obviously unused to company, but he didn't *look* like a murderer. I tugged at my shirt. I longed to unstrap myself but decided it would be too dangerous. Instead I closed my eyes and tried to fall asleep.

'Wake up, damn it!'

'Ouch!' I exclaimed angrily after another hard punch to my arm.

'What about breakfast?' Carter demanded.

'What about it?' I repeated coolly, rubbing my upper arm.

'Earn your keep!' He walked away from me and opened the shutters. 'And once you've made the breakfast you can clean the house.'

'And what're you going to be doing while I work?' I asked, irritated.

'Reading your sci-fi novel. It's been a long time since I read a proper book.'

'That's not fair,' I replied.

'Tough. If you don't like it you can always leave. And if you don't do it you'll be leaving anyway.'

I looked out of the window at the rain. It flowed like mini waterfalls off the leaves of all the trees around. How clever of whoever it was to release into the air a chemical agent which was only activated when it rained. And how extremely clever to ensure that it only attacked human flesh.

'Well?' Carter asked when I didn't respond.

'Why d'you think the rain still only attacks people?'

I asked. 'Why would someone design a chemical to wipe us all out?'

Carter frowned at my question, which had obviously taken him by surprise. 'Maybe they didn't expect the chemicals to remain in the atmosphere for so long.'

'Or maybe they didn't care if they died as long as they could take their enemies with them,' I ventured.

'Hmm,' said Carter, but it was hard to tell whether he was in agreement or just acknowledging what I'd said.

'But that still doesn't explain why the—'

'Never mind the damn rain, what about breakfast?'

'Don't you have any thoughts on the subject?'

'None that I'm going to share with you.'

'What did you do before the war?' I asked curiously. 'You're pretty old so you must've worked at something before all this. Or were you unemployed? You seem well educated, in spite of your bad manners and worse habits . . .'

'All these attempts to get out of making the breakfast aren't working,' Carter said icily. 'And I'm not going to tell you again.'

'All right, all right,' I sighed, getting up. 'I'll cook but I'm not cleaning your bloody house. It was like this when I got here.'

I went into the kitchen and Carter followed me. It was cramped and smelled nose-twitchingly of old, burned food. A wood-burning stove sat self-consciously opposite two huge water tanks which were as tall as Carter, with a diameter of at least two-thirds of a metre each. These tanks had a gap of just under a metre between them, in which a chair had been placed. The kitchen was small enough as it was, without wasting space like that, I thought. The tanks should've been placed next to each other, touching. There were various cupboards, work surfaces covered with rotting bits of food and candle ends, and next to the stove a small sink. I pointed to the door on the other side of the stove.

'What's through there?' I asked.

'The toilet.'

'Where do you keep the food?' I looked askance at the cupboards. Did I really want food out of those dirty, disgusting things?

Carter studied me. 'Between the two water tanks,' he said at last. I frowned as he walked over, moved the chair and lifted the filthy, patchy lino to one side. There was a trapdoor totally flush with the floor.

'The cellar runs beneath most of the house. That's where I keep my food,' Carter said, his eyes burning into me. 'You can go down there and get some, but don't think of stealing anything because I'm going to check you and your bag before you leave.'

I walked across and peered down into the inky blackness that was the cellar.

'What about some light?' I asked.

Carter picked up a candle end and thrust it into my hand, then took a match out of one of his pockets and struck it against the wall before lighting the candle.

Without another word I went down into the cellar. I'd have to find a way of pocketing some bits of candle before I left. I kept a number of useful, useless objects in my pockets: two candle ends, matches wrapped in a tiny scrap of cellophane, a pack of well-used cards, pins, even plasters. They were all things that my mother had given me – and so far I'd never needed to use anything but the cards and the matches. I looked around. I was surrounded by box upon box, swallowed up by the darkness beyond the light from my candle. Before I left I'd also have to try and pocket some food. Carter obviously had plenty.

'Hurry up,' he called after me.

With a patient sigh, I began to search through the tins in the box nearest to me for something suitable to eat.

'Breakfast is served.' I entered the living room, a plate in either hand. Carter was standing by the window, staring out. I placed the steaming plates on the table. My hands can stand really hot things; it's the cold they don't like. We ate breakfast in silence, although I could tell that my host was impressed. Not only did he make appreciative noises as he ate the corned beef hash I'd prepared, he then licked the plate, slamming it back down on the table. There was no 'thank you', not even a 'that was good'.

'What *did* you do before the war?' I asked, annoyed. 'No, don't tell me. Let me guess . . . you wrote books on manners and etiquette.'

'That's not too far from the truth,' Carter said dryly. 'You can tidy up now,' he added quickly, as if regretting the admission.

'I'm not tidying anything – I told you that before.'

Carter smiled suddenly. 'Can you play chess?'

'Yes,' I said cautiously, thrown by the change of subject.

'We'll play chess instead then.' He shrugged. 'It's been a long time since I had an opponent other than myself.'

I could now see why the house was so dirty. The first two games lasted about twenty and thirty minutes respectively and I was thrashed both times. The third game lasted over an hour and I was still beaten, much to Carter's disgust.

'I thought you said you could play,' he said scathingly.

'I can play in that I know the rules. I never said I was a grand master.'

Carter snorted with derision at that.

'I'm no good at strategy games, I never have been,' I told him. In between playing, I made lunch. After the games I made dinner.

And so the first day passed. I asked Carter to show me around the house but he looked at me frostily and didn't deign to answer. When I pestered him further he did tell me that the room next to the living room was a half-empty storeroom, nothing more.

The next day we played yet more chess, then draughts, using the chess pieces as draughtsmen. I was actually better than him at that, much to his annoyed amazement.

'How come you're so good at draughts and so crap at chess?' he asked.

I smiled. 'Draughts is more impulsive. It suits me.'

'What a load of bull!'

'You explain it then,' I challenged.

He couldn't, so he started cheating. Every time I looked away, one of my pieces would mysteriously disappear from the board. When it grew dark we both read for a while. Then he went upstairs and I stayed downstairs. And so the second day passed.

During breakfast on the third day Carter was obviously annoyed. 'I thought you said the rain would only last two days,' he accused.

I sniffed audibly. 'Another two days of rain,' I said slowly. 'I'm sorry I got it wrong before but this time I'm right.'

'Hmm!' he replied sullenly. 'You'd better be.'

'How did you get that scar on your face?' I'd been dying to know since the first time I saw it.

His expression zigzagged faster than a lightning flash. 'You're too damned nosy.'

'Not nosy. Interested,' I corrected. 'I'm surprised anyone got close enough to do that to you. You obviously think I'm more deadly than I look because you carry at least two knives that I know about. That's why I'm interested.'

Carter dropped his fork, which clattered on his

plate. He stared out of the window, his expression sombre and brooding.

'A woman did it,' he said at last. 'A damned woman.'

'What did you do to make her scar you?' The question was out before I could stop myself.

Carter glared at me. 'I was stupid enough to marry her,' he spat. 'No more questions.'

'Where is she now?' I asked.

'Dead.'

A chill dripped down my spine. 'Did you kill her?'

'Hell! No, I did not. Some Marauders got her. Now, I mean it, no more questions.'

'Is that why you hide yourself away . . . because of the Marauders? Don't you miss people, having someone to talk to?'

'No, I don't. In fact, just listening to you makes me grateful for the peace and quiet I get when I'm alone. I haven't talked this much in months.'

'Don't you like people?' I said, ignoring the acid hint.

'No, I don't. I've never met anyone I liked enough to trust, especially when it comes to women. I remember a few months ago when a man and woman asked for shelter from the rain. No sooner had they set foot in my house than the woman started making a play for me. She didn't even try to hide what she was up to from her partner. I woke up that night to find the man in my room, a knife in his hand, ready to separate my head from my neck. Take my advice, Robby, don't trust anyone. Everyone lies and everyone wants something.'

'I don't' – I shrugged – 'unless you count shelter from the rain. I like people, and a lot of people are decent, even nowadays. The only ones I would always avoid are the Marauders – but then everyone avoids them.'

'You're a fool,' Carter said with disgust. 'You won't make it to your eighteenth birthday.'

I shrugged again. Maybe he was right.

We played cards for the rest of the day. Carter had to be cajoled into playing – he said he didn't like cards, but I threatened not to make dinner. After calling me a right little kid, he gave in. It was more fun than either of us expected. We played all the silly children's games my mum had taught me.

Over dinner Carter said speculatively, 'You're the strangest boy I've ever met. I can't make you out at all.'

'I'm not a boy, I'm a man,' I replied.

'Have you ever had sex with a woman?' he asked.

I said scornfully, 'You don't have to sleep with a woman to be a man.'

'But it helps,' Carter said. 'And you still haven't answered my question.'

'No, I haven't,' I answered.

'Maybe that's what you need for your voice to break.'

'Believe me, Carter' – I smiled – 'I don't think that would do much good!'

'I sometimes miss sex.' Carter stared out into the rain.

'Only sometimes?'

'Only sometimes,' he affirmed.

'Don't you miss your wife?' I asked carefully.

'My wife put me off women for life,' Carter said with venom. 'She was incapable of telling the truth, she loved to humiliate me. She damn near emasculated me. She got exactly what she deserved.'

I hesitated before speaking, unusual for me. Carter was so angry, so bitter. His wife was a bitch, he said, therefore all women must be bitches.

'Nobody deserves to be killed by Marauders,' I said quietly. 'Marauders are the sadistic scum of the earth. I wouldn't wish them on my worst enemy.'

Carter sat broodingly silent. He got up abruptly, his chair falling over behind him, and left the room. I didn't see him until dinner time, and even then he didn't say a word to me. I just shrugged it off.

By the fourth day the strappings around my chest had become as uncomfortable as hell. I'd attempted to take them off the previous night but Carter clumped downstairs, accusing me of 'moving about'. We argued briefly until I decided that I was wasting my breath and turned my back on him in an effort to get some sleep. In the dark silence that followed I thought he'd go away and leave me in peace. We both knew I hadn't been moving about. Hell! I'd been trying to keep extra quiet so that I could take off my strappings and padding. Then Carter asked me if I'd like a game of chess. He obviously wanted some company so I reluctantly said yes. He was right. I was far too soft.

That afternoon I was preparing soup in the kitchen when I heard a noise outside the house. I went over to the window, rubbing off the grime which had turned the pane brown, and then I saw them – two of them – moving towards the front door.

Marauders . . .

10

The train . . . I have to get back to the train . . . NOW.

I dredged up the thought from the middle of nowhere, only to find myself snapping back to the present so fast, my head was ringing.

'You brought us out of Roberta's nightmare,' Rachel accused. 'Why did you do that?'

'W-what?' I looked around, almost expecting Marauders to be striding down the carriage.

'We're not safe here,' said Rachel.

I didn't listen to her. I couldn't take in what she was saying.

'The things that happen to Robby – are they real?' I asked.

Rachel frowned. 'Why ask me?'

' 'Cause you know a lot more than you're letting on,' I said impatiently. 'You knew I was sharing these . . . dreams in the first place. So was Robby's nightmare true?'

At first I thought she wasn't going to answer, but I was determined not to say another word until she did.

'Nightmares are sometimes suppressed memories. Some nightmares tell what happened in the past, some tell what will happen in the future, most are nothing more than bad dreams or fears being filed away.'

'But will that happen? The war and the rain?' I asked, appalled.

Rachel shrugged. 'Who knows? Possibly. Probably.'

Unable to take much more, I closed my eyes. I needed to get away, even if it was just in my head. Get out of this carriage, get off this train, go somewhere else . . . Go home.

Dad was in the kitchen, singing tunelessly. But at least he was singing. Deeply surprised, I tiptoed along the hall and stood in the doorway, watching him. Two steaks lay on a plate beside the cooker. Dad bent down and retrieved a frying pan from one of the kitchen drawers. He placed the empty pan over a too-high flame on the hob, still unaware that he was being watched. Turning away to season the steaks, he didn't realize that the frying pan wasn't settled on the hob properly. After a few seconds the pan began to tilt, then fall. I called out and moved forward, my hand outstretched, but I was too slow. Alerted by my cry, Dad spun and tried to catch it, but the handle was away from him. He grabbed at the pan but quickly pulled back his hand as the hot metal beneath his fingers seared his flesh. The pan clattered to the floor as Dad cupped his fingers, cursing up a blue streak.

A lot of noise, less than a little mess and nothing

that a couple of minutes under cold, running water wouldn't cure – that's all it was.

But Dad lost it.

He swore as he snatched up the pan by the handle, then he raised it above his head and banged it down on the work surface. And again. And again.

'Bitch – BITCH – BITCH!' He punctuated each slam with that single word, each one louder than the one before.

I froze mid-way across the kitchen. I wasn't going to stay and watch Dad beat the crap out of the work surface. And I sure as hell wasn't going to try to take the pan away from him either.

Dad spun round to face me, breathing hard.

'You see this, Kyle? You see what your mum has done? What she's reduced me to?'

Somehow the tremulous crack in his voice was worse than his hammering of the work surface. Unable to face him, I headed out of the kitchen, leaving him alone.

Somewhere else . . . Home. Not just a place. It was supposed to be a safe feeling. Except mine was anything but. All I did was open my eyes and I was back on the train. The feeling I'd had as I left Dad alone in the kitchen was still with me. Maybe that was the problem. All the feelings I'd assigned to my mum and dad or our house weren't in those places at all. They were all inside me. That's why I could never escape them.

'Kyle, we're wasting time.' Rachel frowned. 'We need to . . .'

But I didn't hear anything after that. Over Rachel's shoulder I saw that further down the carriage a middle-aged woman was on her feet. She had light-brown, messy hair and her pink lipstick was smudged down towards her chin. She wore black trousers and a dark blue jacket over a light blue jumper. Someone else was on their feet, someone who wasn't hurt. I started towards her, only for Rachel to grab my arm.

'Let her be. You can't help her.'

'What're you on about?' I frowned. 'She's standing up. Maybe she can help us to help some of the others.'

'You don't need her,' Rachel told me. 'You don't need the real world. You need to get out of this carriage and back into the head of one of your friends.'

I scowled at Rachel. What on earth was she talking about? Ignoring her, I turned back to the woman. But what I saw scooped out my insides in less than a second. She was standing on a heap of upturned seats and trying to pull herself up through the broken window above her. The wild look on her face was instantly recognizable. It matched my own expression not too long ago.

'*No! Don't!*' I called out, and pushed past Rachel to race towards her. With a strength amplified by fright and panic, the woman's arms now bore her weight as she kicked her legs clear of the upturned seats below. The scraping, grating sound of the train against the tracks told me what was going to happen next. It was beginning to slide . . .

I grabbed the woman's legs and pulled. She kicked me in the face, splitting my lip and knocking me backwards. I could taste blood in my mouth. The grating noise was getting worse. The woman was more than halfway out of the window. I leaped forward again and seized her legs, determined not to let go this time. I pulled two, then three times, before she let go and we collapsed onto the ground, both panting for breath.

'I've got to get out of here,' the woman gasped. Already she was on her feet. I jumped up. She started to clamber up the seats again, her gaze never leaving the promise of the broken window above. The rain had diminished to mere drizzle now, but even the downpour we had before wouldn't have stopped this woman.

'You can't,' I insisted, pulling her back. 'You'll have the whole train over if you do that again.'

The woman turned suddenly, lashing out with her fists. 'Let me go. Julian and Judith need me. My grandchildren need me.'

'Then stay here until we're rescued!' I shouted at her, losing it. 'Listen to me! If you try to climb out, they'll be scooping all of us off the pavement with teaspoons.'

The woman's hands fell to her side.

'D'you understand?' I was so close to angry tears, I wanted to shake her because she was only doing what I'd wanted to do earlier, what I still wanted to do. I could feel her desperation as if it were my own. The wild look in the her eyes slowly faded.

'D'you understand?' I repeated, struggling to say it more calmly this time.

She nodded. 'I . . . I'm sorry.'

'It's OK,' I said, gulping down the lump of fear lodged somewhere in my throat. 'It's OK. But you mustn't try that again.'

The woman nodded. I wasn't sure if she was even listening; she just kept nodding her head.

'I'm Kyle,' I told her. 'What's your name?'

She carried on nodding. I moved to look her straight in the eye and repeated what I'd just said.

'Lily. My name is Lily.' And as she spoke, the light of reason returned to her eyes. Her voice, her whole demeanour was calmer – thank goodness.

'Right then, Lily. Come and sit with us. We'll wait together for help to come.'

The woman shook her head. 'I'll stay here.'

'I don't think—'

'It's all right, I'll stay here. I need to phone my grandchildren. I want them to know that I'm OK. I won't try to . . . leave again. I promise.'

I looked into Lily's eyes, unsure of what I should do next. I really didn't want to leave her alone.

'And in case you make it and I don't, my name is Lily Channing,' the woman told me.

I nodded but was reluctant to tell her my surname. Strangely enough – especially after my thoughts over the last couple of weeks – I didn't want to think about the possibility that she might need to give my name because I was no longer around to do it for myself.

Lily took out her mobile and started pressing buttons. Was that really the best use of her time? I decided to leave her alone. After all, where was the harm in her phoning her family? I thought about the mobile phone in my trouser pocket. There should still be enough charge on it to make at least one phone call, but who would I call? Most of my friends were on the train with me. I could phone the emergency services, to find out just what was going on and why they were taking so long to rescue us. Or there was always my mum . . .

Lily started cursing at the lack of a signal. I turned and left her to it, still wavering between who I should call. Rachel hadn't moved from her original spot. She stood, her arms folded, looking distinctly un-impressed. She reminded me of all the bizarre things I'd seen since the train crashed. How had she known about the dreams I'd experienced? And how was she able to share them with me? And why was I able to experience them in the first place? I still didn't know the answer to that one. I couldn't forget the rain in Roberta's dream, how destructive it was. It brought to mind another day when the rain fell with a vengeance. My last birthday, spent with my dad.

One sombre month drifted into another and still no word from Mum. On my birthday I opened my eyes to the sight of the rain lashing at my window. It was falling so hard I couldn't see past it. It hung like a heavy curtain of grey on the wrong side of the windowpanes. After a quick shower I got dressed and went down to the kitchen for breakfast. Dad was already there, the obligatory cup of coffee in his hand.

'Morning,' he said without looking at me.

'Morning,' I returned.

I made myself a cup of coffee too. It was all I could be bothered to make. I clinked cups and banged the cutlery drawer and poured in the lukewarm water from the kettle, and all without another word from Dad. Not even a 'Happy birthday, son'. I guess he must've forgotten. We left the house together, forking at the gate, with Dad heading for work and me for school. I turned after a few steps to watch Dad walk away from me without a backward glance. I thought about calling out a reminder, but the bloody-minded part of me thought belligerently that I shouldn't have to. He was my dad, he should remember. Bastard.

Steve wished me happy birthday and Perry threatened to give me one wedgy for every year of my life. I soon told him where he could stick that idea. I spent the entire day in a bad mood. School finished, and I didn't head for Steve's house the way I usually did. For once I went straight home.

I opened the door and listened to the shroud-like silence that now permanently enveloped our house. But as I looked down, my heart hiccupped: we had post. I ducked down eagerly to check out the letters. Just bills for Dad. I checked the answering machine.

Zero messages. I started up our computer and checked for emails. Nothing. Didn't expect any. Didn't want any either.

When Dad came home that night, I'd cooked spaghetti bolognese with sauce out of a jar. I left Dad's in the oven. Usually Dad called out a vague, general 'Hi, Kyle, it's me,' before heading straight into the kitchen. But not today.

'Kyle, could you come down here please?'

How many guesses did I need to figure out what was going to happen next? Answer? Less than one.

'Yes, Dad?' I stopped halfway down the stairs.

'Happy birthday.'

'Thanks.' So he'd finally remembered, had he?

'I'll give you some money later. You can buy your own present.'

'Thanks.' For nothing.

Dad looked up at me, his eyes burning with the light of hope.

'How's your mother? Where is she?'

'How would I know, Dad?'

'Don't be silly. Let me see the card she sent you.'

Ah! Now I knew what prompted his memory. I hadn't been enough on my own. 'What card?'

Dad frowned at me. 'Oh, for heaven's sake,' he said. 'Let me see the envelope then.'

'Dad, I didn't get a card from Mum. No postcard, no envelope, not even a stamp.' I spoke slowly and clearly.

'What did she send you then?' asked Dad.

I shook my head as I looked at him. Dad could hear me but he obviously wasn't listening. He strode over to the phone on the hall table. 'Did she leave a message? How long ago did she phone?'

'Bloody hell on a lollipop stick, Dad!' I flared up. 'No, Mum did not send me a letter, an email or a birthday card. She did not phone. She did not send a carrier pigeon. When are you going to get it into your thick head that she's gone for good? She's had enough of both of us. And I can't say I blame her. Look at you. Look at me. I've had a bellyful of both of us too.'

The light in Dad's eyes dimmed and extinguished, like a candle being slowly smothered before being snuffed out. Hope was Dad's oxygen. But if Mum didn't even get in touch on my birthday . . . He turned away from me, but not before I saw the sheen in his eyes. I turned and took the stairs two and three at a time, heading back to my bedroom. I slammed the door shut behind me just as hard as I could. Then I opened it and slammed it again. I waited to hear Dad yell at me or order me back down the stairs.

Silence.

Sitting on my bed, I waited for the ball of broken glass in my throat to scrape its way down to my stomach. Which part of this was fair? My life wasn't supposed to hurt this much. Clenching my fists, I promised myself in that moment that I wouldn't be like Dad. I'd never be like him. I'd make it so that I didn't need Mum – or anyone else for that matter.

Needing others only brought misery. That wasn't going to happen to me.

Ever.

The next day Dad came home from work at lunch time 'cause he wasn't feeling too great.

The following day he didn't go in to work at all . . .

Dad's isolation was imposed upon him. Now that Mum was back in my life, I was the one imposing silence and hateful looks on her. How strange then that at this moment, more than anything, I really longed to hear her voice. Mum . . . I found it so hard to talk to her now. The words I wanted to say always seemed to get caught in my throat. I used to be able to talk to Mum about anything and everything. Not any more. I couldn't get past the fact that she'd left us. She wasn't there to watch Dad fall to pieces. I was. And all because of her. How did either of us move on from that? She was back in my life but things between us weren't back to normal. We weren't even on the same planet as 'back to normal'.

But who knew when, or even if, any of us would get off this train? If something happened to me, I didn't want my last conscious thought or feeling to be one of regret about my mum. I pulled the phone out of my pocket. Great! Just great! Bashing into things when the train was hit had done my phone no favours. The thing was dead. But someone in this carriage apart from Lily had to have a working phone. I'd just . . .

'Kyle, stop it.'

'Stop what?' I asked.

'You need to focus,' snapped Rachel.

I thrust my useless mobile back into my pocket before letting my hand fall to my side.

'We have more important things to worry about,' Rachel told me, almost belligerently. 'If he catches up with us—'

'Enough with the scary movie crap, OK? Who are you so afraid of? And give me a straight answer this time.'

'The only one any of us should be afraid of,' replied Rachel, looking at me unwaveringly. 'Death . . .'

Silence.

I burst out laughing. It echoed around the quiet carriage, sounding harsh and out of place.

'Death is in this carriage?' I said, eyebrows raised.

'Maybe not this carriage. Yet. But coming through this train – yes.'

'Course he is!' I humoured her.

'And he's looking for you in particular,' Rachel continued.

My sardonic smile held pure disbelief. I couldn't believe I was having this conversation but I decided to play along until help arrived. Goodness only knew what a Christmas cake like Rachel would do if she thought I wasn't taking her seriously. I asked, 'Why would Death be coming after me in particular?'

'Because your dad sent him,' said Rachel.

Which punched the sarky smirk right off my face.

'W-what . . . ?'

Rachel's lips twisted into the semblance of a smile. She had my full attention now and she knew it.

'What d'you mean?' I managed the full sentence this time.

'You heard me,' said Rachel. 'You have to do exactly as I say, or you won't make it off this train in one piece.'

'But why would Dad send Death after me?'

The conversation had taken a sudden ninety-degree turn. It was still the most bizarre conversation I'd ever had, but somehow it wasn't funny any more. Not even close.

'I'm right, aren't I? Your dad is dead?'

My mouth had stopped working. I stared at Rachel.

'And he'd have a reason to hate you? What happened between you and him?'

I shook my head, still unable to speak.

Rachel shrugged. 'You're right. It is none of my beeswax.'

Dad had sent Death after me? He really hated me that much? What was I thinking? Of course he hated me – hadn't he already proved that with his actions?

I shook my head again. This was too freaky. How on earth did Rachel know about Dad and me? I took a stumbling step backwards. If knowledge was power then Rachel had it all and I had none. She obviously knew a lot more than me about what was going on.

'Who are you?' I whispered.

'Someone who's here to help you – if you'll let me.'

'That doesn't answer my question,' I said.

Rachel studied me before she spoke. 'I'm here to stop your dad from succeeding. That's the truth.'

'Is that why I'm having all these nightmares?' I asked Rachel. 'Is Dad messing up my head by sending me those as well?'

'We both know the dreams you've experienced belong to those whose minds you invade,' said Rachel.

'But how is that even possible?'

I just didn't get it. And each time I disappeared inside a nightmare, it became harder to escape from it. With Steve and Miss Wells, it was as if I was watching, a spectator. Hearing what they heard, feeling as they felt but able to step back from it. But not any more. Now, inside each nightmare, it was growing harder to discern where I stopped and my friends started. And with this last one, with Roberta's nightmare, I could still taste the fear that had erupted within me at the sight of the Marauders. I desperately wanted to know what happened next but I was afraid to find out.

I shook my head, muttering to myself, 'They're just dreams. Don't believe them, Kyle, they're just dreams.'

Restless, I started down the carriage towards Lily. Rachel fell into step beside me.

'Isn't that the point?' she asked.

Confused, I stopped and turned towards her.

'On some level, don't your dreams tell you who and what you are?'

I shook my head. 'No, of course not. By definition dreams aren't even real.'

'But if all the things that happen to you, all your experiences, make up the kind of person you are, then doesn't living through a dream do the same thing?'

'But they're not real,' I repeated.

'Who says?'

I thought about all the dreams and nightmares I'd had – and could remember – over the last year. Some were based on or inspired by actual things that had happened to me and my family. But some were as far removed from real life as I wanted to get. Though Rachel was right about one thing. I had been forced to live through my nightmares over the past year. And what had the experience done for me? Bugger all, as far as I could tell. I was no smarter, no braver, no better informed. All my nightmares did was make me even more angry at the world.

'And I've got some advice for you,' said Rachel softly. 'The next time you're in the head of one of your friends, stay put.'

'So I'm supposed to gloat over Joe losing his mind or rejoice over Miss Wells's marriage to God knows what, am I?' I said.

'You're talking about dreams you experienced before I arrived. All I'm saying is it still has to be safer than staying out here,' said Rachel.

'Says who?'

'Says you – if you'd only admit it to yourself. Don't forget, you started jumping into your friends' dreams without any help from me. You wouldn't've started jumping if you hadn't sensed that *he* was after you. We both know you'd rather be anywhere else but here. But you don't have the bottle to stay put once you do it.'

I scowled at her. 'You don't know what the hell you're talking about.'

'If you say so.' Rachel shrugged.

'And if . . . if what you say is true,' I began. 'If my dad really *did* send Death after me, how come you know so much about it?'

Silence.

There! Gotcha! I knew it was all crap.

'I know because I was told.'

'By my dad?'

'No. Death told me.'

It was one of those glass-half-full/glass-half-empty situations. Half of me believed her, or wanted to believe her. But half of me didn't believe a single word and wanted to laugh in her face. It was time to pick a side. Which side should I go with?

'So you're on speaking terms with Death, are you?'

'Something like that,' said Rachel.

'Then why are you trying to help me?'

'I have my reasons.'

God, was she pissing me off!

'Let's just say, I don't want your dad to succeed. I'll do whatever it takes to stop that happening,' she said.

There was something about the way she said it, the total conviction and sincerity in her voice, that made me believe her. In that moment, bizarre as it may sound, I picked a side. Rachel's side.

'Thanks,' I muttered. 'So what do we do now?'

'D'you know this girl?' Rachel asked, pointing at Elena, who lay, eyes closed, on the ground. Beads of sweat decorated her forehead and her top lip.

'Yeah, that's Elena,' I said, squatting down beside her. Her blonde hair had fallen across her cheek. I brushed it back behind her ear.

'She'll do then.'

'Oh, but—'

'Come on. I can tell you like her.' Rachel smiled. 'Are you her boyfriend or is it this guy next to her?'

'She's Conor's girlfriend, not mine. Elena and I are just good friends.'

'But you'd like it to be more.'

'You don't know what you're talking about,' I replied coldly.

'If you say so . . .' said Rachel, that sly grin back on her face. I didn't know which was getting on my nerves more, that smirk or her constant refrain of 'if you say so'.

'Yes, I—' That's as far as I got.

The train gave a sudden lurch and I fell sideways. Putting out my hand to steady myself, I missed the side of the seat I was aiming for and ended up falling across Elena. I instantly put out my hands so that my full weight wouldn't descend on her, but even so my chest still landed on her crooked leg. She groaned but her eyes didn't open. I pushed myself back immediately.

'Ellie, I'm so sorry. Are you OK?'

But I was in trouble. The images had already

started, spinning and ringing in my head. Strange, unsettling images. Of Elena. Laughing at someone. Scowling. The images appeared faster and faster. So fast that I couldn't discern what they were. But they were all to do with Ellie. Her face spun around me, distorted and ugly to look at, like a constantly tilting watercolour of her face, where the paint was still wet and kept running this way, then that, distorting her features. And then Elena's true face was back. But she didn't look like she did on the train. This time her hair was shorter, the way she used to wear it a year or so ago. And she and another girl I vaguely recognized sat in a place of sad silence.

11

Elena's Nightmare

I feel things deeply – too deeply. That's always been my problem, my nightmare. I love too much. And when someone lets me down, I hurt too much. I know it, and yet I don't seem to be able to do anything about it.

Take my friend Katey. She let me down badly – and yet I'd forgiven her.

And here I was, keeping her company when, if I had any sense, I'd be doing something a lot more interesting, like painting my toenails.

'I thought we were friends. I thought we were best friends,' Katey complained.

I sighed. Katey was at it again. What a bore.

'We *are* best friends,' I told her.

'I don't believe you, Ellie . . .' Katey argued.

I sighed again. Katey was really tedious when she snivelled at me. Sometimes she reminded me of a small, yapping dog, snapping at my heels. Katey was my age – thirteen – with huge, laughing, honey-brown eyes set in a pretty, honey-brown oval face. Only she hadn't done much laughing of late – only complaining.

What did she have to complain about? *I* was the one who'd been hurt. I was the one who'd been betrayed by her. Yes, I had forgiven her . . . but I hadn't forgotten. I would never forget.

I tried to placate her. 'We *are* best friends. We have been since we were seven.'

'Then why are you going out with him?' Katey continued.

I took a deep breath, trying to smother the angry impatience rising within me. I didn't have to be here, I really didn't.

'Katey, give me a break. Luke is just a friend. He makes me laugh and we've been to the cinema together a few times. That's all – no big deal. And besides – you're the one who went out with him first. You knew I liked him but you went out with him anyway. And you're the one who didn't have any time for me after you started seeing him – remember?'

'Yeah, and you took care of that,' Katey said bitterly.

'What was I supposed to do?' I asked. 'Suddenly it was you and Luke and I didn't exist any more.'

'And now you've taken up where I left off,' Katey retorted.

'Look, I've had enough of this. I'm going home.' I stood up, glad to be off the chilly brick wall that'd been my seat.

Katey shook her head. 'No, don't. I'm sorry. I'll shut up about Luke.'

I didn't sit down again. Truth to tell, I wanted to go home. Katey was no fun any more.

I looked around, taking in the tall sweet chestnut trees, their leaves green and plentiful. It was a slow, sleepy summer evening. The sun was low in the red-orange sky and somewhere nearby a bird was chirping. It was my favourite time of day – when the day was dying and the night was close to being born.

'So what did you do today?' Katey asked, shuffling to sit properly on the brick wall which surrounded her home.

I gave in and sat down beside her again. 'Not much. Went to school. Went home. Came here to see you.'

I could see that that pleased Katey. A smile lit her face. There was a pause.

'Do you really like Luke?' she asked, watching me.

I shrugged, then grinned sheepishly.

'I liked Luke. I was really stuck on him. But then you already know that, don't you?' Katey said quietly.

'He liked you a lot too. He still talks about you,' I told her.

That really made her day. I sighed inwardly. Lying was such hard work – and so was Katey.

'So what have you been up to?' I tried desperately to disguise my lack of interest.

'I chatted to Mrs Silver. She's just moved in next to me,' Katey replied.

'What's she like?'

'Not bad for an oldi . . .' Katey twittered on while I did my best to make the appropriate noises in the right places. Surprisingly, it didn't take her long to catch on to what I was doing.

'You're not listening to a single word I'm saying, are you?' she fumed.

'Of course I am,' I protested.

Katey glared at me, her expression icy. 'I think you're really mean, Elena. I'm only here because of you—'

'Don't start—' I began.

'Don't start! I spend all day and all night here . . . in this place . . .' Katey swept her arm round in an arc to pan her surroundings. 'I have no real friends, no one to talk to, no one to confide in – except you. You don't even come to see me every day like you promised me you would. And then when you *are* here you can't wait to get away . . .'

'I'm sorry,' I said. 'I just have a lot on my mind at the moment.'

'Yeah, but you can walk away from whatever's troubling you. I can't. I'm stuck here – thanks to you,' Katey said tearfully.

Here we go! I thought. She was always trying to make me feel guilty.

'There's no one of my own age here,' Katey continued. 'You can't imagine how lonely it gets sometimes—'

'Not again, Katey – please,' I pleaded.

Katey opened her mouth to speak, only to snap it shut again without saying a word.

'Katey, I'm sorry. I didn't mean that,' I said.

'Yes, you did,' Katey replied quietly. 'Go away, Elena. You know you want to. Go away and leave me alone.'

'Don't be like that, Katey,' I said. 'I know it's my fault you're here but—'

'There are no buts,' Katey dismissed. 'You couldn't give a stuff about how I feel. All I ask you to do is visit me every evening – that's all. Even if it's only for five minutes. That's not too much to expect, is it?'

I thought about what Katey had said as I walked home. She was right. It was my fault she was in that place. For the first time I thought about what it would be like to be Katey, stuck in one place, with no one to really talk to. I wouldn't like it – not one little bit.

All right then, Katey, I thought. *I'll see what I can do. Then maybe you'll stop blaming me for everything bad that's ever happened to you.*

As I walked home I wondered if I could get a friend to visit Katey with me. But not Luke. Never Luke. Someone else. A mutual friend. It would be a bit tricky, but then Katey wouldn't feel quite so isolated. A strange feeling swept through me. It tightened my mouth and made me clench my fists. Even now, I couldn't bear the thought of Katey and Luke together. After everything that had happened I was still jealous. Another wave descended over me, and another.

Her accident was my fault. And her loneliness – that was my fault too.

So what do I do? Blame myself and, deep, deep down, resent Katey for the way she makes me feel.

I had to do something. We couldn't go on like this.

I fell asleep that night pondering on the problem.

When I awoke I still didn't have the answer.

'Luke, do you remember Katey Fisher?'

'Yes, of course. I remember her very well. It was a shame about her accident.'

I nodded. It was Saturday afternoon and we were in our usual Saturday afternoon haunt – Pizza Perfection. If it wasn't for our group I reckoned the place would go out of business.

'What about Katey?' Luke asked.

'Do you . . . did you like her?'

Luke shrugged, trying to look nonchalant. 'Yeah, she was all right. We got on well together. She was the same person all the time. I liked that.'

I frowned. What did he mean by that? I let it pass.

'Why are you asking about her?'

'I think about her sometimes,' I replied.

'So do I – sometimes. I liked Katey. She was a good friend,' said Luke.

'Ellie, wasn't Katey your best friend?' asked Kendra, another girl from our group.

'Yeah . . .' I nodded, then glanced down at my watch. 'Come on, Luke, we're going to miss the start of the film if we don't move. You did remember to bring the tickets, didn't you?'

Luke frowned at me. '*You*'ve got the tickets.'

I pursed my lips while the others around us started grinning. 'No, Luke, I gave the tickets to you three days ago.'

'No, you didn't.' Luke's frown deepened.

'Yes I did,' I said patiently. 'And you said you were

going to put them under your computer keyboard in your bedroom so you wouldn't forget them.'

'Oh hell! Did I?'

'Luke, you're in trouble!' Perry called out from across the table.

Everyone around us was cracking up by now!

'For heaven's sake, Luke,' I snapped. 'I'm not going all the way to your house and back. I'll wait for you outside the cinema while you go back home for the tickets.'

I stood up and walked out of the restaurant. Luke had no choice but to follow me. I could tell he was behind me without having to look round. I also knew that our friends were watching. I must confess, it gave me a sense of . . . power – like I was a film star.

'Actually, Luke,' I said, once we were alone outside, 'I've changed my mind. I will come back to your house with you if you like.'

My moment as a film star was over. The scene played out for the benefit of our friends could be abandoned now that we were alone. I didn't want them to think that Luke had me wrapped around his little finger! Once a girl gets a rep for being a wet rag she can't get rid of it.

'Yeah, OK.' Luke shrugged. 'I'm sorry about the tickets, Elena. I was sure you had them.'

'It doesn't matter.' I smiled.

As if anything could ever matter except being with him.

We started walking along in silence. I kept glancing

at Luke, unable to believe my luck. I was an item with the hunkiest boy in our school. Somewhere, somehow, I must have done something *right*! We ducked furtively into the alley by the newsagent's – Mr Penn didn't like us using his alley as a short cut – and started walking along the river bank. I loved the river. Sometimes you saw the odd shopping trolley or car tyre floating in the water, but on a day like today it still managed to be one of the prettiest things I'd ever seen. On a day like today the whole world was beautiful.

'Actually, I'm glad you decided to come with me,' Luke began slowly. 'I have something to tell you and I think . . . I think I should tell you sooner rather than later.'

'What is it?' I smiled up at him. He really was gorgeous. Dark brown skin and the darkest brown eyes I'd ever seen. So dark, the irises were almost black. And when he smiled . . . It was like star bursts. And when he kissed me . . . His lips were so soft, so gentle. I was crazy about him. I had been from the time he'd come to our school two years previously – but no one had known. It was secret, like a blazing fire inside an icy-cool cavern. In all honesty I could see why Katey had forgotten about me once she'd started going out with Luke. I'd have done the same thing. Well, at least Luke was mine – now that Katey was out of the picture. I still couldn't feel sorry about that. I'd be a liar if I said otherwise.

'Elena . . . I don't know how to say this without just . . . saying it. So . . .' Luke took a deep breath. 'I don't

'. . . I don't want to . . . go out with you any more.'

I frowned, then smiled up at him, sure he was joking. 'What?'

'I don't want to go out with you any more.' Luke repeated the words without stumbling over them this time. They were obviously easier to say the second time around.

I stared up at him. My smile slowly faded. 'Why?' I asked, my throat tight.

'No reason.'

'There must be a reason.'

Luke shrugged. 'I just think it would be better if we didn't go out together any more. We can still be friends though . . .'

'Is there someone else?'

'No. I just—'

'You're just tired of me,' I interrupted.

We stopped walking. I looked down at the brown-grey river water, dull and dirty even in the afternoon sunlight. What I'd seen before was just through the eyes of imagination.

'Ellie, please try to understand. Be reasonable—'

'Reasonable?' The word burned my mouth.

I stood still, staring into the river. Luke stood next to me. I could sense his uncertainty. He wanted to go. He wanted to be as far away from me as possible. Inside I was choking, screaming. First Katey, now Luke.

We stood in silence for a while.

'Don't get too close to the water, Luke. You can't swim, can you?' I remembered.

'Not a stroke but don't worry. I have no intention of getting anywhere near that lot!' Luke retorted, eyeing the murky, muddy water with distaste.

I looked around, my heart hurting. Hurting so much.

It was peaceful here, but now the world wasn't as beautiful any more. My life was the river. The river was my life. Dark and murky. Filthy . . . disgusting.

'Do you ever wonder what's in there, at the bottom?' I asked.

'No, I don't. And whatever's down there can stay down there as far as I'm concerned.'

Luke's voice grew stronger, more confident, as he spoke. Now that we were off the embarrassing subject of him dumping me, he was happy to speak. All I could think of was that he was deserting me.

First Katey, now Luke.

'Luke, did you tell any of your friends that you're dumping me?'

'I'm not dumping you,' Luke protested.

'Just answer the question please,' I said.

'I didn't tell them we were splitting up – no. I wanted to speak to you first. This is between you and me . . .'

'I see . . .' I said slowly.

Silence.

'Well . . . if that's how you really feel, then I guess— Oh my God! Look at that!' I pointed towards the river.

'At what?' Luke frowned, his gaze following my finger.

'At that! At that!' I said, horrified. 'My God! What is it?'

'What?' Luke moved a step closer and bent forward over the river to take a closer look.

I took one last quick look around.

Then I shoved him.

Luke did a somersault before landing in the water, his arms flailing. He went under immediately. Seconds passed before his head surfaced a little further down the river. He gasped and retched, spitting out the filthy river water. I walked along the bank, careful not to get too close to the water's edge, careful to keep him in sight.

'Ellie . . .' he gasped. His head went under again.

I looked around. This was the most dangerous part. If anyone should come past now . . .

Luke's head re-surfaced. He retched violently, his arms slapping against the surface of the water over and over. He tried to haul his way back to the bank but the water slipped through his fingers and the mud beneath him shifted constantly. I could almost feel the reeds like razor-sharp, icy fingers pulling at his legs and the shifting mud beneath his feet, trying to swallow him whole like a snake.

'Ellie . . . help . . .' he cried. 'I can't . . . I can't swim . . .'

'Yes, I know,' I whispered.

'For God's sake . . .' he screamed.

I took another look around. There was no one in sight.

'*Elena . . .*'

Luke went under again – only this time he didn't reappear.

I watched for a while to make sure he wouldn't come up again. I could hardly risk that. That had been my mistake when I pushed Katey into the river. I'd left too soon and someone else had come along and seen her floating in the water. Luckily for me, Katey died without regaining consciousness – otherwise I might have been in trouble.

Nope, it looked like Luke had definitely gone down for good. I walked back to the cinema. I made a big show of checking my watch every couple of minutes while the queue of people behind me moved slowly into the foyer. Marching in, I asked every member of staff I saw if my boyfriend Luke had phoned or left some kind of message for me. But no, he hadn't. I stormed back to Pizza Perfection.

'Is Luke in here?' I asked, furious.

'No. I thought you two were going to see a film?' Perry replied.

'So did I. I've been stood up. The film's started now,' I fumed.

I stayed in the restaurant with the rest of them until the evening. They didn't find Luke's body until four days later. It was spotted floating face down in the river, all swollen and bloated. When they told me he'd been found, I cried and cried. For days I was inconsolable. It was as if a part of me had died too. I mean it. Luke was . . . Luke was my love. He'd always have a place in my heart. I know that because I feel things so deeply.

'Hi, Katey, how are you?' I smiled.

'I'm fine, Elena. And yourself?'

'Not bad.' I shrugged. 'Not bad. Well, Luke, aren't you going to say hello.'

Luke turned his head away from me. His face was ashen, his eyes huge and staring like he still couldn't quite believe what had happened to him. He's looked better! I thought with distaste.

'I'm glad you're here, Luke,' I said. 'It's good to see you.'

He looked at me, then turned away.

'I know you're upset, but you'll get over it.'

Honestly! What was I supposed to do? Luke had tried to leave me, desert me – just like Katey when she'd first started getting serious about him. So I had to do something . . .

Besides, Katey wanted a friend and Luke was the ideal candidate – now that he didn't want me any more.

He'll forgive me. He has to.

After all, apart from whingeing Katey and some other boring old farts in this cemetery, who else has he got to talk to?

12

I scrambled away from Elena and sat down, facing her. I still couldn't believe it. Elena couldn't have done that. No one could be that . . . ice-cold. But I couldn't deny what I'd just seen. Elena and Katey. Elena and *Luke*. Had she really done that to him? Had she deliberately pushed him into the river? I had to be cracking up, losing my marbles and then some. What other explanation was there?

Steve in the army?

Joe in a mental hospital?

Roberta fleeing from acid rain and worse?

Miss Wells married to . . . Well, that was just too ludicrous. And could Elena really be the stone-cold killer I'd just seen? I mean, she'd have to be some kind of serious psycho to take out anyone who got in her way like that. But I couldn't deny that I'd been inside her head. It was almost like I became her – her every action and thought singing crystal-clear through me. One dream later and I knew her inside and out. The terrifying thing was she had a emptiness inside her where her conscience should be.

But, thinking back, I still remembered how distraught she had been when Luke died. Was that really just an act? A way to gain sympathy from the rest of us and remain the centre of attention for weeks, even months? The whole thing sounded too Machiavellian to be anywhere near the truth.

And yet . . .

That's what I kept coming back to.

And yet.

I needed to think, to pull myself together. Elena's story was something in the past, something that had already happened. Luke used to be one of my mates. I remembered going to his funeral. I didn't know Katey but I was there when the head told everyone about her accident. So suppose what I'd seen was true? This last encounter had unsettled me more than I could've imagined. Seeing the world through Elena's eyes had tilted my perspective. Before Elena there was still a part of me that could believe that none of this was quite real. There was no *proof*. But now . . . I guess it boiled down to the fact that I believed what I'd seen about Elena. For some inexplicable reason I *believed* it. And I couldn't just sit back and do nothing. I couldn't let her get away with it . . .

Hang on. I was getting way ahead of myself. My first priority was to get off this train. If and when that happened, then I could set about finding some way of proving or disproving what I'd seen. I wouldn't be able to trust myself or anyone else until I did. The trouble was, if Elena's story was true, then anything could be true. And if anything could be true, suppose *everything* I'd seen on this train was true? What then? What else was I going to learn about my friends? What secrets did they keep locked inside in their dreams or nightmares that just a look or a touch from me could unlock?

But I didn't want to learn any more about them. This was definitely a case of too much information. I looked along the carriage. Lily was sitting down now, staring into space. What would her nightmare be? Was she living through it now? What was playing in her mind – something from her past or something coming in the future?

'Well, that was different!' said Rachel from behind me. 'Your friend Ellie's a piece of work. You didn't suspect any of that, did you?'

'Of course not. I thought she was . . . I mean . . .'

Rachel regarded me speculatively. 'You're not a very good judge of character, are you?'

'Elena had . . . has everyone fooled,' I said with more than a little resentment.

'Not Steve,' Rachel pointed out.

Which was true. Steve had never really liked her, though he could never explain why.

'How often do you get people wrong like that?' she asked.

I didn't answer. Rachel smiled at me, a strange knowing light in her eyes.

'Oh, and Kyle, you can't keep jumping in and out of

your friends' heads like that.' She frowned. 'It isn't safe for either of us when you do that.'

But I hardly heard her. Something else was going on.

A shimmer was beginning to appear, entering our carriage from the third carriage.

'He's here,' Rachel said, horrified. 'I thought we had more time. We have to go.'

'*Kyle, wait for me . . .*' The voice was as close as it'd ever been.

Rachel tried to pull at my arm but I couldn't move. My blood had frozen inside me. My lungs had seized up completely. She pulled me backwards. I stumbled and almost fell against her.

'Kyle, move,' she hissed at me.

The shimmering light at the far end of the carriage was growing bigger as I watched.

'Kyle, don't look at it. You mustn't look at it. That's how he gets his strength,' said Rachel, but I hardly heard her.

'*Kyle!*' she screamed at me.

At last I managed to drag my gaze away.

'Who's he?' Rachel said urgently, pointing at one of my friends.

'Perry,' I whispered. 'That's Perry.'

'He'll do,' said Rachel. 'Take us away from here. *Now!*'

With all my heart I wanted to be away from here.

One blink was all it took to get my wish.

13

Perry's Nightmare

I don't know what it was that made me take a second look at the girl in the mask. Maybe it was the mask itself; shaped like a diving swallow with wide almond-shaped slits cut in the swallow's black wings for the eyes. The swallow's tail and wings were edged with what looked like tiny, sparkling green emeralds, which caught the light and dazzled. Maybe it was the girl's dress, of Grecian style and the same emerald green as the mask edging.

Or maybe it was what was behind the mask, in her warm eyes, which were the same colour as the emeralds. Green eyes laughing . . . at me? *With* me? I wasn't sure.

To be honest, I'd been about to leave. The fancy dress party had failed to ignite and although a few people were dancing, most were standing around in small groups trying to make themselves heard over the relentlessly loud music.

Except for her.

She stood alone, watching me, watching all of us

156

with that strange, slight smile on her lips. Taking a deep breath, I arrowed across the room towards her. I wanted to reach her before another guy saw her. I admit it, I was intrigued. I noticed with satisfaction that the mystery girl watched as I crossed the crowded room. She smiled. With encouragement? With amusement? I couldn't tell.

She's probably laughing at this ridiculous costume, I thought sourly.

Why had I let myself be persuaded into wearing a pirate's outfit? I felt ridiculous.

But who dares and all that, I told myself, battling on. I could never remember the end of sayings, just the beginning. My friends Kyle and Joe were good at remembering quotes. Joe's memory was a little too good. It meant he bore grudges. Why was I thinking of Joe when I had a beautiful girl in my sights. At last I stood before her. And all the things I'd anticipated saying to her flew from my head and out the nearest exit.

'Hello, Perry,' the girl said.

I groaned. How I loathed my name! Perry as an abbreviation just about made it to passable. But my name as written on my birth certificate ... Bloody awful!

'I see you know my name,' I said, rueing a romantic mother who loved classical stories.

'I asked about you.' She smiled.

Yes! I'm in! I couldn't help grinning. 'Why?' I asked, though I reckoned I already knew the answer.

The girl shrugged. 'I thought you looked ...

interesting. More interesting than most of the boys here.'

'I'm glad you think so.'

'And I *love* your name.'

'It's kind of you to say so.'

The girl shook her head. 'I'm never kind.'

A shiver of anticipation trickled down my spine. She was flirting with me! 'What's your name?' I asked.

She seemed to consider my question carefully. 'My name? My name is— No! You guess it!'

'Like Rumpelstiltskin?' I laughed. I hoped she was suitably impressed with my literary prowess. It wasn't everyone who knew Rumpelstiltskin!

'I'll make it easy for you,' the mystery girl told me. 'My name begins with M.'

'Will you dance with me while I try to guess it?' I asked, hoping against hope that I wasn't about to get shot down in flames.

'Of course. I'm not going to let you out of my sight until you guess it correctly,' said the girl.

Even though her lips were turned upwards in the semblance of a smile, there was something in her voice, some indefinable note, which made me pause for the first time.

'Who *are* you?'

'That's for you to find out.' She smiled again, taking my hand. 'I thought you wanted to dance with me.'

'Let me see your face,' I said.

'Not yet,' the girl replied. 'Later – when you're ready. But not yet.'

'I don't understand. I'm ready to see your face now,' I argued.

'Not until you guess my name,' she replied firmly. 'Guess my name and I'll give you a night you'll never forget.'

Was that a threat or a promise? But then she smiled joyously and led me out for a dance. A new song began. The girl started to dance, her movements liquid and sensual. Somehow, thank God, I managed to keep up with her. It was as if her carefree spirit had wrapped itself around me as well. I knew we looked good. I knew I'd never danced better. Steve, eat your heart out! And this girl was deliberately dancing as close to me as she could get. She smelled lovely, a hint of flowery perfume which was subtle rather than overpowering. Warmth radiated from her. I could feel her breasts through her dress as she pressed against me. I could feel her hips against mine. I tried to shift away slightly, before I embarrassed myself. The mystery girl looked up at me, smiling mischievously.

'Am I making you uncomfortable?' she asked.

I shook my head, trying to think of the most boring things I could to take my mind off what was happening to my body: geography and jelly, party political speeches and Jessica in my class, who had no conversation whatsoever. It was working! I risked a glance around. All eyes were on us as we moved together.

But a strange thing was happening. As I danced, the music grew louder and wilder, until my head was spinning. And the mystery girl swayed in my arms, smiling at me . . . laughing at me as she danced away, then back towards me, then spun me round and round. Suddenly it stopped being fun. My eyes were like a camera lens, zooming in and out too quickly. I was beginning to feel dizzy, nauseous. I wanted to stop dancing but the girl held my hands tightly and whirled me round and I couldn't break free. I tried to speak, to stop her, but the words spun out of my mouth and away from me without making any sense. And still the music continued.

'Guess,' the girl ordered.

'What?' I gasped, trying to catch my breath.

'What's my name? Guess.'

'Maria.'

'No.'

'Mary, Melanie . . .'

'No.'

'I . . . I must stop . . .'

'Guess,' the mystery girl demanded.

'Marsha, Mariella, Margaret . . .'

'No.'

'Please . . .'

'Guess my name.'

I breathed out name after name after name and the music got louder and wilder until everything around me was a rushing blur – except for the mystery girl. She was like the hub around which chaos revolved.

'Melody, Meggie, Marcie, Madonna, Megan . . .'

'No, no, no,' the girl laughed.

I didn't know which was spinning faster now – the blood in my body or the room around me.

'Guess.'

I went through every girl's name beginning with M that I could think of, but to each guess the girl laughed delightedly and screamed, 'No.'

'I . . . I can't think of . . . of any more. I've got . . . to stop . . .' I could hardly get the words out. My lungs were about to implode, my blood roared inside me. Another fraction of a moment and I would collapse.

'*Stop!*'

Abruptly the music stopped.

'Are you all right, Perry?' The girl's eyes were glinting.

I looked around, gasping frantically as I fought to regain my breath. No one was taking the least bit of notice of me. Didn't they hear me shout for help?

'Are you all right, Perry? Is something wrong?'

'You . . . you . . .'

'Yes?' prompted the girl.

I blinked heavily as my lungs filled and my heart slowed. 'What just happened?' I asked.

She frowned. 'We were dancing and you were trying to guess my name. Then you suddenly stood still and started staring at me.'

'I did?'

She nodded. I ran my fingers through my already ruffled hair. I looked around again, searching for a sign on someone's face that they knew what I'd just been through – but there was nothing. I felt really, really sick.

'I . . . I need some air. I'll go outside for a while.'

'Shall I come with you?' the girl asked lightly.

I looked at her. Everyone else faded away. I felt as if I were at a crossroads, as if the answer to her question was vital. I shook my head to clear it. Now I was off in my own head, imagining things. That was my mate Kyle's trick!

'Just say if you don't want my company.'

'No . . . I mean, yes, yes, I do.'

The girl linked her arm with mine. 'Let's go this way, though the kitchen and out the back rather than fighting our way to the hall.'

'But what about the girl whose party this is? She might not like us traipsing through her house,' I said doubtfully.

'She won't mind.'

'You don't know that.'

'Yes, I do, 'cause you're talking to her,' she laughed.

I frowned at her. 'But I thought this was the party of some girl called Emma?'

'M, not Emma. Everyone assumes M is short for Emma but it's not. It stands for the letter M. Very few people know my real name. And I'm still waiting for you to guess it.'

M led the way through the dining room and the kitchen and down some stone steps to the back garden – if you could call it that. It was so big, it looked more like a small park! The moon was full and high, bathing the house and the grounds beyond in a cold white light. The night air was warm and smelled of freesias and roses and the faint hint of orange blossom, like my mum's air freshener. I looked out over the vast lawn before me. There were flowers everywhere. Hedges broke up the huge expanse of grass, and far across it I saw what seemed to be silvery lights glinting. I sensed rather than saw that M was watching me.

'I hope you don't think I'm gate-crashing,' I said, after an uncomfortable pause. 'Naima invited me. She said you wouldn't mind.'

'And she was right. In fact I told her to invite you,' she soothed. 'Come on, let's walk down to the lake.'

'There's a lake? Wow! This is some house!' I whistled.

'I like it.' M smiled.

I realized that the dull silvery glint I could see across the lawn had to be a part of the lake.

'So where're your mum and dad?' I asked.

'Gone,' she replied simply.

What did that mean? Gone for the night? Gone on holiday? Gone for good? I decided not to push it. If I was real lucky I might get a kiss, or more, and I didn't want to ask painful, personal questions and ruin the mood. A soft breeze began to blow. M pulled the hair-pins out of her hair until it fell free of its formal Grecian style, cascading down her back. She shook her head and laughed.

'I prefer my hair loose and free.'

'It looks better that way.'

'I think so.'

We walked across the lawn towards the lake. The wind was beginning to pick up now. It snatched at M's hair, tossing it around her face. I kept stealing glances at the girl beside me. She was so beautiful. I could hardly believe that she wanted to be alone with me. What would she do if I casually draped an arm around her shoulders? What would happen if I wrapped my arms around her and kissed her? God only knew, that was what I was longing to do. We rounded a high hedge which partially hid the lake from the house. I gasped. I'd had never seen so many statues in one place. They were all around the lake shore and beyond.

'Where did you get all these statues?' I asked.

'I made them,' M said.

There was no pride or modesty in her voice. She was merely stating a fact.

'You *made* them? I'm impressed.' I took another look around. 'What're they made of?'

'Stone.'

'Do you mind if I take a closer look?'

'Be my guest. This is where I come when I want to be alone with my thoughts,' M said softly. 'And I like to have all my men around me.'

'All your men?'

'Each statue is of a man,' she replied.

For the first time I saw that she was right. There were statues touching other statues, statues running, walking, kneeling, praying. Statues of men laughing, crying, raging, hiding their heads behind their hands. Statues of surprised men, disbelieving men, amazed men, even a couple of men laughing – and all in a variety of dress. Some contemporary, but most in period costume from across the centuries.

Suddenly all the emotions, all the attitudes over-whelmed me so that I had to look away. I turned to M. She was real and vivid. She was just what I needed to calm my imagination, which seemed to be working overtime tonight. I looked back at the house. We were now too far away to hear the music, and the lights were just tiny candle-flames through the hedge. I turned to gaze out across the lake. I felt strange, dizzy again, only this time M and I were standing still while the wind howled and the rest of the world spun away.

I shivered. I began to feel distinctly anxious. The water in the lake jumped and splashed in time with the wind's harsh whistling. I looked around, my sense of unease growing. Then I noticed that none of the statues were set on a plinth. They were all free stand-ing, on their own legs or knees – a few on their backs. I walked over to the nearest statue. I reached out to touch the jacket. It was clearly a leather jacket, but stone hard, stone cold. Frowning, I looked into the man's face. The expression was bewilderment. The attention to detail really was amazing.

'How d'you get them to stand up without a base?'

'Guess my name and then I'll tell you.'

And the wind grew fiercer.

All at once a peculiar thought struck me. Icy fingers began to stroke all over my body.

'Your name . . .' I turned my head slowly. 'Your name is . . .'

M had taken off her mask. Her whole face was alive and glowing with joy. 'I knew you'd get it,' she laughed happily.

The wind died. Not a murmur, not a whisper of it was left. But still M's hair writhed and slithered around her head.

'Medusa . . .' It was the last word I ever said.

'Congratulations, Perry! Or would you rather I called you by your full name? And it's such a romantic name. A name that always brings out the best in me.' Medusa's laugh tinkled like a tiny bell in the still evening air. She stepped up to me, the newest statue in her garden. 'Perry, I know you can hear me deep inside your stone tomb. All my statues are alive, deep inside . . . for a while. Get used to your new home, Perseus – you'll be here for a long, long time. Sooner or later your heartbeat will slow, and then it will cease. But I think in your case it will be later. Much later. But, Perseus, I can guarantee one thing: you'll pray it was otherwise . . .'

And with one last satisfied smile, she ran across the lawn and up the stone steps to rejoin the party.

14

Ha! I actually laughed out loud. And the sound snatched me up and dragged me back to the train. I didn't know about the other visions but I *knew* what I'd just seen about Perry wasn't true. Medusa! Medusa was just a legend. She didn't really exist. And even if the legend had an iota of truth to it, Medusa sure as hell didn't exist nowadays. Perry's encounter *had* to be imagination.

Why were some of my visions so real, while others, like those of Miss Wells and now Perry, seemed so . . . far-fetched? Medusa! What next? Wolverine running for American president?

'What's so funny?' asked Rachel.

'You are,' I told her. 'D'you know, you actually had me going until Perry's dream.'

Rachel looked at me but said nothing.

'What is it? Some kind of hypnotism trick?' I asked. 'You're good – I'll give you that.'

'I'm not trying to trick you,' Rachel denied softly.

'But you really expect me to believe that Medusa

comes after Perry just 'cause of his name? Please!'

'The dreams you take us into are nothing to do with me,' said Rachel. 'And I told you before, some dreams show what is to come; some are just dreams, nothing else.'

'Look, I don't know what your game is but I'm not playing,' I told her belligerently.

Now that I knew it was some kind of hoax, I was determined to focus on the task at hand – like getting the hell off this train.

'Which game would you prefer to play?' Rachel asked me coldly. 'Mine or his?'

And she turned me round to face the end of the carriage. Where the shimmering light was before, there was now the translucent, misty form of a man. At least, I think it was a man, but it was more like a ghost forming before my eyes than anything else.

Ghosts and shadows . . .

They were on my list of things that scared me the most.

I wasn't out of this nightmare yet.

'Now, d'you want my help or not?' Rachel asked.

I couldn't speak, could hardly think. All I could do was feel the fear inside eating me up as I watched the shadow struggle to become more tangible. And it was a struggle, I could see that much.

'Get us away from here, Kyle,' Rachel whispered.

'How?'

'One of your friends. Lose yourself inside the dream of one of your friends. Then he'll never find you.'

I turned and looked at Perry, at Steve, at Joe. But I couldn't think myself into their dreams again. It was as if their minds had closed a door against me. Beside me Rachel was beginning to breathe more heavily, as if panic were beginning to set in with her too.

'Kyle, hurry . . .'

I backed away, stumbling as I did so but managing to remain on my feet. Out of the corner of my eye I saw Roberta. I thought of her dream and found the way was still open to jump back into it. So those were my choices. The Marauders from Robby's head or that *thing* at the end of the carriage. No contest. That apparition was after *me*. Against the Marauders, Robby stood a chance – even if it was only slim. What chance did I have against Death? I closed my eyes and leaped. And somewhere along the way, Rachel leaped with me.

15

Roberta's Nightmare

Marauders!

The midnight-blue overalls which covered their entire bodies struck fear into my heart. The Marauders were the only ones – that I knew of, at any rate – who could survive the rain. And it was because of their uniform. I'd never met anyone who knew how they did it, or where their uniforms had come from in the first place. There were rumblings about the Marauders being someone's private army but no one knew whose, or even if the rumours were true. Marauders arrived without warning and left destruction and chaos in their wake. I ran for the trapdoor between the water tanks and let myself into the cellar, careful not to fold the lino right back so that it would flop over the trapdoor once I had closed it. The last sound I heard was banging on the door, then the sound of wood splintering. I didn't wait to hear any more.

Down in the cellar I forced myself not to panic, although I thought my heart would explode out of my chest. I felt for the knife I always kept on me, reassured by the cool feel of it in my hand. I was armed at least. But hell! I'd never killed anyone before. I'd never had to. What I'd said to Carter was a lie. There was muted shouting and crashing above me. I looked up as if trying to see through the ceiling. Carter . . . Was he all right? Had they killed him yet? I should've stayed with him – but if he was dead then I'd be dead too by now. What could I do that Carter couldn't? I was smaller, younger, not as strong. More muted sounds. I wasn't even sure if they were voices. Now everything was quiet. In some ways that was worse than hearing noises.

Looking through the darkness, I decided that the wisest thing would be to keep out of sight until the Marauders left – or came down into the cellar, whichever happened first. Slowly I felt my way along, arms outstretched, to what I thought would be the ideal spot behind two columns of boxes that I remembered. Very carefully, so as not to knock them over, I inched my way around them. In the space behind the boxes I could stand up straight without being seen from the trapdoor and I had just enough room to kneel but not to sit. I felt safer, but not safe. I counted the time passing by listening to my heart hammer.

Did I doze off? I'm not sure, but I was suddenly keenly aware of the sound of the trapdoor opening. The half-light created by the open door spilled to just in front of the boxes I was hiding behind.

If they came down into the cellar . . .

'How much food do you have down there?' The Marauder's voice was harsh, rasping.

'About enough for six months, maybe a year,' Carter replied.

I pursed my lips in relief. With Carter still alive maybe I stood a chance.

'And it isn't contaminated?'

'Only some of it.' Carter had informed me on my first day that none of the food was contaminated. I understood why he lied.

'Bring us some food,' the same voice demanded. 'And no tricks or I'll peel your flesh myself.'

'I'd better go down with him, Captain. He might have weapons stashed down there,' said another voice.

'Good idea,' the captain agreed. 'Abel, make sure you watch him closely until I return. I'll search the rest of the house. There may be others hiding, in spite of what this man says. Once we've eaten we'll tie him up and you can help me fix the comms box so that we can contact the others. This building will make a good base.'

'What about him?' Abel asked.

'What about him? He has no value except as a cook.'

'He said some of the food was contaminated.'

'He lied. If it was tainted, why would he keep it? I'll wait until the chief arrives. He can decide what he wants to do with this one. Until then he can feed us.'

If it was down to Carter's culinary expertise to save him, he wouldn't stand a chance. I heard footsteps moving in different directions. One set came down the cellar steps, walking in my direction, then stopped.

'If you have anything of value hidden,' the Marauder Abel said silkily, 'tell me where and I *may* persuade the captain to let you live.'

'*May* don't make it,' Carter said.

'*May* is all there is. Think carefully. A chance of life against no chance at all. It seems reasonable to me.'

'That's because you're on the persuading side of that knife. Try seeing it from my position.'

More footsteps. I could see them now, to my left. Abel had most of his back to me. Carter was just visible beyond him. I poked my head out from the side of the top box. Carter's face was bloody and bruised and swollen. An almost imperceptible start told me that he'd spotted me. Anxiously I licked my lips, wondering what I should do next. Carter moved closer to Abel, who rapidly backed away, waving the knife in his hand. Carter stepped forward again. I shook my head frantically. Once again Carter stepped forward and once again Abel backed away in my direction. By now the Marauder was less than a metre away from me.

'If you move again, I'll kill you,' Abel said harshly.

I sidestepped the boxes and crept towards the Marauder, every bloodcell in my body screaming at me to get back, to duck down and hide. Ignoring every grain of sense I had, I moved slowly and carefully, desperate not to make a sound, but Abel must've heard me, or sensed me. His head whipped round. He immediately turned back to Carter, but although he was fast, Carter was faster. He lunged forward, throwing his arm around Abel's neck while his other hand covered the Marauder's mouth. Abel struggled like hell, making Carter spin so they were both facing me. Abel didn't keep still for a single second. I stood petrified, my knife in my hand. Carter tried to get a grip around Abel's throat and head, but every time he tried to adjust his grip, Abel tried to yell out a warning to his captain.

Carter hissed at me, 'Do it. For God's sake, do it. I can't hold him much longer.'

I took a deep breath and, after briefly closing my eyes, thrust the knife into Abel's stomach, twisting it upwards towards his heart. My hands were almost instantly wet and warm. I pulled out my knife, more reflex than considered action. I stared into Abel's eyes, which were wide with a strange surprise. Carter let the Marauder slip to the ground. I knew he was already dead but Carter wasn't taking any chances. He twisted the man's neck, then pulled the body to one side of the boxes where it wouldn't be seen. He cursed when he found that Abel, unlike most Marauders, had no gun. I looked down at the body, my heart still fearfully pounding inside me. I'd killed someone. I'd actually killed someone. Even though I knew it was us or the Marauders, I still wanted to cry. *I'd killed someone . . .*

'Carter, I'm going to be sick,' I whispered, my hand over my mouth.

'Not yet, boy,' Carter hissed at me. 'Wait until we've killed the other one.'

You had no choice, Robby, I kept telling myself. *It was him or you.*

The thought helped some, but not much. I swallowed hard, then went on swallowing until the bile that kept filling my mouth stayed down. We crept up the steps to the kitchen, where Carter armed himself with a knife in either hand. I wiped my sticky red hands on a rag that was probably supposed to be a tea towel. I kept wiping them – still faintly red but now dry – on my jacket as we crept upstairs, staying away from the middle of each step to avoid the creaks and groans of the wood beneath our feet. I'd never been upstairs, but I was too frightened to be curious. The captain was moving about in one of the rooms. Carter turned to me, pointing at himself.

'Your bedroom?' I mouthed silently.

He nodded. Quickly but silently he moved to the other side of the open door. He pointed at me, then inside his room, indicating that I should go in first. I mean, sod that for a game of soldiers! I shook my head angrily, not impressed with his idea of using me for bait. Carter started making threatening faces. I shook my head again, but he looked like he was about to leap across to where I was standing and throttle me, so I tiptoed into the room when the captain had his back to me, hoping that Carter's plan was a good one. The man was searching through an old-fashioned chest of drawers, snorting with disgust when all he found were clothes – and not terribly clean ones at that.

A floorboard creaked under my foot and I froze. Too late. The captain turned sharply. One look at me and he rapidly reached for the gun around his waist. In a heartbeat it was out of his belt and already moving upwards, pointing towards my chest. And I couldn't move. All I could do was watch death rush inexorably towards me. But something whizzed past me and I watched as, almost in slow motion, the captain clutched at the knife that had just sliced its way into his chest, before crashing to the ground. Carter didn't wait for me. He ran over, relieving the captain of his gun before turning furiously back to me.

'What the hell did you think you were doing? Were you going to stand there and watch him kill you?'

I didn't speak until I was sure I wasn't going to disgrace myself by throwing up. 'Sod off, Carter!' I snapped. 'I knew you had my back.'

'You shouldn't've relied on that. Suppose I didn't?'

'But you did. So what's the problem?'

'You are, Robby. When're you going to learn that you can't rely on anyone but yourself? You can't trust anyone else.'

'I trust you.'

'More fool you then,' Carter snapped. 'Now I want the truth. How much longer is the rain going to last?'

'Another twenty-four hours.' I sighed. 'Then I'll be on my way.'

Silence.

'I promise, this time tomorrow the rain will've stopped.'

'Look . . .' Carter seemed uncomfortable. 'You don't have to go tomorrow. You can stay an extra few days if you like.'

Surprise widened my eyes as I stared at him. 'If you don't mind, I'll take you up on that. I'd rather wait until the Marauders have moved on.'

'Fair enough.' Carter's face grew hard. 'But you still sleep downstairs, and no tricks. This time I'll be sleeping with a gun.'

'Well, when you blow your foot off or worse, don't look to me for sympathy,' I said.

Carter smiled reluctantly. We stripped the dead man of his overalls, then went down into the cellar and stripped off Abel's too. Carter repaired the front door with some wood from the cellar, using one of the Marauder overalls as protection from the driving rain.

The next few hours were tense. Even though we closed the shutters, we didn't dare risk lighting any of the candles and we moved about as little as possible. At every moment I expected to hear a bang at the door or a window shattering. We hardly spoke. Dinner was kidney beans in chilli sauce, warmed up but not really heated on a camper stove. My sleep that night was fitful and fretful but at last the morning came. And no more Marauders. I hoped that the two dead men were an advance scouting party, or maybe a breakaway group.

Next day we waited for a few hours after the rain

had finally stopped, then buried the bodies behind the house. By the time we'd finished I was in a state. I was smelly and dirty and longed to take off my damned strappings. I hadn't dared loosen them during the previous night, fearing the arrival of more Marauders. It seemed to me that I'd spent most of my time in Carter's house afraid for one reason or another.

Two days after the rain had stopped, Carter and I walked for over an hour to the nearest river. I didn't want to go with him but he insisted. I dreaded getting there. Totally unselfconscious, Carter stripped naked and jumped into the icy water.

'Come on in then. The water's lovely!'

'I . . . er . . . I think one of us should be on guard in case the Marauders haven't moved on yet,' I suggested.

'Good idea,' Carter called back. 'I'll get clean then act as lookout while you have a swim.'

How was I going to get out of this one? Carter dived down into the water and disappeared. I lay down on the riverbank, closing my eyes against the sunshine. I kept remembering the look on Abel's face when I stabbed him . . .

I must've drifted off to sleep because when I opened my eyes, Carter was kneeling over me and I instinctively knew that he'd been there for a while. I stared at him, wondering anxiously at the angry, sombre look on his face. Oh my God! He didn't know, did he? He hadn't guessed?

'What's the matter?' I frowned, uncertain.

Carter's breathing was deep, audible. He stood up

quickly and strode off towards the house. I opened my
mouth to call him back – after all, he was supposed to
act as lookout while I swam – but then I thought better
of it. This way was much safer. It was OK - he didn't
know or he would've said something. Eagerly I
watched him leave. Now I could bathe in peace and
without having to reveal the truth to him. Even my
fear of the Marauders faded into insignificance at the
prospect of taking off my strappings at last. I
undressed, then washed the strappings and padding
and left them on large rocks by the riverbank to dry. I
rinsed Abel's blood off my jacket and then jumped into
the river, my knife still in my hand. The water was so
freezing it stole my breath away – but it was wonderful. Luckily, only the rain was lethal. Once the rain
stopped, after about an hour the water reverted to
'normal' and was safe again.

Mum once tried to explain the science of it to me,
but I didn't really understand. Science was never my
strongest subject. It had been some new chemical
weapon designed by X to wipe out Y. Only the
weapon, unlike the faction that made it, hadn't been
quite so choosy and had entered the upper atmosphere, spreading around the country and maybe
beyond. Mum told me the chemicals were only
neutralized after a certain period of time at ground
level. So those of us who were left watched the rain
and waited for the day when the man-made chemical
would be burned out or washed down or made safe in
some way. But in the meantime no one went out in the

rain. I still remembered when the rain wasn't my enemy. I didn't even have to close my eyes to see myself walking, dancing, singing in the rain. I swam to and fro, the knife between my teeth. After at least half an hour I clambered out and got dressed, reluctantly restrapping my chest and wrapping the damp padding around my waist. After that I headed back to the house.

The days fell into a semi-regular pattern. I went to the river every morning, either making an excuse not to accompany Carter or going by myself when he didn't want to go at all – which was usually the case. I did all the cooking and Carter did what he called the cleaning, which wasn't worth much. We played cards and chess, at which I got better and Carter got worse. Sometimes I'd look up from the chessboard to find him watching me, the strangest expression on his face and his mind obviously not on the game. Such was life for about three weeks. Easy in an uneasy sort of way. I knew I should move on but my life had taken on some semblance of normality and I was loath to give it up. My stay with Carter was close to being the longest time I'd ever spent in one place since the civil war began.

One evening I asked him, 'Why don't you have any books of your own? The way you read and re-read my books, I would've thought you'd be surrounded by them.' I sighed inwardly as Carter's face took on the same hateful, vengeful expression it always did when he was about to mention his wife.

'The back room used to be full of them. Shelf after shelf of books.'

'What happened to them?' I asked. The back room was totally empty.

'My wife made a bonfire of them. I was meant to be away for two days but I came back early and caught her burning the last batch.'

'Why on earth did she do that?' I asked, scandalized. Books were now like gold dust. In fact, books and gems were the new country-wide currency. No one valued anything else.

'Apparently I cared more about my books than I did about her. So she and her lover decided to teach me a lesson.'

'What happened?'

'I got this scar on my face.'

My blood ran colder. I wanted to ask what had happened to his wife and her lover but I was afraid of the answer so for once I kept my mouth shut. As if guessing my thoughts, Carter smiled – a hard, bitter smile. I looked away.

On good days Carter would talk to me. But sometimes it was as if he couldn't bear to even look at me, to be in the same room as me. He would disappear out of the house after gruffly asking if it was going to rain. Then I wouldn't see him for hours. We still played chess, but when Carter was in a mood I never spoke. He inevitably became furious with me when I talked too much. It took me longer than it should have to realize what the problem was. Carter was lonely, so lonely he was only just beginning to realize it himself.

One evening, a few hours before the rain I'd predicted was due, I went to the river for my last swim for the next three days. The air was fresh and clean and I felt more relaxed than I had done in a long time. Carter had gone off somewhere, so I was looking forward to an uninterrupted swim. But first I lay down in my favourite spot, a few metres from the water and the midges, and closed my eyes. The calm I felt was so rare and new that I couldn't help smiling. I really ought to be thinking about moving on but I was so tired of travelling. Hell! I was just tired! Sometimes I wondered if it was worth surviving like this, existing like this, but only sometimes. Life was special – Mum had drummed that into me and I believed it. Some of the time. Most of the time.

I lay still, enjoying the peace and not thinking of anything in particular. But then the whispered sound of breathing made me open my eyes. Carter's face was only a few centimetres away from mine. He kissed me before I could stop him, but as soon as I pushed at his shoulders he let me go.

'What the bloody hell d'you think you're doing?' I gasped. Ohmigod! Carter had kissed me! *How had he guessed?* How did he find out? I'd been so careful.

Carter ran his fingers through his hair. 'I'm sorry. I . . . hell!'

It was the look on his face that stopped me from leaping to my feet and running. He was angry and appalled, but not with me.

'You're . . . you're gay!' I breathed with relief.

All this time I'd been safe and never knew it. The irony of my situation struck me and I started laughing. In fact, I roared with laughter. Carter sprang to his feet and, after a bitter look in my direction, marched off. Guiltily I stifled my giggles. I wasn't laughing at him. My laughter was just a release. I was *safe*. For the first time since my mum died, for the first time since the war, I was safe. But how could Carter know that? I shrugged. Never mind. I'd explain it all to him when I got back to the house. Carter was gay! Maybe that was the cause of the trouble between him and his wife, or maybe his wife had put him off women for life. No, it didn't work like that. But hell! What did I know? Carter was gay. That was all I cared about. It struck me that he had never told me his wife's name. I'd have to ask him when I got back.

I finished my swim and walked quickly back to the house, not bothering to strap my breasts down as I usually did. Carter was in the kitchen. It looked as though he was making dinner, but it was difficult to tell because he had his back to me. If he *was* making dinner, then I was in trouble.

'Carter, I—'

'Rob, I want you to leave. I want you to leave this house now,' Carter interrupted, his back still towards me.

'But it's going to rain before morning,' I protested.

'Then the sooner you leave the sooner you'll find shelter somewhere else.' Carter still didn't turn to face me. 'You can use one of the Marauders' suits.'

'If I get spotted wearing that thing by anyone who's not a Marauder, I'll be torn apart as I'm on my own. And if I stumble across Marauders, once they find out that I'm not one of them, I'll get torn apart anyway.'

'You'll just have to take your chances like everyone else,' Carter said stonily.

'Carter, is this because—?'

'No, it isn't,' he denied harshly.

'But I understand. Really I—'

'There's nothing to understand.' At last Carter swung around to face me, his expression furious.

I grinned at him. 'You should've told me, Carter,' I said lightly. 'I couldn't care less about your . . . sexual preferences. But if you'd told me sooner I wouldn't have had to strap down my breasts and pad out my waist. You have no idea how uncomfortable—'

'You're a woman!' he said incredulously, staring at my body.

'Every cell!' I beamed again at his statement of the obvious. 'My name's Roberta, but I call myself Robby. Before my mum died she told me it wasn't safe to travel around alone as a girl. That's why I pretended to be a boy . . .' My voice trailed off as I watched Carter. He was rigid with fury.

My smile faded. 'I didn't mean to deceive you. I mean, well I guess I did deceive you deliberately but only because you're a man and I didn't know you were—'

'You damned liar!' he roared.

'I never lied to you,' I said, annoyed and suddenly nervous. 'You never said to me "Are you a woman?" and I never said "No"!'

Carter took a step towards me. I took a hasty step backwards.

'I don't see what you're so angry about,' I snapped. Carter was frightening me. The look on his face was like nothing I'd ever seen before. 'Unless of course you're disappointed that I'm not a man . . .'

Mistake!

He grew even more angry at that. I stepped back again, only to bash into the water tank behind me.

'Oh, for goodness' sake! Don't look at me like that. I'm not your wife.'

Another mistake.

He stood in front of me, his eyes burning into mine. My heart pounded in my chest as I stared at him, desperately trying to figure out my next move. Without warning I darted to my right, hoping to run round him.

That was my biggest mistake.

He grabbed my arm and pulled me round to face him. Instinctively I knew I should've held my ground and tried to reason with him. He started shaking me hard, his face contorted with rage. He wasn't Carter any more, I wasn't Robby. He was just a furious, deceived man and I was the girl who'd deceived him. His fingers were biting into my arms like raindrops.

'Carter, let me go,' I tried to demand through chattering teeth. He shook me harder at that, before

185

suddenly releasing me. Out of the corner of my eye I saw his hands, clenching and unclenching. I started to take a step backwards but he was too fast for me. He made a fist and punched me just as hard as he could across my face. I dropped like a stone. The rusty nail taste of blood was in my mouth and everything around me had turned brilliantly, blindingly white. I blinked, then blinked again, too stunned to even cry. Colours started appearing before my eyes again. Dazed, I looked up. My dad was staring down at me, breathing hard.

His face was a blur of shapes, swirling in my head like wet paint, but it was definitely my dad. Except now the shapes were beginning to solidify. And it wasn't my dad. It was Carter. How strange that I'd never noticed just how alike the two of them were. Disgust swept over Carter's face as he regarded me. Without saying a word, he turned and slammed out of the house.

I told myself to get up, but I couldn't control any part of my shaking body. It was five minutes before I managed to get my breathing under control. And at least another five before my limbs began to obey me. But once I'd staggered to my feet, I managed slowly but surely to get some momentum behind my movements. I washed my face and rinsed the blood out of my mouth. My tongue felt like it was two sizes too big. I touched it gingerly, then examined my fingers. They were covered with blood. I must've bitten my tongue when . . . when . . . I spat in the sink and rinsed the blood away. After that I just swallowed it. I couldn't waste any more time waiting for my tongue to stop bleeding.

I got dressed quickly, my chest strapped and the padding back around my waist. I took the matches out of my pocket, picked up my novel and set fire to it. The flames danced upwards as I held the book. I waited until they seared my fingers before leaving the burning book on the wooden table. I went into each of the downstairs rooms and set fire to whatever would burn. I left my final match on the bottom step and walked slowly out of the house, ignoring the flames crackling all around me. I walked some metres away before turning to watch it burn. The sky was now a dusky blue-black, a perfect backdrop for the conflagration. I watched the flames grow higher and higher each moment, licking hungrily at the sky. I sniffed the air, satisfied, sad.

'That's for you, Mum,' I whispered.

I heard running behind me, but I didn't turn round. I continued to watch the house. The flames were lovely, blood-red, blood-orange, blood-yellow. The heat warmed me. I wrapped my arms around myself.

'What've you done?' Carter stood beside me, incredulous. And afraid.

I didn't flinch away from him. We watched the fire together, the house a mass of flames now. It was almost impossible to discern the original structure. I sniffed again.

'It's going to rain within the next few hours – and sooner rather than later too,' I whispered.

'But without shelter, *you'll* die.'

'So will you.' I turned to face him for the first time. 'As my mum used to say to me, Carter – such are the times we live in.'

I turned back to the blaze, unable to keep the tears from streaming down my face.

The fire lasted for over an hour, crackling, then dying before our eyes, without another word passing between us. And the rain was closer. Very little of the original structure remained in place as the fire died down. Most of the house was razed to nothing but carbonized rubble. I turned slowly and started to walk away. I wanted to be alone when the rain started, but Carter grabbed my arm, turning me round to face him.

I flinched out of his grasp, my fists clenched. But only for a moment. If he wanted to take his revenge by killing me, then he'd be doing me a favour. Being caught in the rain would be a slow, excruciating death.

'Robby, what d'you want me to say? I'm sorry . . . I'm so sorry . . .'

I stepped away from him.

'Oh hell,' Carter said harshly. 'Look, I . . . I don't want to die. I don't want you to die either and we . . . we can survive this. We can *both* survive this.'

I looked up at him, saying nothing. It was strange how ghostly-silver his face looked in the fading moon-light. Gaunt and ghostly. Did I look as strange?

'If we . . . if we can clear the rubble from over the cellar door, we could stay down in the cellar until the rain stops.'

Still I said nothing.

'But I can't do it without you. Hell! Even with you we might still die, but with your help maybe . . . maybe we stand a chance. You've survived this long . . . Surely you don't want to die like this . . .'

And we watched each other – silently.

16

The look that passed between Roberta and Carter was filled with such hopelessness that I couldn't watch any more. I really couldn't. I wasn't able to deal with what their expressions were saying to each other. I pulled away – and found myself back on the train. And what's more I was grateful for it. The rain was at last beginning to ease.

'I don't understand how I'm supposed to stay inside these dreams when they always end so . . . They end,' I said. 'I mean, there's nowhere to go after the dreams are finished.'

'Yes there is,' Rachel said softly. 'You can accept your fate, just as all your friends and your teacher have to accept theirs.'

I stared at her.

'That's the main reason why you keep falling out of their dreams – you won't accept the inevitable,' she continued.

'Nothing's inevitable. We all have choices.'

'Who're you trying to convince – me or yourself? Roberta had the right idea.'

'What d'you mean?'

'Well, it's all pointless, isn't it?'

I didn't even try to disguise the shock I felt at that moment. 'Not necessarily,' I argued finally. 'Some things are worth dying for, but aren't there more things worth living for?'

'We both know you don't really believe that,' said Rachel. 'Your dad did what he set out to do. And you'll do the same. The train, school, your friends, it's all meaningless. Haven't you reached the same conclusion recently?'

We exchanged a look then, a look that told me she knew *exactly* what had been going through my head over the last few weeks.

'So all I have to do is accept my fate or the fate of my friends, and then what?' I asked.

'Then you'll find what you're looking for.'

'And what's that?'

'Peace.'

Peace . . . That word sounded so good.

'And how exactly do I go about accepting my fate?'

'You enter a dream and you stay put.'

Oh, was that all? She made it sound as easy as breathing.

'I couldn't stay in Robby's dream, OK – and don't give me a hard time about it,' I said as she opened her mouth to give me a hard time about it.

'I won't, but that thing will,' said Rachel, pointing down the carriage.

The mist now had mass. It was forming itself into

something frighteningly solid. Well, I'd seen enough, thanks. I certainly didn't want to find out what Death looked like in the flesh. Time to pick a dream and stay put. Conor . . . I hadn't been inside his head yet.

'*Kyle, wait for me . . .*'

Yeah, right! The whisper inside my head came from the dark mist at the other end of the carriage. Nothing on earth could've kept me in that carriage. I focused on Conor, Rachel took my hand and we leaped.

17

Conor's Nightmare

Before Nan got ill, everyone said she was cuckoo. She certainly had what my dad called 'views' on certain subjects. She didn't like any swearing in her bedroom. She swore like a career soldier in the rest of her house, but not in her bedroom. And she didn't believe in leaving her curtains shut after nine in the morning. She said it was an insult to the sun. In cold weather she'd go out into her garden to feed the birds with her bra around her head and tied under her chin. She said it kept the cold off her ears better than any woolly hat. But we didn't mind any of that because, well, it was kind of funny. My nan rode a motorbike and horses, did a parachute jump for charity, kept two pet rats in her living room – except when she knew Mum was visiting her; then the rats would be kept in the shed at the bottom of the garden. Mum hates all rodents. So you see, Nan was pretty fearless. Except for one thing.

She couldn't stand dripping taps.

Mum and Dad warned me and my sister, Sorcha, to make sure we always turned off the taps in Nan's house properly. I remember once, when I was only seven or eight, I left a tap dripping on purpose. Not a fast drip, just a slow and steady *plink, plink*. I wanted to see what Nan would do. She eventually got up from her armchair in front of the log fire and headed for the bathroom. I held my breath, but I didn't have to wait long. Nan absolutely freaked. She went berserk. She ran out of the bathroom screaming and crying and darting around frantically like a kite in a high wind.

'Go away! It's not my fault. It's not time,' Nan shrieked as she spun round and round. I watched, terrified yet fascinated.

It took Mum and Dad ages to calm her down, and when we got home again they both raged at me for a good half-hour, made me write a sorry note to Nan and then stopped my pocket money for a month. I never tried that experiment again. It wasn't until I was much older that I even dared to broach the subject. It was one time after school when I popped in for a quick visit. Nan had had a hip-replacement operation and it was taking her a long time to get over it. In fact, for the first time she looked her age. We usually played a game of football or dodge ball in her garden but she obviously wasn't up to it. So we played a couple of games of backgammon (Nan's favourite) and then dominoes before I plucked up the courage to ask her.

'Nan, why don't you like dripping taps?'

Nan opened her mouth – to rant at me, I think. But then her mouth snapped shut. She regarded me. 'D'you really want to know?'

I nodded.

Nan was silent for so long, I wondered if she'd thought better of telling me. But then she said quietly, 'Conor, some people don't believe in anything they can't see, can't hear, can't think about. Some people don't believe in anything they don't *want* to think about. Well, I used to be one of those people. I didn't believe in Heaven or Hell, or demons or angels or anything like that. Shows what little I knew. I thought believing in things like that was like believing in the tooth fairy or Father Christmas.'

'But you believe in all that now?' I frowned.

'I believe in ghosts, Conor.' Nan's laugh was bitter and brief. 'And if ghosts exist, then so can all the other things we don't yet understand.'

'You don't really believe in ghosts, do you?' I asked sceptically. This had to be a wind-up.

'Conor, I know they exist,' said Nan. 'I *know*.'

'How?'

Nan stared into the fireplace, watching the orange-yellow flames dance and sway. A faraway look came into her eyes. 'Why not?' she muttered to herself. 'Why not?'

She turned towards me. 'Conor, I'm going to tell you something I've never told anyone before.'

I waited without speaking through another long pause. I didn't want her to change her mind. Nan sighed, then she began.

'I used to go to Ashville Secondary School. My best friend was a boy called Eddie. My teacher was Mrs

Tate. Mrs Tate was tall and thin, with strawberry-blonde hair and almond-shaped blue eyes. I used to sit at the end of the second-to-last row in the class, closest to the window. And that's how I spent most of my time, watching the world stroll past my window. Mrs Tate always used to say to me, "Amy, you should spend less time daydreaming about other worlds and more time living in this one. This life isn't a dress rehearsal, you know."'

'Is that why you do all those really exciting things?' I asked, remembering Nan's various adventure holidays like abseiling and orienteering.

'Partly. A small part,' Nan replied.

'What's the big part then?' I asked.

'Mrs Tate arranged a day trip for the whole class to see a pantomime at the local theatre as a Christmas treat. We were all going to see the play in our last week at school in that autumn term.' Nan smiled sadly. 'I remember it seemed to snow every other day that December.'

' "This outing will be extra special because we'll have the chance to meet the actors and actresses after the performance and ask them lots of questions," Mrs Tate said.

'We were all so looking forward to it. Most of us had never been to the theatre before.

' "You're going to love it, I promise," Mrs Tate told us enthusiastically. "*Jack and the Beanstalk* is a great pantomime. And what's more, I've got reduced price tickets – less than half price. The price includes the coach trip there and back. We'll have a trip across the river into town – won't that be great?"

'And just like that, she assumed everyone was going to go. And she was almost right. Everyone in the class signed up for the trip and all the money was paid. Except mine.' Nan took off her glasses and absent-mindedly cleaned them on her skirt before continuing. 'I had no money. My family couldn't afford it, so I couldn't go. It was as simple as that. And I was the only one in my class who couldn't go. D'you have any idea what that felt like, Conor? I don't suppose you do. My clothes were always clean but never new. My shoes were polished, but always bought second-hand. My sister and I never went hungry but we were never stuffed full either. Our mum did her best, but money was always too tight.

'I remember handing in the letter about the pantomime trip to Mum. "Mrs Tate wants all of us to go to see *Jack and the Beanstalk*. It's not too expensive – she managed to get a huge discount on the price of the tickets. Can I go please?" I asked her.

'Mum read the school letter, her head deliberately lowered as she read. I glanced at Alyson, who was glaring at me, sparks flying from her eyes. The look said that I should know better than to ask – but I've always believed, *Don't ask, don't get*.

' "I'm sorry, Amy . . ." Mum began, still not looking at me.

' "Mum, please," I begged. "Everyone else is going. I don't want to be the only one who doesn't go."

' "I'm sorry, Amy," Mum said more firmly, raising her head to look at me this time. "I can't spare the money to let you go to this."

' "It's not that much," I pleaded. "And I'll get a job as soon as I can and pay you right back."

' "Amy, a penny is a lot of money if you don't have it," sighed Mum. "Alyson needs shoes and the electricity and gas bills have just come in. I'm afraid we really can't afford it."

'I tried to bank down the slow flame building into a fire inside me. But it wasn't working. The fire was growing, raging inside and it had to get out somehow.

' "I hate this house and I hate the way we live," I exploded. "I'm so sick and tired of not having any money. We never go anywhere, we never do anything – so what's the point? I might as well just go to bed and not come out ever again. I might as well just *die*."

' "Amy, don't be ridiculous," Mum dismissed.

' "It's not ridiculous. I never go to the pictures with my friends at the weekend because I never have any money," I yelled. "I never go to any of the parties I'm invited to because I can't afford to buy any presents. It's not fair."

' "Where is it written that life is meant to be fair?" Mum asked angrily. "Don't you think I'm as fed up as you are about never having any money. I'm doing my best, Amy."

' "Your best isn't up to much!" I shouted.

'Mum looked at me, just looked at me – and all the hurt and pain in her face extinguished the flames inside me in less than a second. She turned and walked into her bedroom.

'Alyson turned to me and started slow clapping. "Well done, pig-face. Well done."

'I stormed into the bedroom my sister and I shared and slammed the door. I'd known from the time I was given the consent form that it was a waste of time, but that still didn't stop bitter disappointment from gnawing at me.

'And it was even worse when my friends found out that I wasn't coming. Mrs Tate asked me for my consent form and I had to tell her that Mum hadn't signed it and wasn't going to.

' "Doesn't she want you to see this pantomime?"

' "No, it's not that." I rushed to defend Mum. "It's just . . . we can't afford it."

' "Oh, I see," said Mrs Tate.

'I just wanted a hole to open under my chair and swallow me up. All my friends turned to look at me.

' "But you should go," said my friend Eddie. "Everyone else is going. You belong with us."

' "Yeah, we should all go together," Yvonne added.

'Even Mrs Tate asked, "Amy, is there any way you could come?"

' "No, miss," I replied, wishing they'd all just shut up about it. I was feeling bad enough already and they were just making it ten times worse. Eddie was right, I *did* belong with them, but I just didn't have the money. Didn't he understand that if I could've gone, I would have?

'When the day of the theatre trip came, I bunked off school. I wasn't going to go and sit in another class so everyone would know that I was too poor to even go on a day trip. Alyson tried to tell me that being poor was nothing to be ashamed of, but that was what my head knew, not what my heart felt. So I bunked off.'

I frowned at Nan. 'I still don't understand why you don't like the sound of dripping taps.'

'I'm coming to that,' Nan snapped. 'Have some patience. Now, where was I? Ah yes! I spent the day in the library and walking around the town centre. I seem to remember I went to the park and stayed in the adventure playground until school was over, and then I went home. Mum didn't know what'd I'd been up to that day, so that was the end of that – or so I thought.

'You see, I didn't know what had happened because I didn't listen to the news that night – that was for boring grown-ups. I went to my room to do my home-work, Alyson was out and Mum was busy using the sewing machine – so the radio was off all night. I skipped breakfast and headed off for school quite early. There were only a few people hanging around when I arrived and they were obviously very upset about something but I didn't know them to talk to, so I headed for the library until the bell rang.

'When at last I walked into my class, all my class-mates were sitting in their places already. All of them – including Eddie, who was always late. That, if nothing else, should've told me that something was very wrong.

' "Hi, Eddie." I smiled, slipping in my seat next to his. "How was *Jack and the Beanstalk?*"

'Eddie turned towards me and he looked so sad. "Amy, what're you doing here?" he asked. His voice was so strange, kind of cold and far away and gurgly.

' "I'm *supposed* to be here, Eddie. It's my classroom too – remember?"

'Eddie turned to look back at Mrs Tate. I looked around. No one was laughing or chatting or whispering. Everyone was deadly silent. The hairs on the back of my neck began to prickle.

'Mrs Tate turned to me. "Amy, you must leave now," she told me.

' "No!" shouted Eddie. "She belongs with us!"

' "She belongs with us!"

' "She belongs with us!" The whole class was chanting now.

'What on earth were they all talking about?

'All at once, everyone in the class turned to look at me like I'd suddenly sprouted another head or something. But the frightening thing was, they all turned at the same time and looked at me in the same way. I mean, *exactly* the same way. The prickling sensation at the back of my neck grew. I looked at them and they looked at me and not one of them was smiling. And worse still, not one of them made a sound. I began to tremble inside, waiting for someone to say something, anything. The sound of the door opening had me practically jumping out of my skin.

' "Amy, you can't stay here," said Mrs Corbin, the headmistress.

' "That's what Mrs Tate said." I frowned. "Why can't I stay? I know I didn't come to school yesterday but—"

'The headmistress looked shocked. "Amy, that's not funny."

' "What's not funny?"

'I looked around. Everyone in the class was still watching me, not the headmistress.

' "Eddie, what—?" I began.

' "That's in very poor taste, Amy. *Enough!*" Mrs Corbin shouted at me.

' "She can't see us," Eddie told me.

' "What?" I exclaimed. "I don't understand—"

' "Amy, we're going to close the school for the rest of the day." Mrs Corbin walked over to me and put her arm around my shoulders. "I know this must be hard for you but—"

' "What's hard for me?"

' "Losing your friends like that," said Mrs Corbin.

'I looked around the class at all my mates, then back at the headmistress. I still didn't have a clue what she was talking about.

' "Come on, Amy. I'll phone your mum to come and pick you up," she said.

' "Mrs Tate, what's going on?" I cried, truly bewildered. I turned to my best friend. "Eddie, is this some kind of joke you're all playing?"

' "Amy, our coach overturned on the way back from

the theatre. We all ended up in the river," Eddie told me. "And we couldn't get out."

'The moment Eddie uttered those words, the clothes of each person in the class began to drip, drip, drip. Great big puddles of water on the floor. I just screamed and screamed and screamed . . .'

There was no sound in Nan's room except the ticking of her clock on top of the telly.

'And that's why you hate the sound of dripping taps, because it reminds you of what happened?' I managed to gasp out.

'No, darling,' Nan told me wearily. 'When a tap drips in my house, my friends from school and Mrs Tate all come and stand before me. They stare at me and say nothing and their clothes just drip onto my carpets – except nothing ever gets wet. And I'm so tired of them watching me. I'm so tired . . .'

'Why do they watch you?' I asked, turning my head this way and that, as if to see them standing in the same room as us. 'What do they want?'

Nan smiled. 'They want me to join them. I should've been with them and somehow I think they feel cheated. They won't rest until I'm with them. So I'll jump from planes and I'll ride motorbikes and I'll hike up mountains, but I'll never, ever do any activity that involves rivers, lakes or the sea. Not while they're waiting for me. They're never going to let me go and I—'

Out in the kitchen, we both heard the sudden but unmistakable sound of a tap beginning to drip . . . I looked around the room but could see nothing. Nan stared, her eyes wide and frantic. And then she started to scream.

I ran to the kitchen to turn off the tap, but no matter how tightly I turned it, it continued to drip. And in the living room Nan was still screaming.

'Nan, I can't turn it off!' I shouted. 'Nan? *Nan?*'

Then the screaming stopped. Somehow that was worse. My heart in my mouth, I ran back into the living room. Nan was still sitting in her chair, her eyes wide open. But she wasn't breathing and I knew in that instant that she'd never breathe again. And the thing that will haunt me until I'm old and grey was the fact that her clothes were soaking wet and drip, drip, dripping onto her favourite armchair and the carpet below.

18

How horrible. Poor Conor's nan. Poor Conor. His grief struck me hard. I knew exactly what he was going through. He really loved his nan and I felt like a voyeur spying on his grief. Of course I couldn't stay. I had to get back to the train.

I could feel Rachel trying to pull me back into Conor's dream but I couldn't stay. I just couldn't.

'Kyle . . .'

I raised a finger to shush her. I could hear something. From above came the welcome sound of an approaching helicopter. Now that the wind and rain had died down, they'd come back to rescue us. And not a moment too soon. I didn't even have the nerve to look directly down the carriage. Out of the corner of my eye, I could see a more solid shape than ever before, but I wasn't going to turn my head for a proper look. It was was wet and squelchy underfoot, and I'm sure all the water beneath us wasn't helping us to stay on the bridge. A different colour helicopter came into view and hovered above. Waving my hands above my head, I waited eagerly to see a paramedic descend. But instead a TV camera appeared, its lens trained straight down on me. I couldn't believe it. A TV camera. We could all die at any moment and the best the gits in the chopper could do was train a camera on us. I'd felt a lot of things since the crash, but this was the first time I'd felt burning anger. Well, if they wanted a spectacle, they weren't going to get it from me.

Clambering over debris, I studied the faces of my friends, trying to jump into someone's mind and away from the intrusive TV camera. Then I saw Naima. Hell! I didn't want to invade *her* dreams. I couldn't stand her and she was so damned selfish and spiteful, her dreams would probably be worse than Elena's – but what choice did I have? I closed my eyes – and hitched a ride on the nightmare running through Naima's head. And for once I didn't feel Rachel with me. I searched around for her but she'd obviously decided not to follow me. I turned my attention back to Naima, dreading to think what I would find. When I opened my eyes I saw something I never, ever thought to see on Naima's face. A sadness, an intense but contained grief that made me start with surprise. Even with everything I'd seen before now, it still took me a couple of seconds to realize that I wasn't looking at the Naima of here and now. The girl with the saddest eyes I'd ever seen was yet to come. The girl with the saddest eyes was at least a decade away. Maybe even two. A moment later and I was no longer looking at Naima; I was inside her head looking out.

19

Naima's Nightmare

Dying was a great disappointment to me. I had expected burning, choking flames and demons and screams of rage and pain. I had *hoped* for soothing music and welcoming light and smiles and flowers; but what I got was Payne's Cemetery. Payne's Cemetery was really two cemeteries divided by a line of solid, majestic oak trees. On one side – my side – were the bodies of us 'People'. On the other side were the bodies of those we called the 'Others'. On my first day dead, when the sun had just set and the evening sky was a suffocating purple-blue, I awoke to find myself buried next to Mrs Statson, probably the biggest gossip anywhere, alive or dead. She had been my boss for more years than I cared to remember so I knew how vicious her tongue could be.

'Well, well, Naima! So you're dead too,' she said smugly. 'I'm surprised you didn't die before me, the way you always carried on. Look who's here, everyone.'

Maybe I *was* down in Hell after all.

'Well, child,' Mrs Statson urged, 'what happened to you? What did you die of?'

'Loneliness, Mrs Statson.' I smiled. 'I missed your gossiping tongue so much.'

'Don't get smart with me, Naima.' Mrs Statson frowned. 'You always were no better than you should be.'

'Well, you'd know all about that, wouldn't you?' I said sweetly.

Eternity next to this woman? God forgive me my sins!

'Never mind Mindy Statson. She has the fastest tongue on either side of the oaks.' I looked at the man who had just spoken. I recognized his face, although I didn't know his name. He worked – or used to work – in the garden of one of the Others. In fact, if memory served, he was quite a famous gardener, constantly sought after in the City. He had a rugged, interesting rather than handsome face and shoulders almost too broad for his short height.

'Naima, you have to understand something,' he said. 'The first rule of this place is that we each tell what brought us here.'

'Why are you here?' I questioned. By this time more and more People were gathering round, staring at me, the newbie. A few I recognized; most I did not.

'I died of a heart attack,' he said.

'And what is this place?' I asked. 'Heaven? Hell? Or somewhere in between?'

208

'We don't know,' he replied. 'It's not too bad though . . . once you get used to it.'

That could be said for anywhere in the universe.

I looked up at all the faces staring down at me before scrambling to my feet. I don't like to be looked down on.

'Are you in charge here?'

The man smiled before replying. 'In charge of what? There's nothing to be in charge of.'

'What's your name?'

'Oliver.'

'Hello, Oliver.' I thought about holding out my hand, but then decided against it. After all, this wasn't a party.

'We're still waiting to hear how you died,' Julia Greeg piped up from behind him. I never did like that woman. She was responsible for whipping up the mob that killed my best friend Raven. Raven believed in live and let live, even when it came to the Others, and she made a lot of enemies because of those beliefs. Julia Greeg managed to convince a few drunken hotheads that Raven was a fraternizer – worse than a murderer in our colony. They went to her home and torched it, aiming to make Raven homeless. None of them realized that Raven was fast asleep inside. The smoke made sure she didn't wake up. The flames made sure she didn't get out.

'Is Raven here?' I looked around the crowd eagerly. At least Raven's presence would make this place bearable.

'No,' Julia said smugly. 'She didn't make it here.'

'She didn't miss much,' I spat back.

I remembered that Julia Greeg had been knocked down and killed by a hit-and-run driver. Everyone knew that the driver had to be one of the Others – they were the only ones who could afford to drive in our colony – but not exactly which one. Or if anyone did know, they certainly weren't saying. Not that it would have made much difference: the driver would be tried by his peers and found not guilty. After all, it was only one of the People who had died and we People didn't matter. My only regret about Julia's death was that I hadn't been the driver.

Julia marched forward and grabbed my arm. 'How did you die? We won't ask you again,' she hissed at me, her cold breath fanning my face.

I looked down at her arm, feeling her bony fingers clutching at my flesh. 'Move it or lose it,' I said quietly. She removed her hand immediately. Julia may have been a coward but she was no fool.

'I'm here . . .' I spoke slowly to the eager faces crowding around me. 'I'm here because I killed one of the Others.' It was the truth but I didn't tell them to get their approval, I just wanted them to hear it, then leave me alone. Some cheered, some smiled, every hostile expression disappeared. The atmosphere changed immediately. I was instantly one of them. I was *accepted*. I listened to their eager questions firing at me – questions I wasn't ready to answer.

'Which one . . . ?'

'What happened . . . ?'

'Which of the Others was it . . . ?'

'Why only one . . . ?'

It went without saying that I'd paid the ultimate price for taking out an Other. There was no way in the world I would survive after that. No one was terribly interested in how I'd died, just why. Maybe this *was* Hell after all.

'Leave the girl alone,' Oliver bellowed. 'She's only just got here.'

Silence. Oliver might say he wasn't in charge but they sure respected his orders.

'Well, girl, you can't have been as bad as I thought if you took out one of the Others.' Mrs Statson smiled. This was the first time I'd ever done anything right in her eyes. She belonged to a Resistance movement that I considered a waste of time and I had told her as much when I came to work for her. She'd never forgiven me for that when we were alive. After all, I should've been a prime candidate for recruitment. My mother, a singer, was taken to the City to perform for the Others soon after we joined the colony, only I never saw her again. Then my dad had been killed in a hunt organized by the Others a couple of years later. He had to work as a beater, driving the nesting birds out of their gorse nests and up into the air for the Others to shoot. Only a stray bullet ate its way into my dad's back, killing him instantly. Just a bit of sport for them, a day out. But one moment I had someone and next moment I was alone.

With my background, I should've been begging the Resistance to take me in – I guess that's how Mrs Statson saw it. She didn't understand that all I wanted to do was keep my head down and get on with my life. I didn't want to make a stand, cause any fuss, stand out in any way. She said that made me a coward, too afraid to stand up for what I believed was right. I told her that made me smart and liable to live longer than her or anyone else in the Resistance.

I was no fan of the Others but I was no fan of Mrs Statson either. And the Resistance movement just didn't interest me – at least, that's what I told myself at the time. The thing was, Payne's Cemetery didn't interest me either.

I walked away from all of them towards the edge of the cemetery, ignoring their whispers behind me. I had to get out of this place. Eternity here would drive me crazy. The cemetery was bordered by a low, white, wooden fence, which gleamed in the cold, silvery cemetery light. The light spilled a metre or two beyond the fence, but I could see nothing past that. I peered, trying to stare my way into the darkness beyond. It was enveloping, almost welcoming. And it was away from Payne's Cemetery, which was all I cared about. I lifted one foot and stepped over the knee-high fence. I gingerly placed my foot down on the ground beyond. I was unsure what to expect but the earth was solid beneath my feet.

'It won't work,' Oliver said quietly from behind me.

I ignored him and swung my other foot over the

fence, only to find myself somehow back on the cemetery side of it. I tried again and again and again – and got precisely nowhere. With each step outside I'd be back inside the cemetery.

'You're wasting your time,' said Oliver. 'I've tried. Hell, I've been here for ever but still a day doesn't pass when I don't try to get out.'

I turned to look at him. 'So we're all stuck here?'

'That's about the size of it.'

I looked around. 'What about getting out from the other side of the oaks, past the graves of the Others?'

'I don't know. I think this fence runs all the way round the cemetery but I can't be sure. Besides, the Others would never let any of us get far enough into their side to find out. But I don't think they can leave any more than we can. Otherwise they wouldn't still be here.'

'Does no one ever cross over to their side?'

'Never,' Oliver stated firmly. 'And if you want to stay healthy, I wouldn't try it.'

'What could they do to me? Kill me? In case you hadn't noticed, they've already done that.'

I'd only been dead a few days before I lost track of time completely. Time was a measure against which I had nothing to hold. I sometimes glanced over to the side of the Others, past the oaks, but I never saw him. I wondered if perhaps he searched for me as I searched for him . . . if he was even there. But it wasn't as if I could ask anyone for information about him. I didn't talk to anyone really, except Oliver. They all wanted to know every little detail of how and why I'd killed one of the Others, which one I'd killed and how I'd died and I wasn't prepared to open myself up like a book for them to read. They wouldn't like the answers anyway.

One late evening I sat just outside a circle of us People discussing the Others – again – but I wasn't really paying much notice. The Others seemed to be the only topic of conversation anyone had. And it was the same old boring diatribes I'd heard when I was alive being aired yet again. But then – of all people – something Julia said caught my attention.

'I'm telling you, there's something very strange about their zenerths. They say their music is unique – in a secret tradition handed down throughout the generations – but the zenerths are like nothing I've ever heard before.'

'Don't let your imagination run away with you,' an old man across the circle from her snapped. 'Their music is as disgusting, as depraved as they are. They beat on those drums and dare to call it music.'

'I never said it wasn't disgusting,' Julia retorted. 'I just said—'

'I think the zenerths produce some of the finest music I have ever heard . . . from anywhere.' Although Oliver's voice was quiet, it seemed to carry across our side of the cemetery. Suddenly not a sound could be heard.

'How can you say that?' Mrs Statson's voice

exploded into angry indignation, shattering the stunned silence. 'The zenerth is one of *their* instruments. How can you possibly say that it produces fine music?'

Oliver shrugged. 'Because in my opinion it does. Just as I can look at a house burning and admire the form and beauty of the flames but abhor the violence and destruction it causes.'

'Surely one can't be separated from the other?' someone else demanded.

'Why not?' Oliver shrugged again. 'You all know how I feel about the Others, but you have to admit, their zenerths are like nothing any of us have ever heard or seen before. And when one of their skilled musicians plays a zenerth, they can make you laugh or make you cry or any emotion in between.'

I stared at Oliver without really seeing him. The arguments flying around me faded to a slight buzzing which could've been inside my head. I was no longer in Payne's Cemetery, no longer dead. Instead I was back. Back in the past. Back with *him*.

I could see it now, the five-sheet zenerth taking pride of place on the wall. And he stood below it, proud of its lines, its colours. This was a particularly unusual zenerth: some of the sheets were held in square and oval frames as well as circular. The largest sheet was forty centimetres square, and formed the base. This sheet, held taut in its wooden frame, was overlapped by a smaller oval frame, which in turn was anchored between two circular frames. Another large oval frame touched most of the others at some point and formed the top of the instrument. Hidden immediately beneath the four topmost sheets were metal strings of different lengths and stretched at different tensions. He took it down and started to play it, stroking and tapping first this sheet then that one, coaxing the low, sweetly sad music from the top four sheets and a low beat from the base until all the sheets filled the air with music and all I had to do was close my eyes for my mind to be filled with lights and colours in an eurhythmic pattern. Then he began to sing to me, accompanied by the zenerth, which he stroked and caressed. I was mesmerized.

'Naima? Naima, are you all right?'

Dazed, I looked at Oliver. 'Yes. Yes, I think so,' I said, confused.

'Come with me,' he suggested. I stood and followed him to the fence which defined our prison. He sat down with his back against the fence and motioned for me to sit beside him.

'Pete and Julia and Mindy Statson – in fact all of them here – are exactly the same.' Oliver sighed, deep contempt in his voice. 'Sometimes I wish I'd behaved slightly better or slightly worse when I was alive – anything so that I didn't have to end up here. But you're different. You're not like them. Yet. I can see it in your face. You and me, we're more alike – kindred spirits . . .'

216

'Surely you and I are here because we *are* like them,' I replied.

It didn't take a genius to work out what was going on, and the Others beyond the oaks on the other side of the cemetery were probably exactly the same as us. We were two wings on the same bird. Oliver didn't say anything. He just glared at the others milling aimlessly away from us.

'I . . . I killed Baris,' I admitted suddenly. 'I . . . I murdered him. That's why I died—'

'Baris!' Oliver said, aghast. 'The colony leader's first born?'

'The one and only. I picked up his gun . . . and shot him dead . . .'

Oliver regarded me. I looked ahead, through the oak trees to where he might be watching me . . . even now. I could feel the curiosity burning through Oliver but he didn't speak and I appreciated that.

'He told me how the zenerths are made and then he took down a five-sheet zenerth he kept on the wall and started playing it for me.' Still I didn't look at Oliver, my eyes picking through the darkness past the trees. 'You're right, Oliver. The zenerths do make a very beautiful sound. And d'you know why? The sheets are our skin. The skin of us People . . . talented singers, poets, writers – anyone the Others feel will suit their purpose. The Others kill our artists and preserve their skin to make their instruments. It has something to do with the way those chosen for each zenerth are killed. Each set of People is carefully selected . . . They have to complement each other . . . And they have to be killed in a special way, so that their skin isn't damaged.' Without looking at him, I knew I had Oliver's full attention. 'Baris told me all about the process. He was proud of how clever the Others are. In fact he delighted in telling me how clever.'

At last I turned towards Oliver. He was staring at me, profoundly shocked.

'I suppose I should be grateful,' I said, close to tears. 'I'm here, trapped in this cemetery, but independent still and with a mind of my own. My skin isn't part of some musical instrument, waiting for the hand of one of the Others to bring me to life . . .'

I bowed my head, struck by the sad irony of what I'd just said, but then I dismissed my thoughts with a slow shake of my head.

'I don't understand,' Oliver whispered. 'How do they . . . ? Where does this happen . . . ?'

'The best and most creative talents are always taken into the City to perform for the Others – we all know that. Only they aren't allowed to perform as themselves – they are *transformed*. That's the word Baris used – transformed. Once our musicians and artists are selected, we never see them again, and yet it's still considered an honour to be chosen. Only top-ranking officials and a few involved in the manufacturing process for the Others know the truth. Our musicians and artists don't live in ease in the City, the way we always thought; they're killed for their skin; slaughtered to make music. Baris said their zenerths are traditional instruments, always made from the skins of their enemies.'

'And that's why you killed Baris?' Oliver asked me quickly.

I bent my head. 'Yes. When he started playing his zenerth for me, when he was so proud of it . . . something snapped inside me—'

Oliver didn't wait to hear any more. He jumped up, calling everyone to him. His voice was loud, relentless. I scrambled to my feet.

'Oliver, no. Please don't tell . . .'

But Oliver looked straight through me. I doubt if he even heard what I said. What I'd told him had been for his ears alone, I didn't want it shared, but I realized now that I had been mistaken in confiding in him. Helplessly I watched as he told everyone my secret. There was a hushed silence when he finished; some people stared past the oaks, but most stared at me.

'Three cheers for Naima!' Julia shouted. 'Three cheers for the woman brave enough to kill the son-of-a-bitch!'

I clenched my fists behind my back as they cheered me, my nails digging deeply into my palms.

Was he over there, watching this?

Julia came over to me when the cheering had finished. 'Did you get a chance to tell anyone else the truth about the zenerths? Any of us who are still alive?'

I shook my head. 'The security guards found me kneeling over Baris's body. They kept me there until his father arrived . . . and then his father . . . his father killed me . . . right there and then . . .'

I remembered his gun pointing at me. I remembered waiting for the blast to tear right through me. I heard the shot. Before the sound could even begin to fade, my whole world turned a blinding, searing white and my body became colder than blue ice. Colder than I'd ever thought possible. The next time I opened my eyes, I was in Payne's Cemetery.

Julia frowned deeply. 'We have to find some way of alerting those who are still alive to what's going on. There must be some way out of here! We have to find it now, to warn them. It's a shame you didn't spread the word before they killed you too.'

'A lot of our artists don't go to the City to perform for the Others,' I told her. 'They hide where the Others will never find them. Our art won't die out.'

'No thanks to the Others,' Julia retorted.

'No thanks to the Others,' I agreed.

I remembered the look of surprise on Baris's face when I shot him. Surprise, then disbelief, then hatred. I hadn't cared then. I hated him so much. I hated him for not understanding, for confirming that he was indeed one the Others and not different, not special as I had always thought . . .

Angry calls and whistles filled the night from our side of the cemetery.

'You bastards . . .'

'Scum . . .'

A line of People stood before the oaks, screaming at the Others. The Others were shouting back, just as angry, as filled with hate as we were. I walked over to stand in the middle of the crowd – and saw him, Baris, on the other side of the oaks. Even though I'd been looking out for him, to finally see him was still a shock. He was just as I remembered, tall, over six feet, with a broad forehead and thick eyebrows over intelligent eyes. He had such a strong face. I still remembered how I'd stared at him the first time I saw him. And he caught me staring and smiled, a smile which turned into a grin at my blushing confusion. Totally unlike the way he looked at me now, loathing burning in his eyes.

So he still hated me. I was glad. If he hadn't hated me then I wouldn't have seen him again. But then I saw it . . . and disbelief tore through me like the gun blast that had ripped into my body and ended my life. Baris had his zenerth slung across his body, his hands resting lightly but possessively on the instrument. His father must have buried him with it, Baris's pride and joy. We stared at each other. Baris looked at his zenerth, then back at me, and his hands fell slowly to his sides.

'Listen to me. *Listen to me!*' I shouted. Gradually the cemetery quietened. 'I killed Baris because he owned a zenerth, because he played it in front of me and was proud of it. And then his father killed me. I think Baris and I should finish what we started. A fight to the end, right here, right now. I won't mind going to Hell if I know he's there with me.'

'I agree,' Baris replied slowly, his low, deep voice rumbling through me the way it always did.

'Naima, let me fight for you,' Oliver demanded, stepping forward. From the abhorrence on his face I could see that Payne's Cemetery was where he belonged, just as we all belonged here, whether we admitted it to ourselves or not.

'No, Oliver. For once I'm going to fight my own battles. Baris is mine.'

'Just as you belong to me,' Baris replied. The hatred in his familiar voice rushed through me. I could see him so clearly; he could see me. For the first time we saw each other for what we truly were.

'And where I'm going, I won't need this any more,' Baris added gravely.

We all watched as he walked towards the cemetery fence. He unstrapped the zenerth, looking down at it for several moments. I wondered what he was thinking. Once I would have said without hesitation that I knew. Suddenly he threw the instrument over the fence. It spun further and further away from us, spiralling into the darkness. I never saw or heard it hit the ground. My eyes were once again on Baris as he turned and walked back.

A silence of anticipation settled on both sides of the oaks. Baris moved forward until he stood just over his side of the line. I moved to stand opposite him. We were touching distance apart. He hadn't changed at all. Strange, but somehow I had expected to see more of a difference in him.

I remembered all the times we had lain in bed after making love, just holding each other. He told me that he loved me, that we would go away . . . away from the colony, even though it was strictly forbidden for us People to travel without all kinds of permits. But there were ways, Baris assured me. We'd travel to another country where we'd both be accepted, where we'd find some happiness. He'd bribe whoever he had to, pay out any amount of money to get us away. It would take all the money he had, and once we were in a new country, life would be difficult: we'd both have to start again with nothing, but at least we'd be together; we'd have each other, Baris promised me – and that was all either of us cared about.

I'd packed my few belongings and gone to his house as I did each morning since I'd started working there as a housemaid two years before. Today was the day; it was all arranged. Baris had hired a car and we were going to drive across the country to a minor border crossing where he had already bribed the guards to let us through. It would take us over three days of hard driving to get there and any number of things could go wrong between now and then, but I refused to dwell on any of them. Baris and I were going to be free, and whether it was for a day or a lifetime, it'd be worth it.

Baris's security guards let me through as usual, without checking my holdall. I finally made my way to Baris's bedroom, avoiding more guards and Mrs Statson's replacement, who was just as bad, if not worse, but I had snuck through the house to Baris's room so many times before that I wasn't anxious. Baris and I had been lovers for over a year now, a deep secret that neither of us dared reveal to anyone, otherwise we'd both be condemned and I'd probably 'disappear' one night, never to be seen again.

We sat down on the edge of his bed, his arm around me as we whispered about our future.

'No second thoughts? No regrets?' Baris asked.

'None.' I smiled. 'What about you?'

'None,' he replied.

'Did you get everything we need?' I asked eagerly, knowing that even if he said no it wouldn't really matter.

'Most of it is in the car already, but take this,' he said, picking up the gun from his bedside table and pushing it into my hands.

I recoiled from the weapon. 'What's this for?'

'In case we run into any guards or police patrols on our way. I'll have one as well, but it'll be better if we're both armed.'

'Do I have to? I mean . . .'

Baris smiled, hugging me closer to him as he put the gun firmly into my hand. 'Once we're out of this country, there'll be no need for guns, Naima. I promise.'

'And no one will follow us?'

I wasn't important enough to follow, but I was so afraid of Baris being pursued and brought back and punished. And I loved him too much to see any harm come to him.

'By the time anyone thinks to come looking, we'll be long gone.'

'Yes, but what if your father decides to come home early?' I worried. I couldn't get rid of the nagging feeling that something was going to go wrong. 'Or what if—?'

But Baris just laughed. 'You're never happy unless you've got something to worry about. We'll be fine. The car's outside, the tank is full, I've got money and I love you. So what could go wrong?'

'Nothing,' I replied, and we kissed, putting all the love and passion we felt for each other into every touch.

We took one final look around his room, the room where we had first been together. Then Baris saw his zenerth, high up on the wall. He smiled eagerly, telling of the nights when he would play for me while we travelled. I said it would be too dangerous to take it but he insisted.

'I love this thing most in the world, followed by you!' he teased.

Then he told me all about this strange musical instrument and I couldn't understand how he could profess to love me and yet own such a thing. For the first time I saw him as he really was.

A different perception.

A different morality.

Different . . .

Looking at Baris's face now, I could see that he was remembering too. We'd had so much to look forward to. Together. Even now I still didn't understand exactly what had happened. How could dreams turn to dust so quickly? When I shot him, he fell to his knees, his hands over the gaping wound in his stomach. The bewilderment in his eyes as he looked at me sank into deep, abject hatred. He took a while to die. Being gut-shot is a slow, very painful death. And as he died, we watched each other, neither of us saying a word. He'd died hating me . . . I'd died hating him, and both for the same reason.

Now Baris grabbed my hands in his and a cry rose up from both sides, before the tense silence fell again. What would he do? Close his hands over my throat for all eternity? What would I do in his shoes? I looked at Baris, waiting . . .

But then he smiled at me. Such a sad smile.

Just as sadly, I smiled back.

'I love you,' he whispered.

'I love you too,' I replied softly.

He did still love me, I could see it in his eyes. Just as he could tell by looking at me how I felt about him. Wrapping our arms around each other, we kissed. We had to make it last, make it count before all the others forced us apart. From far away I could hear all those in the cemetery roaring at us, but they didn't matter any more. Nothing mattered except us. Baris was a murderer – but so was I. He came from a race of murderers who couldn't see that what they were doing to us was wrong. Maybe Baris had realized exactly what the zenerth meant to me when he threw away his most prized possession. I didn't care about that any more. We were damned, Baris and I . . . damned to each other. Damned because we loved each other, and nothing could or would ever change that now.

When we stopped kissing, we held each other tightly, our eyes closed as we waited for the rest to descend on us and rip us to pieces.

But nothing happened.

'Baris . . .' I said uncertainly, opening my eyes.

I didn't dare look round. I didn't dare look at anyone but him.

'Come with me,' said Baris.

We walked towards the cemetery fence together, our arms linked, our eyes focused only on each other and nothing else. I could hear the roars of fury around me, but they were distant, totally external.

We stepped over the fence and carried on walking.

20

They made it out of the cemetery. They *made* it. And where they were going I couldn't follow. For the first time in what felt like for ever, I smiled. And it felt so strange, so alien, it faded almost before it had begun. Musical instruments made out of human skin? I knew Naima's nightmare was in the future, but no way could that come true. Could it . . . ? Who was I trying to kid? I mean, every time I thought something monstrous like that couldn't happen, never in a million years, the daily news on the telly invariably proved me wrong. I didn't know what country Naima was in or what colony she and her family had joined, but what did that matter? And I'd been wrong about Naima not caring about anything or anyone but herself. She was just very good at keeping her feelings deeply hidden. I could understand that.

So Naima had fallen for someone and killed him.

And everything I'd seen had been her life after death.

Who was Baris? What kind of man was he? What

type of person would use the skin of other people in that way? I'd thought that kind of thing had stopped with the Nazis in the Second World War. Obviously not.

Listen to me! Thinking about warring ghosts like they were normal, everyday things. I was thinking about too many things. My head was still buzzing with each vision I'd seen. My head felt like an over-saturated sponge, but what was leaking out was *me* – my sanity, my sense of my own thoughts and feelings. I had too many of the thoughts and feelings of my classmates to have much room left for my own. It took all my concentration to focus on something else. Not Rachel, not my friends, and definitely not that *thing* at the end of the carriage. I looked up again. Was the TV news helicopter still there? It was, and its camera was still trained on me and Rachel.

Were they transmitting right this very second? Was it a live feed going out on all channels nationwide as I stood looking up at it? Maybe Mum was at home, watching me now. Well, it sure as hell wasn't the moment to wave. But everything I was hoped that Mum could see me, that she knew I was OK. For now. If Mum were standing in front of me, what would I say to her? What would I do? I knew what I wanted to do. I wanted the last couple of years to never have happened. I wanted Mum and me to hug like we used to, for everything to go back to the way it was before. I didn't want to hate her any more, but I didn't know how to stop.

Time to escape again and stay put this time. Whose dream hadn't I visited yet? The black woman in the camel coat, the stranger. Her nightmare would be something completely new, something I'd never seen before because I didn't know her. I could escape into her head and never come out. Death would never find me inside her head. And it was as easy as closing my eyes.

21

The Stranger's Nightmare

1985
Waiting.

I've been waiting all my life.

Exactly a year ago today my daughter Miriam walked down the dusty brown road from our township to school, swinging her orange string bag in her hand. Afternoon came and went. As did evening. As did night. I sat and waited for her throughout the night, then the next night . . . and the next.

Waiting.

I never saw her again.

I learned a few days later that she had been detained by the police.

'But why?' I asked.

Miriam's friend Joshua looked down at the ground. He couldn't meet my eyes.

'Miriam stood still when they began to whip us,' Joshua said quietly. 'I've been hiding ever since in case they came back for me. I tried to send you a message . . .' His voice cracked and faded, a temperamental radio being taken further and further away from me.

'She stood still?' I asked.

'She didn't move.' Joshua looked up, his eyes burning. 'You should have seen her. You would have been proud.'

'Proud?' I balked at that strange word.

My daughter was gone. Proud?

'I have to go now,' Joshua muttered.

I barely heard him. My daughter was gone.

Gone.

I sank to my knees and wept, silently, in case my daughter felt my distress . . . wherever she was. I could not add my grief to hers. But I never gave up waiting. I never gave up hoping that one day she would walk through my door.

Waiting.

A month later I had to seek domestic service.

'How can you hire yourself out to be a slave – worse than a slave, a nothing?' my son Gabriel asked angrily.

'Tell me what else to do to put you and Ruth through school,' I snapped back. 'Do you think I want to go? Do you think I want to leave you? Think again. I do it so that you and Ruth will not have to live your lives as I have lived mine. You will have something better. Education is the key that opens any door—'

'*I* wouldn't do it,' Gabriel interrupted with contempt. 'I wouldn't be a slave.'

'You would if you had children, if you wanted the best for them.'

I was tired, so tired of trying to make Gabriel understand. But at least he spoke to me. Ruth, my youngest, had barely said two words since I'd told them that I was going to be a maid.

'If having children means living like an animal, worse than an animal, then I'll never have children,' Gabriel said.

I smiled. 'Children are the one thing you'll ever have that no one, not even this government, can deny.'

'They killed my brother!' Gabriel shouted. 'Our father hardly ever sees daylight working down the gold mines from dawn to dusk. Now Miriam has disappeared and we'll never see her again. You're a fool—'

I slapped him, hard. 'Don't you ever say that again. Don't you even think that your sister isn't coming home.'

Gabriel scowled at me, fighting to hold back the tears that shimmered in his eyes.

'Gabriel . . .' I stretched out my hand.

He ran out of our shack. I sighed. Maybe I'd been too hard on him but he had to be taught not to give up. He had to be taught to wait.

The road to Madam's house was long and hard and dusty. The hot earth scorched my feet through the thin soles of my shoes. But I kept walking. I promised myself as I walked to Madam's house that I would ask about my wages as soon as I saw her, but my courage deserted me in her tomb of a house. I knew that Madam wouldn't appreciate questions about money. And I needed this job.

So I didn't ask.

I'll wait until I've worked the month, I thought. *I'll wait.*

I rang the bell. The door opened almost immediately. Madam stood there, her face set, her green cat eyes looking down at me.

'Come in, Adeola,' she said at last.

I entered the house, out of the sunshine into the cool dark.

'I want you to know that you're easily replaced,' Madam said as soon as I set foot past her front door. 'If you can't do the job, there are at least a hundred others who can. If you don't want the job, there are at least a hundred others who do. And another thing: when you come into this house you're to use the back door. Do you understand?'

'Yes, Madam,' I murmured. Of course I understood.

'My son's room is across the hall from yours. You're to feed him, dress him, make sure he wants for nothing. You're to keep the house clean and cook all the meals. Do you understand?'

'Yes, Madam,' I answered. I've understood all my life.

Oh, Ruth, Gabriel, how I love you. How I miss you already.

* * *

First Day

I prepared lunch for Madam. Two lamb chops, peas in real butter, boiled potatoes. She stood over me the entire time. The smell of the food made my stomach churn. I hadn't eaten since the evening before. I had had to set out early in the morning to walk the long, long way to Madam's house and I was so tired, so hungry by the time I got there. Madam ate her food in the kitchen.

'You can have some lunch too,' she said as she sat down.

I looked down at her plate. 'What am I to have, Madam?' I asked.

'You may have a plate of beans and some tea as it's your first day. Tomorrow your lunch will be bread and jam and tea.' She cut into her lamb chop.

Later that evening, as I was preparing dinner, Madam's husband arrived with their son.

'Peter, this is our new maid. She's going to be your nanny,' Madam's husband said to the small blond boy clutching at his hand.

Peter couldn't have been more than five or six. His cheeks were round and chubby. His arms and legs and stomach were fat and soft. I thought of Ruth at home, her arms and legs thin and hard like pencils, her stomach bloated from malnutrition. I looked up from Peter to Madam's husband. I liked him less than I liked Madam but I smiled tremulously.

I needed the job.

'Why is she here?' Peter asked.

'Your mother needs some help around the house now that she's pregnant,' Madam's husband said. 'Now, Peter, it's time for bed.'

Madam's husband looked at me. 'Take him to bed,' he ordered, his eyes chewing me up and spitting me out.

I held out my hand, which Peter took after a moment's hesitation.

'Come on, Peter.' I smiled. 'You can show me to your room.'

Peter smiled up at me. 'It's this way. You can follow me.'

I looked at him, forcing a smile.

My children . . . Oh, Ruth, Gabriel, I love you so much. I miss you. My eyes creep and creep back to the long, hard road that took me from you. The same road that will bring me back to you. But I must wait to see you. I must wait.

First Week

The house was empty. Madam had gone to see her doctor. Madam's husband had gone to work. Peter was with a neighbour.

Peter . . . What a strange child.

He followed me everywhere, like a puppy. And when his parents weren't around he'd help me with some of the chores. I made the most of it. I knew it couldn't last. But for now he liked me and I didn't mind him. After all, he was just a child.

I was vacuuming the upstairs when I heard the

236

sound of a car pulling up outside. I was halfway down the stairs when the front door opened.

'What are you doing?' Madam's husband snapped.

'I was just coming to answer the door. I was vacuuming.' I kept my voice low and soft. Even the volume and tone of my normal voice are not my own in this house, in this country.

Madam's husband closed the door and leaned against it. He looked at me speculatively.

'Think yourself lucky that you're with us and not most of my friends,' he said at last. 'Their maids use brooms or a dustpan and brush. They're not allowed to touch the vacuum cleaners.'

I didn't know what to say so I said nothing. He spoke as if I should be grateful that he and his wife allowed me to clean their house and eat their bread and jam and mealie meal and samp. I turned round so that he wouldn't see my face.

'Where are you going?' he asked.

I turned back. 'To finish the vacuuming,' I replied.

He stared at me but said nothing.

'May I go back to it?' I asked.

He shrugged. 'That's why you're here.'

I vacuumed their bedroom, larger than my shack several times over. I vacuumed Peter's room, around his double bed, under his chair, around his wardrobe. I paused by the window, leaving the vacuum cleaner switched on. I looked out over their pool, over their back garden. I felt homesick and heartsick and, oh, so tired.

Miriam, are you still alive?

My heart tells me yes. My head tells me no. Which should I listen to? I want to slam down every police worker in the country. I want to tear down their prisons, bulldoze their walls until I find you. First Daniel, my eldest, shot in the back while running away from them, and now you, my daughter. Is that why you didn't run, Miriam? I'm trying to understand. Trying desperately . . .

'We don't pay you to gaze out of the window.'

I jumped at the voice of Madam's husband behind me. I turned. He was standing in the doorway watching. I began to vacuum furiously.

I needed this job. I would give neither him nor his wife an excuse to fault my work.

'Turn that thing off.'

I turned off the vacuum cleaner.

'Come here.'

I walked slowly towards him, my heart pounding. A key turned in the lock downstairs. Madam was home early. Madam's husband looked at me; then, without warning, his open hand came up to slap my face just as hard as he could.

'Get back to work,' he hissed.

My face stinging, I went back to the vacuum cleaner without saying a word.

First Month
'These are your wages. You've been satisfactory . . . so far.'

I looked down at the money in my hand. I wasn't surprised. I was disappointed, but I shouldn't have been. I should have known better.

'Is there a problem?' Madam asked.

I shook my head.

'Because of course you do get food and lodging. Besides, if I paid you any more I'd have to pay tax on it, directly out of your own wages, I might add, so you'd lose out in the long run.'

I clenched my hand around the money. To be told that my low wages were for my own good I was used to. To be expected to believe it tore into me like talons. I'm not a fool.

I may keep silent, waiting . . . but I'm not a fool.

I went home that afternoon, for the first time since I started working for Madam. It took three hours to walk home but I was feather light. Every step along the dusty road brought me closer to my reason for carrying on; every step brought me closer to my reason. I ran the last few metres to my mother's shack. Ruth and Gabriel were both there. I hugged them, drank and smelled and tasted them until my senses were flooded. A month, a whole month had passed since I'd seen them. Ruth and Gabriel and I talked until it was very late – about their school, their friends, their lives without me.

I told them of some of my life at Madam's house. My duties, my food, Peter. Ruth was young. She accepted everything I said at face value. Gabriel was different. He watched me, his eyes burning black, but he said nothing.

After my children went to bed I sat up with my mother talking, telling the truth, until at last I fell asleep in my chair. All too soon Mother was shaking me awake.

I washed in the dark by the standpipe. I kissed my children while they slept and began the long journey back to Madam's.

First Year
It is hard, so hard. I have been here six months and it feels like six centuries. I have seen my children six times – that is the hardest of all to bear. I am on my guard all the time. Outside I simmer silently; inside I boil and rage.

Madam's baby was a girl. They called her Charlene – a name with no character, no background, to my way of thinking. Madam doesn't lift a finger to do anything for Charlene. She sees her child for about an hour every day. I try not to feel sorry for the child. She sees her mother more often than my children see me and she'll probably grow up to be just like her mother, but for now she's innocent and I tell myself that she can't help who she's born to . . . yet.

Madam's husband still won't leave me alone. Just the sight of him makes me feel physically sick. He keeps touching me. The last time he pushed me against a wall and touched my body all over. It is like a game to him. He has even started touching me when Madam is elsewhere in the house. I just close my eyes and endure. I need this job. Peter is a consolation though.

He still follows me everywhere. He sneaks me biscuits and bits of meat from his plate. Of course, when it's stew I can sneak for myself. Stew meat can't be missed in the way that chops or chicken legs can.

I miss my children so much. I thought maybe the ache would get easier, less sharp, but instead it just gets worse. And the road taunts me. Beckoning, beckoning all the time. I hear it calling, even in my sleep. I long to walk it, with no thought in my head of ever turning back.

On my last visit home Gabriel said, 'You care more about Peter than you do about us. You're with him a lot more. We never see Father, we hardly see you.'

'But you know why—' I began.

'You give in too easily!' Gabriel shouted. 'You don't fight. You should *fight*!'

'I work so you and Ruth will have the strength to fight,' I pleaded.

'You work because you're too afraid to do anything else. You're afraid to fight. Then you blame me and Ruth for your cowardice. You are a domestic, you are a slave. You are nothing.'

I couldn't speak for the tears, sharp as broken glass, in my throat. What could I say? How could I explain that I am waiting.

Last Night
Last night, for the first time, Madam's husband visited my bed. I lay there waiting for him to finish, waiting

for him to leave so I could vomit. The door opened and in walked Peter, rubbing his eyes.

Madam's husband didn't realize at first that his son had come in and carried on moving on top of me.

I watched Peter, he watched me, both of us visible in the light of the full moon outside my curtainless window.

Watch your father, I thought as I stared at Peter. Watch how your father uses me because your mother won't give him what he wants. Watch how he uses me because he can. He chews me up and spits me out.

I waited for Peter to speak. I willed him to speak, to understand.

I waited.

'Dad?' Peter whispered.

Madam's husband turned his head. 'Go back to your room, Peter. I'll be right there.'

Peter looked at me and I knew my consolation had disappeared. Madam's son hated me. I was nothing now. He was his father's son.

Today
'Kaffir. Dirty, stinking kaffir.'

I tried not to mind. I tried not to hurt inside but I did. Madam and her husband had gone to have dinner with some friends, leaving me to look after Peter and Charlene, who was upstairs asleep in her cot. Throughout the day Madam's son said barely two words to me. Once his parents had left he sat in the kitchen watching me. Slowly, deliberately he picked up an egg from the work surface and dropped it on the floor. Without a word I cleaned it up. He dropped another. I cleaned it up. He dropped another. I looked at him. He spat at me before running up to his room. I followed him, wiping the spit from my face. He lay on his bed, staring up at the ceiling.

He sat up as I came into his room.

'Kaffir. Dirty, stinking kaffir.'

'Peter—'

'Kaffir.'

He hated me. I hated him. There sat my oppressor, my children's oppressor. I walked over to Madam's son. He was strangely quiet. He just watched me. I pushed him back against the bed.

You blame me and Ruth for your cowardice . . .

I picked up a pillow.

You work because you are afraid to do anything else . . .

I put the pillow over Peter's face.

You're afraid to fight . . .

Peter kicked against my arms but suddenly I was strong, as strong as the world and everyone in it. His screams were muffled by the pillow but I could hear them. They answered the screams and echoes in my own head.

You are nothing . . . nothing . . . nothing . . .

Slowly, so slowly, Peter stopped struggling. Still I held the pillow against his face. When at last I removed it, his eyes were open and he was staring at the ceiling.

I closed his eyes.

There was no respect, no dignity – just screams. Loud, long screams filling my mind. Will they never stop?

You are nothing . . .

Now

I am walking home. Home is where I belong. I don't think I'll make it – they'll catch up with me first, but it doesn't matter. Each step weighs like lead around my neck, breathes like baby's breath around my heart. The road that beckoned me before now ignores me as I walk on and on. On and on and on . . . I'm walking home.

I'm not waiting any more.

22

Dazed, I stared at the woman, my eyes big enough to swallow her up. Her forehead was lined but her cheeks were smooth. She had a round face, her cheekbones high and prominent. Her hair was more black than grey but the grey was obvious. In her time she must've been beautiful, but the world had ground her down until her face held only a trace of what she'd been before. She was still wedged upright between the seat and the floor, and still unconscious, her eyes closed – but it didn't matter. I could see through her closed eyes to the pain that was her life, the guilt and loneliness that'd been hers since she escaped South Africa. She was so tired of running and hiding. Her fatigue flowed out of her like water from a faulty tap. I didn't have to wonder if her nightmare was real. If she'd been awake, I wouldn't have had to ask. Nor did I need to stay in her head for confirmation – not that I could have stayed. The stranger's desolation ate into her every second of every day. Not a day went by when she didn't think about her children – or Peter. How could

I stay in her nightmare? The woman was lonely and alone, with nothing but her grief, and I wasn't strong enough to share it.

I steeled myself to glance down the carriage. A man stood at the far end. The solid, dark, faceless vision of a man who stood like a three-dimensional shadow, watching me. Death wasn't a skeleton with a scythe, he wasn't a bag of bones in a hooded mask, he was a normal, everyday, faceless man. Death was faceless and silent, the way I'd always imagined. If I had any courage at all, I wouldn't have turned away from him. But I couldn't look. I didn't want to die. Over the last few months I'd been wondering about it, especially after what happened to my dad, but leaping into all these nightmares had messed with my head so much that I wasn't sure what I believed or what I wanted any more.

'That's what this is, Kyle. That's all life is,' said Rachel from behind me. 'Nothing but selfish people doing self-centred things.'

Before this morning I might've agreed with her. But not any more. 'That's not true,' I replied. 'There are such things as hope and love and decency. There's even such a thing as live and let live.'

'Have you seen much evidence of that on this train?' Rachel sneered.

'Maybe not so much,' I admitted. 'But I'm jumping into nightmares, not daydreams. I'm living through other people's worst fears. Fear makes us all do things we wouldn't normally.'

'Is fear what made your dad send that thing after you?'

I turned to look at the apparition. He started to raise his arms as if reaching for me. I immediately turned away, my heart trying to batter its way out through my ribs. It took all I had not to turn and race away just as fast and as far as I could.

Death was reaching out for me . . .

'You can still win, Kyle,' said Rachel. 'You can still beat him.'

But how could I beat Death? I looked around, trying not to show the fear I felt. Kendra! I hadn't been inside her head yet. Kendra wouldn't be another Elena. Her dream would be nothing like that of the stranger. I'd hide out in her head until Death passed me by and entered the first carriage. After all, it didn't take a genius to figure out what was going on. He was moving from carriage to carriage, collecting . . . I squatted down next to Kendra and took her hand.

A spasm jolted my entire body, like I'd touched a live, electric wire. I was inside Kendra's head, looking through her eyes, though her gaze kept darting here, there and everywhere like a frightened rabbit. But at least this leap had worked. Maybe this would be the dream I could lose myself in – and even if it was just for a little while, hopefully it would be long enough.

23

Kendra's Nightmare

'Kendra, we're all going for a drink after work. Would you like to—?'

The sudden ringing of the phone on my desk made me jump.

'Gosh, you're twitchy,' laughed Arif. 'Guilty conscience?'

I dredged up a smile. 'Something like that.'

The phone continued to ring.

'Aren't you going to answer that?' he asked.

No. I know who it is and I don't want to talk to him . . .

But the thoughts in my head were prisoners. No way would I ever let them escape for Arif or anyone else to see. I picked up the phone, knowing full well what I'd hear.

'Hello? Kendra speaking.'

Silence. Someone was at the other end all right. *He* was at the other end; listening, breathing, waiting.

'Hello?' I tried again.

He still refused to speak, the way he always did. I put down the phone.

'Wrong number,' I said, smiling at Arif to lighten my words even further.

'So do you want to come to the wine bar later?'

'I—'

The phone began to ring again. I picked up the receiver.

'Hello?'

Silence.

Him again. If Arif hadn't been standing there, I would've shouted at him to leave me alone. Or pleaded. Or wept bitter, reluctant tears. Tears which would reveal just how much he was getting to me.

'Kendra?' Arif's voice brought me back to where and how I was.

I put down the phone. 'Someone playing silly buggers,' I dismissed. 'Can't make it tonight. Sorry. Some other time? Anyway, I'd better get back to work.'

I turned away from Arif, willing him to leave before my phone started again. He took the unsubtle hint and headed back to his desk. My phone began to snarl at me again, each ring jagged like sharp teeth. I glanced up. Arif was heading back to his desk but his head was turned towards me. And even though his face was in profile, the frown on it was unmistakable. I picked up the receiver.

'Yes?' I snapped.

'That's a charming way to answer the phone,' said my mum.

I sighed. 'Sorry, Mum. It's been one of those days.'

'It's not even ten o'clock yet,' Mum pointed out.

'Shows how bad it's been then, doesn't it?'

'Hmm! Anyway, I'm phoning to remind you about dinner tonight. And I'm cooking all your favourites, so don't bother cancelling on me.'

'I wasn't going to, Mum.'

As if! Dinner at Mum's meant a few blessed hours away from my own flat. Away from *him*. My neighbours would probably throw a party to celebrate my absence.

'Is Zach still giving you grief?' asked Mum.

'Nothing I can't handle,' I replied.

'You mean he's still—'

'Haven't seen or spoken to him in days,' I interrupted.

'You're sure?'

'Of course I'm sure. He's got the message now.'

'About time. See you later, love,' said Mum.

'Bye, Mum.'

I put down the phone. It started to ring. I picked it up.

'Hello?'

Silence. I put down the receiver. Today was going to be a long day, just like yesterday and the day before that and every day for the last month.

I walked through the reception area of my building, my heartbeat now audible in my ears. The lunch-time ordeal was about to begin. After a quick reconnaissance through the glass doors, I took a deep breath, opened them and stepped outside. The warm spring air stroked at my face. It was a beautiful day, but it was like something seen out of the corner of one eye. I was too busy looking for him instead.

Sometimes when I came out for my lunch, he'd be on the pavement waiting for me. Sometimes he liked to show himself. Most of the time he didn't. When all this first started, if he was there I'd ignore him and just walk past without saying a word. And when he wasn't I'd breathe a deep sigh of relief as I headed off to buy my sandwiches. But on those occasions I'd get the inexplicable feeling that I was being watched, followed. I'd turn suddenly to catch him out before he could duck out of the way or hide behind another pedestrian. Sometimes I actually saw him following me. I tried ignoring him, confronting him, reasoning with him – but nothing worked, because he wanted nothing. Except me.

'I love you, Kendra. Come back to me,' he'd say softly.

No, Zach. No, Zach. No, *Zach*.

Leave me alone. Please, please leave me alone. I want to move on with my life. I want you to do the same. No, Zach . . .

That was when we first broke up. But the phone calls and standing outside my apartment building and waiting for me outside my work premises and the emails alternating between abusive and pleading had all taken their toll. Strange, the power of words. Four words to be precise. Sent to me every hour on the hour, twenty-four seven. He must've written some kind of program to send out the message automatically. I bought myself some anti-spam software and blocked every address of his that I could think of. But email addresses are ten a penny so it didn't work. And on top of that, the letters and the post-it stickers on my car started. Four little words.

You belong to me.

Once I came home, and the moment I set foot in my flat I knew something was wrong. I went into the living room, the bathroom, the kitchen, the spare bedroom, then finally my bedroom. Nothing had been taken. Nothing had been touched – except my bed. My duvet was on the floor, my top sheet pulled back and my fitted sheet, the sheet I slept on, was still wet from his stains. It took more than a few horrified moments for me to realize what I was seeing. I spun round, my heart charging. Was he behind me? Behind a door somewhere, waiting for me to come home? Waiting to . . .

I ran from the flat and out of the building, then immediately called the police.

Once I'd explained that I didn't think *he* was in my flat any more, the police had sure taken their own sweet time arriving. Two male officers finally arrived after more than half an hour has passed.

'Has anything been taken?' asked one, while the other wandered around my flat.

'No. Not as far as I can see.'

'The door isn't damaged,' the officer pointed out.

'Zach must've picked the lock or something,' I replied.

'Does he have a key?'

'I made him give back his front-door key when we split up but he might have made a duplicate before he did,' I said.

'Well, as nothing has been taken and nothing has been damaged, there's not a lot we can do.'

'Look what he did to my bed.' I pointed furiously, my cheeks burning with anger and more than a little embarrassment.

'But for all we know it could've been done . . . with your permission, at your request,' said the officer. 'When you two were together maybe . . .'

'And I'm telling you we are not together and haven't been for weeks,' I insisted.

But I was wasting my time. It had taken them more than thirty minutes to arrive. It took them less than five to leave. I stripped the bed and put the sheets in a bin liner. I was never going to sleep on them again. After phoning around for a locksmith, I turned the mattress and remade the bed. But once it was made, I sat down on the edge of it and sobbed myself into a headache. The phone began to ring. Like some kind of Pavlovian reaction, I stopped breathing. My breath actually froze in my lungs.

'Hi, sweetheart . . .' Zach's voice was low and soft. 'Did you like my present? Just a little something to show you how much I love you.'

'You are a sick bastard, Zach!' I screamed at him.

'I love you,' he whispered as I slammed down the phone. I knew then that Zach was never going to let me go.

I finally went to bed, dreading him. My front door lock had been changed, but I was so desperately afraid that even a new lock wouldn't be enough to stop him. I fell into a fitful sleep and woke up terrified, more than half expecting Zach to be standing over me with a knife or maybe even a gun in his hand.

If I can't have you . . .

When Zach and I first split up, my good friend Gina tried to tell me that what he was doing was romantic. She doesn't see it that way any more. None of my friends or family see it that way. Only Zach thinks it's romantic – at least, that's what I assume is going on in his twisted head. Only Zach believes that, in time, I'll come to realize just how much he loves me and go back to him.

He's not outside my office building today. But it doesn't matter, because my head is full of him and my eyes are looking out for him and my ears are waiting for his voice to call out my name with that way of his.

'*Kendra* . . .'

Whichever way I turn, I can see no way out.

So I guess, if he hasn't won already, then he's winning. Because Zach is my whole, miserable life and my whole, miserable life is Zach.

It had started . . . I could set my watch by the incessant ringing of my doorbell. Nine p.m. without fail. Day in.

Day out. Maybe if I just sat quietly, in the dark, he'd go away. Maybe he'd think I was out. Maybe he'd think I'd moved.

Maybe . . .

'*Kendra* . . .'

I jumped, then hugged myself as if he could hear me jumping. Why wouldn't he leave me alone?

'I know you're in there . . . I just want to talk to you . . .'

'Go away, Zach,' I screamed silently at him. 'Mrs Guy upstairs is going to give me hell for this.'

I'd only met her for the first time that morning. Strange that I'd lived in these flats for almost six months and it was only under these embarrassing, ridiculous circumstances that I'd met the middle-aged, blonde woman who lived directly above me. But then I didn't know any of my neighbours. I barely had a nodding relationship with the woman who lived across the hall.

I replayed that morning's conversation over in my head. Mrs Guy's words rang out, clear as a bell and just as hard to ignore.

'How much longer do you expect this to continue, Kendra?'

I said, 'I don't know what you mean, Mrs Guy.'

I thought: *Mind your own business, you nosy old cow. I don't need you to contend with as well as Zach.*

'I'm directly above you, and as the flat opposite to you is empty, I'm the one who has the most to put up with here. How much longer will I, and everyone else in this building, have to put up with your boyfriend pressing on your doorbell until all hours?'

I tried to control my temper – and failed miserably.

'For as long as *I* have to put up with it,' I said coldly.

'It's not just the ringing of the doorbell that I'm down here about either. I hear him shouting for you. Every night it's the same thing.' Mrs Guy folded her arms across her chest, flattening her breasts. 'Why don't you tell him to stop?'

'I've tried, Mrs Guy. I don't like him ringing my doorbell any more than you do.'

'Well, I'm not the only one to mention it, you know,' Mrs Guy told me.

'I don't doubt it.'

No one would dare ring her doorbell till all hours.

She frowned. 'If you really want to do something about it, why don't you call the police?'

'I've tried that too, Mrs Guy,' I said patiently. 'They can't ... won't do anything until he actually does something destructive.'

'Is that what they said?'

'That's what they meant.'

'Well, I'm not prepared to put up with it for much longer. If you won't do something about it then I will.'

'Be my guest.'

I didn't mean to but I slammed the door in her face.

Now he's beating at my door. *Go away, Zach. Why won't you go away?*

'Kendra, I just want to talk to you. Open the door.'

And he kept at it, slamming his fists against the door over and over again. Minutes came and went and the rhythm of his drumming and calling out didn't slacken once.

'Kendra, open this door—'

But all at once the pounding stopped. I froze. Around me the darkness echoed with the sound of the sudden silence. In a way the silence was almost worse. Silence can contain anything your imagination can conjure up.

'Kendra, please . . . please, darling . . . open the door. I need to talk to you . . . please, darling . . . I just want to talk to you . . .'

I stood up slowly. My feet, my legs were no longer mine.

'Please darling . . . just let me in . . .'

I swayed slowly, like a snake in a basket weaving to the sound of the snake charmer's music.

'Please, darling . . .'

I walked slowly, softly towards the door.

God, I was frightened . . .

Don't open the door, Kendra. Don't be so stupid.

Slowly, softly, I moved forward. I just wanted it to be over. I just wanted him to leave me alone.

'I can see you, Kendra . . . Please open the door . . .'

Soft, seductive words. Breathed rather than said.

I hugged my arms even tighter around me. My arms were mine. My legs were his. I was almost at the door.

Don't open the door, Kendra . . .

It was almost as if there was an invisible cord between Zach and me – a cord at which we were both dragging and heaving. A tug-of-war (or was this love?) for my body, my soul, my destiny.

And I was losing.

I put my hand out towards the doorknob.

'I want a word with you, young man.'

I froze again. Mrs Guy's voice was ice water thrown into my face.

'Why don't you leave Kendra alone?'

'What happens between Kendra and me is none of your business.' Zach was furious. He knew, as I knew, that the spell was broken.

'Yes it is my business when you prevent me and everyone else in these flats from sleeping.'

'If you didn't listen at bloody key holes then you'd get to sleep faster,' Zach fumed.

'Don't take that tone with me, young man,' Mrs Guy said.

I wanted to laugh. I wanted to scream with laughter. Go get him, Mrs Guy!

'You ought to be ashamed of yourself. What do you hope to achieve by pestering Kendra every evening? Is she supposed to come back to you when you wear her patience thin? Is she supposed to feel sorry for you?'

'*Mind your own business!*' Zach yelled.

I knew this wasn't the real Zach outside my front door. Zach is . . . was the gentlest, friendliest, kindest man I'd ever known. He never said a cross word to me or anyone, he never argued. When we were together he always let me make the decisions. Always. He never bought anything unless I said it was all right. He couldn't even buy a sandwich without getting my OK first. He never had an opinion or a thought of his own without asking for my approval – and that was the trouble.

I grew uneasy, then unhappy with our relationship, and it took a while before I realized why. Zach was wearing me down. I had enough trouble being me, without having to be him and me at the same time. So it got to the stage when I grew tired of trying and that's when I purposely set out to rile him, to provoke him, but even then he never rose to the bait. He'd smile or shrug or tell me he loved me – as if that was the solution to everything. Once I really believed it was. Now I knew different.

So, as calmly, as carefully as I could, I told Zach that I no longer wanted to go out with him.

'It's not you,' I told him. 'It's me. I just . . . I just feel we need a break from each other. I need some time, some space.'

At first Zach just laughed it off. He thought I was joking. When he realized I was perfectly serious, his smile faded. And the new Zach appeared. The Zach who was a stranger – a dangerous stranger.

'Why don't you leave the poor girl alone! Go on! Hop it!' Mrs Guy urged. 'Your sort make me sick.'

'What sort would that be?' Zach asked.

I held my breath.

'The bullying, domineering sort who thinks that

might is right,' Mrs Guy shot straight back at him. 'The sort with such low self-esteem that the only way you can feel good about yourself is to make others feel worse. You're pathetic.'

'Go to hell.'

'I'm going to stand right here until you leave this building,' Mrs Guy said icily. 'If you're going to keep me up all night I might as well spend it on the stair-well. At least it's cooler out here than in my flat.'

'You interfering, old—'

'There'll be none of that language either, thank you very much,' Mrs Guy cut in.

Silence.

Then, to my intense surprise, I heard the sound of Zach's retreating footsteps thundering down the steps.

'Kendra . . . Kendra, are you there? Can I come in?'

Reluctantly I opened the door. I could guess what was coming.

'Mrs Guy, if you've come to complain again then I—'

'What d'you mean – complain?' Mrs Guy frowned. 'Look, can I come in?'

I stepped aside, closing the door behind her as she walked into my hall. I didn't offer her a seat.

'I didn't come to complain or to lecture you,' Mrs Guy began. 'I want you to know that I'm your friend – whatever you may think of me. And you need a friend. I won't take up too much of your time. I just came to give you some advice.'

Here we go! I thought with a sigh.

'Don't let that man – or any man – bully you or terrorize you into going back to him. If you don't want to see him again, then don't.'

I stared at her. That was the last thing I expected to hear.

'You've got to stand up for yourself. And I know what I'm talking about. A while ago I walked out on my abusive husband. He pestered me into going back to him in the same way as your boyfriend. He'd ring my bell at all hours, he'd wait for me outside this apartment block, he'd pester my friends, until in the end I gave in and agreed to live with him again – against my better judgement, I might add. But I was so tired of the whole sorry mess. Well, it was a mistake. A mistake I'm still paying for. So stand up for yourself, Kendra. You've got to be true to yourself. If you want him back, that's one thing. But if you don't, then tell him so. And don't let him persuade you otherwise.'

And so saying, Mrs Guy left me staring after her as she went out of the door. I sat up all night thinking over what she'd said. She was right. I was close to giving in to Zach. I was so tired. Tired of his constant harassment. I just wanted some peace and it seemed like giving into Zach was the easiest way to get it. But where would I be if I gave in? Right back where I'd started. And something told me that it would be harder to leave Zach a second time. He'd never let me leave him a second time. I finally drifted off to sleep in the early hours of the morning, still thinking about what Mrs Guy had said, still wondering what I should do.

Saturday morning, at nine o'clock precisely, the doorbell rang. And rang. And rang. Zach again. He was twelve hours earlier than he should have been. I marched to the door in my pyjamas without even putting on my dressing gown and flung it open. I caught Zach's look of surprise at my action.

'Yes? What do you want, Zach?' I said angrily.

'Can I come in?' he asked quietly.

'No, you can't. You and I have nothing to say to each other.'

Zach regarded me. Then he turned on his most beguiling smile. The one I never used to be able to resist.

'I just want you back,' he said. 'Doesn't all this prove that?'

'You can't have me,' I replied. 'When we first split up I wasn't sure if I'd done the right thing, but now I know I had a lucky escape. Do you really think I'd come back to you after the way you've hounded and harassed me? Do you really believe I'd let myself be bullied into staying with you? Let me tell you something – and like all clichés it's absolutely true – I wouldn't come back to you if you were the last man on the entire planet. So you can ring my bell until your finger drops off and it still won't get you anywhere. I'm not going to let you ruin my life any more. You are not a part of my life, Zach, and you never will be. So leave me alone and move on.'

And I slammed the door in his face. I held my breath as I waited for his response. I was elated and excited and terrified all at once. But the best thing of all was I wasn't scared of Zach. No, I was scared of myself. I really didn't know I had it in me. I would never have found out either if it hadn't been for Mrs Guy. I listened to the sound of Zach's footsteps walking slowly down the stairs.

I couldn't believe it. I'd won. I'd done it. Grabbing my key off the hall table, I ran out of my flat and up the stairs to Mrs Guy's. I rang her doorbell, bobbing up and down with excitement. A tall, good-looking black man I'd seen around occasionally but had never spoken to opened the door.

I smiled at him. 'Can I speak to Mrs Guy please?'

'Who?'

'Mrs Guy. She lives here.'

'No one lives here except me and my girlfriend, Tricia Clarke,' the man said. 'I'm Sam Filey.'

I checked the flat number on the wall. I was at the right flat.

'Mrs Guy doesn't live here?' My smile faded. I still couldn't take it in.

'Sam, who is it?' A woman of about my age came to the door. 'Oh, you're from downstairs, aren't you?' She smiled. 'I'm Tricia.'

I smiled back, uncertain. 'I'm Kendra . . . Kendra Boland. I . . . I was after Mrs Guy. I thought she lived here.'

'Mrs Guy?' Tricia frowned. 'The only Mrs Guy I know lived in this building about five . . . no, six or seven years ago.'

'Where is she now?' I asked, an icy hand stroking my back.

'Well, I heard' – Tricia lowered her voice – 'I heard that she left her husband in Cornwall and came to live up here in London. He followed her up here and persuaded her to come back to him. Then, on the day they were due to return to Cornwall, there was a huge quarrel and her husband . . . well, her husband battered her to death on the stairs over there.'

I stared at Tricia, hoping against hope that she was winding me up.

'That's impossible. I saw her this morning.'

Tricia and Sam exchanged a look.

'I did see her this morning,' I persisted. 'She's in her late forties, slim build, blonde collar-length hair.'

Still Tricia and Sam said nothing.

'You must think I'm crazy,' I said, running my right hand through my braids.

'Of course not. But we know you've been under some stress recently.' Tricia smiled. 'I tell you what, why don't you come to ours for lunch later?'

'Good idea,' Sam agreed.

Surprised by the gesture, I reached for my automatic refusal. 'I wouldn't want to intrude—'

'It's not an intrusion,' said Sam. 'We'd love you to come. Say one o'clock?'

I thought about it. 'Well, I do have some shopping to do first, but OK then. I'll bring a bottle of wine.'

I smiled again and went back downstairs, my smile fading to nothing as I returned to my flat. I didn't understand at all. I knew what I'd seen. Mrs Guy was real. She was as real as I was. I slipped on my sandals, grabbed my bag and left the apartment to go to the shops. As I walked across the gravel forecourt I had the feeling that I was being watched. I turned back and looked up at the windows.

There, on the second floor, watching me, was Mrs Guy. She smiled at me and waved. I waved back before I realized what I was seeing. The sunlight glinting off the window where Mrs Guy stood made me squint. When I looked again, she had gone.

24

Thank God Kendra's dream had a happy ending. She was going to be all right. Whatever happened to her, she was going to make it – if her dream came true ... when her dream came true. Strange, but at first I thought all the dreams were just my mind playing tricks on me. Now I knew better. Of the dreams I'd seen that weren't set in the past, most were possibles, a few were probables. Kendra's felt like a probable – but at least she'd survive.

'Why didn't you stay in Kendra's head?' asked Rachel. 'Her dream turned out OK.'

'But it was *her* dream, not mine,' I replied.

I must admit, I had been tempted, but the idea of being nothing more than a mere spectator in someone else's life ... well, that just didn't work for me. If I went too far down that road, who knew when or even if I'd ever be able to find my way back.

'It doesn't have to be for ever, you know,' said Rachel.

How on earth had she guessed what I was thinking?

'You have a very expressive face.' She answered my unspoken question.

It doesn't have to be for ever . . .

But it would be if I lost my way, and that would be so easy to do.

I looked down the carriage towards Death. He was becoming less ephemeral and more real with each passing second. But that was strange in itself. Why wasn't Death real to begin with? Why was he taking so long to materialize? Surely that wasn't the way Death worked? Or did he always play these kinds of games first, killing his victims slowly, nanosecond by nanosecond, as the dread inside them grew fiercer?

Well, no more.

I was going to prove to everyone, as well as to myself, that I could do this. No more running and hiding. I started walking towards him.

'Kyle, no!' Rachel called out. 'Don't be a fool.'

I kept walking. With each step, it felt like my legs were slowly dissolving, but I willed myself to keep going. When I reached Lily, to my surprise she grabbed hold of my hand.

'Thank you for helping me,' she whispered.

'It was no—'

But her hand was prickling against mine, sending a swarm of stings shooting up my arm and across my entire body.

I didn't want this to happen again. I was ready to

meet Death, not jump into another dream. But I was given no choice. Lily was in her bedroom and I was there too, looking through her eyes – watching the world as the world watched me.

25

Lily's Nightmare

I knelt down, feeling every weary second of my fifty-three years. I tugged at the bottom drawer of my dressing table but it refused to budge. Rocking open the drawer was a slow, frustrating process. My knees were beginning to hurt, even though the carpet beneath them was good-quality, thick wool. Shifting my weight, I sat down, carefully stretching my legs out in front of me. I looked around the bedroom. How many years had I spent in this house, in this bed? More than twenty. Almost thirty.

I smiled at the Christmas decorations my grandchildren had insisted on putting up for me. Paper-chains and tinsel boas and glittering baubles covered the walls and hung down from the overhead lampshade. I hadn't wanted my bedroom decorated, but as usually my beloved grandchildren had won me over.

'Oh, come on, Nan. It's Christmas,' Julian pleaded.

'Please, Nan,' Judy joined in. 'It'll make your room look so pretty. Please.'

And of course I gave in. When had I ever refused my grandchildren anything? I ran my fingers across my tear-filled eyes. This wasn't helping.

'Keep searching,' I told myself. I had to find some clue as to why this had happened. I turned back to the open drawer. Diaries. Diaries of different sizes, colours, shapes. All my private diaries, holding each secret thought and fear. The yearly diaries I'd faithfully kept since my sixteenth birthday, when I'd received my very first one. I'd never shown them to anyone. I'd never wanted to, never dared to. And I'd never re-read them. Once a page was written I never returned to it. What was the point? Writing the truth, but never reading it, was my way of burying the past. And starting a new page each day had been somehow symbolic, not to mention therapeutic.

But now I needed to see them, to read them.

I looked down at the diary on the carpet beside me. My current diary had only a few pages left before the end of the year. But I would only make one more entry – and that was for today, Christmas Day.

I took my diaries out of the drawer. Opening them one at a time, I carefully laid them out in a line on the carpet next to me. There were so many of them that it took some time to arrange them in chronological order. I shifted again so that my back was against the dressing table. I had thirty-seven diaries on either side of me.

That was when I felt a frisson of anxiety. The gateway to the past was now open. All I had to do was walk through.

But this wouldn't be like arguing with my memories. They were old and frail, as I now was, and could easily make mistakes. But my written words – I couldn't argue with them.

I ran my fingers over the oldest diary. The blood-red velvet was skin-smooth and almost warm to touch. My fingers moved to the next diary, then the next and the next. I saw the one I wanted, a small diary, palm sized, with a raspberry-pink cover, decorated with yellow flowers. I held it to my nose. It still smelled of playing cards and old spices. I opened it.

14 February

I'm happy, happy, happy. Alex met me outside the Italian restaurant. He was holding a dozen long-stemmed red roses. He ordered champagne with the meal. It was wonderful. Then, guess what? He handed me a small box and asked me to marry him. I tried to stay calm, I really did. I thought to myself, Lily, act like you get a marriage proposal every month at least!

But I couldn't. I leaped up and hugged him right there in the restaurant. I didn't care. I'm so happy I want to scream and scream and never stop. So what if Alex is thirty-three? I like older men. They are so much more mature. Besides, I'm only ten years younger than him. That's not such a gap. And Alex is wonderful. He says that we can get married exactly a year from today. How romantic!

He loves me. Me!

And the only itsy-bitsy fly in the ointment is that he wants us to start a family as soon as we're married. When he said that I got a peculiar stirring in my stomach.

I'd rather wait a while before starting a family. But never mind. We'll cross that bridge when we get to it.

He loves me. No one has ever loved me before.

I think I'll never again be as happy as I am now . . .

There was a dull thud as I slammed the diary shut. I could hardly hold it, my hands were trembling so much. Putting the diary back in its place, I picked up one for the following year.

16 October

I hate this. I hate this so much. And Alex doesn't care. He has no idea how I feel. All he keeps talking about is how wonderful it will be when the baby arrives.

I've made a colossal mistake. The biggest mistake of my life.

Alex wants children. I don't. I love him desperately, but the thought of this thing inside me terrifies me. I should never have got pregnant, but Alex wanted it so much. I knew the instant I conceived. A hollow, nauseated feeling bit down deep inside me. The feeling hasn't got any better. In fact, it's worse. Something repulsive and alien has been planted in my body and slowly but surely is taking me over. I'm no longer in control; it is. It dictates when I should eat, when I should sleep, even when I should pee.

I'm going crazy.

I fight against it, but it is too strong. It's got to the stage now where I can't bear to look at any part of my body, except my face. At least my light-brown hair and my grey eyes are the same. My cheeks are a little thinner, but they're still mine. Nothing else is.

I lie in bed at night, clawing at my hideously swollen stomach while Alex lies gently snoring beside me. I feel like a balloon that's about to pop and there's nothing I can do about it.

I envy Alex and resent him like hell because of it.

I'm trying to suffer in silence, but then I find myself feeling even more bitter towards him. Why should I be the only one to suffer?

I hate this.

I swear that this pregnancy will be my last. Never, not even for Alex, will I go through this again. Another pregnancy and I can kiss my sanity goodbye. If it hasn't gone already.

26 December

It's over. At last. The thing was born quite easily on the day before Christmas Eve. It was born within two hours of my contractions starting. The pain wasn't too bad and it slipped out of my body like a greased eel. That made it worse. The whole process disgusted me. I didn't want to take the baby when one of the nurses handed it to me. It was bloody and slippery and smelled foul. I only took it in my arms because Alex was standing there, tears of joy in his eyes.

He never cried for me.

'We'll call her Nicole, shall we?' he whispered.

I looked down at Nicole lying in my arms. I was so revolted I could feel my stomach churning.

'Isn't she perfect?' Alex beamed. 'Look, she's got your eyes. She's got my nose though. Isn't she lovely?'

Everyone around me was telling me what a lovely baby I had. Wasn't she an angel? Adorable? I looked down at her scrunched-up, screaming face and I couldn't see it. I really couldn't see it.

And I think . . . I think Alex knew I couldn't.

She doesn't even look like Alex. She looks like me. The same almond-shaped eyes tilting up slightly at the outer corners and extra long fingers and toes. Alex has short, pudgy digits. Nicole couldn't even get that right.

I shut the book slowly, put it carefully back in its place and picked up the next one in line: a full-sized A4 diary with a blue vinyl cover.

12 May

I feed her when I have to, clothe her when I have to, change her nappy when I have to – that's it. Alex, of course, is the complete opposite. He worships the ground Nicole crawls on. If she starts crying at night, he's up and at her side in an instant, her first sob somehow penetrating even his deepest sleep. But his snores deafen me if I cry at his side.

Every day he tells Nicole how beautiful she is and how much he loves her. Humiliated, I said to him tonight, 'Why don't you say that to me any more?'

'But, Lily, you know that already,' he replied.

I'll never ask that again.

It's all her fault. I'll never forgive Nicole for spoiling

what Alex and I had. She's turned me into the invisible woman.

I shut the diary and let it drop from my hand. For several moments I sat still, staring at one diary in particular, the diary which marked my thirtieth year and Nicole's sixth.

'I can't . . .' I muttered. Yet even as I spoke, I reached out to the grey-leather-bound, paperback-sized diary which I'd sworn I would never touch again.

1 December

What am I going to do? I'm losing it.

Today I lost my temper with Nicole. 'Mum, is Dad going to die?' she asked me.

It was as if every muscle in my body was immediately pulled taut. God forgive me, but I slapped her. She looked up at me as if she'd never seen me before. I didn't mean to do it. It's just that . . . she put into words something that I wouldn't even let myself think. Silent tears spilled down her cheeks.

'Nicole, I'm sorry . . .' I started to say.

She turned her back on me and walked out of the living room.

Alex, don't you dare die. What will I do without you? You're only forty, for God's sake. No one has a heart attack at forty. What am I going to do?

Nicole's sixth birthday.

I wish I was dead.

I stared down at the blue ink on the yellowing page, smudged by my tears all those years ago. Fresh tears splashed down the page. My life hadn't been so bad. There had been good times, happy times. So why were all the clues tied up in the moments of despair and misery? It didn't make sense. I closed the book and put it back in its place, then allowed my fingers to skim over the covers of the next few diaries. It was all coming back now. The years of carrying on, though I never knew why. The years spent burying grief, living my life on autopilot. The years of shutting out my daughter until, at eighteen, Nicole had left home, never looking back. Then the slowly building guilt and shame and loneliness.

I looked at the diaries at the end of the line. The ones that covered the previous three years of my life.

The last two years of my life.

These diaries contained the final clues. The pointers that had been there, ready to be acted upon had I but noticed them. I picked up the diary of two years ago.

25 December

I have always dreaded Christmas, but I must admit, I was really looking forward to this one. And I wasn't disappointed.

It was wonderful.

My first Christmas with my grandchildren. Nicole still hasn't told me what happened between her and her ex-husband Robert, and of course I can't ask. It's not my place to ask Nicole her business. I'm just grateful that she turned to me three months ago. I realized I was her last resort but I didn't mind about that. I feel I have so much to make up to her, but I haven't a clue where to begin. I don't think we'll ever have the mother–daughter relationship that most of the women I know seem to enjoy, but if we could at least be friends then I'd happily settle for that.

But thank you, God, for my grandchildren – they're so perfect. I'm totally besotted with them. Why? Maybe it's because I didn't carry them. Writing that makes me feel uneasy, but if I can't be truthful in my own diary, then where can I?

I remember the very first time I saw them. A jolt of happy recognition rippled through me. Julian is a miniature Alex. Even Judith looks like Alex; a small, sleek, feminine version. They both have his cat-like eyes, his lazy, crooked smile. They're seven-year-old angels. The resemblance to their grandfather really is uncanny. He would have adored them. That thought makes me a bit sad, but I really feel I can't be too unhappy today, even though I still miss Alex terribly.

This morning was the best. I was in the kitchen when I heard the twins crashing down the stairs. Thinking that Nicole was still in bed, I went into the living room to be with them. They were so enthusiastic and eager they made me laugh. They knelt down in front of the Christmas tree.

'What is it, Nan? What is it?' Judith asked. She sniffed at the large box-shaped present I had bought them.

'Open it and you'll find out,' I said.

Nicole came into the room and sat down on the sofa, watching them. I knelt down next to Judith and Julian as they tore off the wrapping paper.

They did everything together.

When the wrapping paper was strewn all over the floor, Julian sat back on his heels.

'It's a cage,' he said, surprised.

'It's a hutch,' I said. 'And you'll find what goes in it in a cardboard pet carrier in the cupboard under the sink.'

The twins almost knocked me over in their haste to get to the kitchen. 'Be careful with it,' I called after them.

The living room was eerily silent after they had left. The hair on my nape began to prickle. With a frown, I turned. Nicole's eyes were narrowed slits as she regarded me.

'Why, Mum?' she said.

'Why what?' I asked.

'Why do you . . . ?' Nicole's voice trailed off.

'Go on,' I prompted.

'It doesn't matter.'

I don't know which one of us felt more frustrated. Nicole turned away from me.

'You've got lots of photographs on your windowsill,' she said. The subject change was too abrupt to be even remotely subtle. I turned to look at the windowsill as well. There was the wedding photo of Alex and me, Alex by himself and two photos of Julian and Judy, hugging each other and pulling faces for the camera. Terribly sentimental, I know, but I love looking at my photographs – especially when I'm alone.

'Look, Mum, look!' Julian ran into the room. He was closely followed by Judy, who walked with measured, careful steps, a grey rabbit cradled in her arms.

'Nan, it's a rabbit,' Judy said, her eyes sparkling.

'I know, dear. I bought it for you – remember?' I teased.

'What's his name?' Julian asked.

'Her name is up to you and your sister,' I told him. 'You choose.'

'Let's call her . . .'

Julian and Judy looked at each other.

'Cloudy,' they said in unison.

'She's just the colour . . .' began Julian.

'Of a cloudy day,' finished Judy.

They're always doing things like that. Sometimes I'd swear they can read each other's minds.

Nicole had bought each of them a burgundy turtleneck jumper, some puzzle books and one of those pocket computer games, but they spent all day playing with the rabbit. I was a bit uncomfortable about that. I caught Nicole looking at me once or twice, but she didn't say anything. She looked disapprovingly at the rabbit as the children played with it. I tried to get them to play with the things Nicole had bought them, but she stopped me, saying, 'Let them play with Cloudy if they want to. They can play with my stuff any time.'

I do hope Nicole didn't feel too badly. That certainly wasn't my intention.

Well, that's Christmas Day over. All in all it hasn't been too bad.

Chaos reigned in the house this morning. For some reason, Cloudy bit Julian. I think Julian was more scared than seriously hurt, but he was crying and Judy was crying and their mother was panicking like a good 'un. Nicole kept insisting that she should take Julian to the local hospital for a tetanus injection. Have you ever heard the like? For a little rabbit nip!

'That rabbit is dangerous!' she shouted. 'It ought to be put down.'

I didn't mean to but I laughed in her face. Anyone would think we were talking about a ten-ton Rottweiler, not a two-pound rabbit. In the end I lent her my car and she drove Julian to the hospital. Judy insisted on being with her brother, of course. I was alone in the house of the first time since Christmas Eve. For the first ten minutes I cherished the peace and quiet, but after that I just wanted them all back. I missed them terribly. They have only been in my life for a few months, but already it feels like they've always been here. I just wish that Nicole and I had been closer when she was younger. Then Judy and Julian would've been a part of my life from the time they were born. When I think of what I missed, I feel a kind of ache inside. But then I think of all the future years we'll have together and that's enough to make me smile with contentment.

When I went down to breakfast this morning, Nicole and the twins were already in the kitchen. They weren't exactly whispering, but their voices were very low. They went silent the moment they realized I was in the room.

'Mum . . . I've got some bad news,' Nicole said slowly.

'What is it?' My heart started to beat faster.

Please, God, don't let them leave, not now I've found them.

'It's . . . it's just that . . . Cloudy is dead,' said Nicole. 'I came downstairs this morning and she was lying on her side in the cage. I don't know what she died of . . .'

Relief washed through me, followed by a backwash of guilt. Cloudy's death didn't begin to compare with losing my family. I looked Julian and Judy.

'Are you two all right?' I asked.

They nodded.

'But our rabbit is dead,' sniffed Judy.

'Never mind. I'll get you another one. We'll pick it out next week, as soon as the pet shop is open,' I said.

'Promise, Nan?' Julian said.

'Promise.' With a smile, I crossed my heart and hoped to die.

Luckily it seemed that the twins hadn't grown too attached to Cloudy in the few days they'd had her.

I looked at Nicole. To my surprise, she lowered her gaze and turned away from me. I hadn't seen that look in a long, long time but I still recognized it. She was hiding something.

'Where's Cloudy now?' I asked.

'In the garden,' Nicole said. 'I thought we should bury her.'

'Yes please.'

'Oh let's.'

The twins hopped up and down with excitement.

'You two got over your grief quickly.' I frowned.

'Well, Cloudy is dead now . . .' Judy said very seriously.

'And we can't bring her back.' Julian shook his head.

'She was dead when we came downstairs for our breakfast. Wasn't she, Julian?' Judy asked her brother.

Julian nodded.

I looked at Nicole. She was glaring at her children, her face set. Sometimes Nicole is too hard on them. I must admit, I did think it was a bit gruesome of them to be so eager to see Cloudy buried, but children bounce back so quickly, don't they? And besides, they've probably never seen anything buried before. Poor Cloudy. I wonder what happened to her?

Nicole took me to one side later on in the day and asked me not to buy another rabbit. God forgive me, but sometimes I can't help thinking that she can't stand to see her children happy. She's always watching them. She doesn't even trust me enough to let me look after them for more than a couple of hours at a time.

I placed the diary, face down, on my lap. I reached for the next one. A big, black leather-bound diary that had been a present from my work colleagues when I'd taken early retirement. This diary would be the most damning of all. All last year's secrets were contained within its pages – secrets which I had written out but which, paradoxically, I'd been unaware of – until now.

I just had to give it to them today. Besides, a puppy isn't like a rabbit. I couldn't hide it in a box under the sink until Christmas Day. So as soon as Julian and Judy had come downstairs for their breakfast, I told them what I'd bought them.

'OK, you two,' I began. 'You remember what happened to Cloudy last year?'

'Cloudy?' Julian frowned.

'The rabbit I bought you,' I reminded him.

Their memories sure were short!

Judy and Julian looked at each other before turning back to me and nodding slowly.

'Well, because of what happened last year, I decided to get you another pet. So I bought you a certain something that's out in the garden shed,' I said.

'Can we get it now?' Judy asked excitedly.

'After your breakfast,' I told her. 'And that's not an excuse for gobbling down your food.'

Ignoring me completely, the twins were halfway through wolfing down their scrambled eggs and beans on toast when Nicole ambled into the kitchen, rubbing her eyes.

'Good morning, Nicole. And many happy returns,' I said.

'Mum, Mum, guess what? Nan's bought us a pet for Christmas,' said Julian.

'Only we can have it now,' Judy added.

Nicole stared at me.

'Is something wrong?' I frowned.

'You didn't . . . tell me you didn't get them another pet,' said Nicole sombrely.

283

Shocked at her tone, I stared at her. 'What's the matter?' I asked. 'It's only a puppy.'

'A puppy. Hooray!' the twins shouted. They stood up, their breakfast forgotten, and headed for the back door.

'You two aren't to go out there until you're dressed warmly and wearing your wellies,' I said. 'It's freezing outside.'

They rushed up the stairs.

'I wish you hadn't, Mum,' Nicole said quietly.

'Why ever not?'

'I don't want this puppy to end up the way the rabbit did,' Nicole replied.

I stared at her. 'Why on earth should it?'

Nicole opened her mouth, only to close it again without saying a word. She pursed her lips as she looked at me.

'Nicole?' I said uncertainly. 'Is there something wrong?'

Nicole shook her head slowly.

'Oh, before I forget,' I said, 'I didn't have a chance to buy you a birthday present. What would you like?'

'You don't have to get me anything,' Nicole said.

'I know I don't have to. I want to.' I smiled.

Silence.

'Do you know what I'd like? What I'd really like?' Nicole said at last.

'Tell me.'

'I'd like my photograph on the windowsill. Just one photograph with me in it.' The words were choked with bitterness.

I stared at her. I started to protest . . . then I realized she was right. All the photos on my sacred windowsill, and she wasn't in one.

'You'd love it if I was really out of the picture, wouldn't you? Julian and Judith can stay, of course, but me? I could go to hell for all you care. All my life I've been waiting for you to love me. And then I realized I was aiming too high. So I thought I could settle for you just liking me. But I'm nothing to you, am I? Just the anonymous woman who gave you your precious grandchildren.'

Shocked, I struggled to get the words out. What words? Any words. Any words that would let her know just how wrong she was. I might have felt like that a long time ago, but not now.

But I couldn't speak. The words were a frenetic jumble in my head.

'Nan, are you and Mum not friends any more?' Judy asked from the door.

I hadn't even heard them come down the stairs.

'Of course we are.' I forced a smile onto my lips. 'Your mum and me just have a few things to sort out, that's all. Now off you go and play with your puppy.'

Julian and Judy slowly left the room, casting backward glances at us as they left.

'Nicole, you're wrong—' I began.

'Mum, I don't want to talk about it.' Nicole sighed, heading for the door herself. 'I just wish you hadn't got them another pet without consulting me first.'

And I thought Nicole and I had been doing so well recently. I'll have to do something to put us on a better footing. She's so wrong though. I do care for her. She forgets – or maybe she just doesn't know that I'm still learning too.

Well, Nicole and the twins will have the house to themselves on Boxing Day. I'm spending the day with my friend Rebecca, who lives in Oxford. It's quite a drive so I'll have to set off early. I think maybe I've been crowding Nicole by always being underfoot. It struck me a while ago that if she wants to be alone with the twins then she has to leave the house with them, now that I no longer work. I'll have to watch that next year. It will be one of my New Year's resolutions. I will give Nicole more time alone with her children. I have to remember that they're her children, not mine. Maybe I'm trying to make it up to Nicole through them.

I think about that sort of thing a lot these days. The whys and wherefores of the past. Nicole and I still aren't close. I guess we'll never be. That saddens me. I do care about her, really I do. And what I feel has nothing to do with Julian and Judy. I just find that sort of thing very hard to say. I never had any trouble saying those things to Alex, so why do I find it so difficult to let Nicole know how much I care about her? If Alex was still alive, maybe Nicole and I would be closer. He would have stopped me making so many mistakes.

God! I'm going to worry myself into an early grave if I carry on like this.

27 December

The puppy is dead. I can't believe it. First Cloudy, then Joey. When I tucked Julian up in bed tonight, he was still crying.

I got back from Rebecca's house this morning, and even before she said hello, Nicole told me that Joey was dead and that she'd already buried him.

'What did he die of?' I asked.

'He just died,' Nicole told me, storming out of the room.

He just died? What does that mean? I couldn't get much out of Julian or Judy either. They were too upset at Joey's death.

Judy did say something that made me think though. She said, 'Mum was really angry with Joey.'

'Why?' I asked.

''Cause you bought him for us,' she replied.

'That's why she was mad at our rabbit,' Julian said.

And then they both nodded up at me several times.

I can't believe . . . Does Nicole really hate me so much that she would kill a rabbit and a puppy? Just to get back at me?

I won't believe it. The twins do have very active imaginations. I'm sure that there's a perfectly reasonable explanation for Joey's death. I just wish I knew what it was.

So the clues *were* there. All the time. They were glaringly obvious. I turned the diary over and placed it on the floor. I should've noticed them, I should've realized. Then maybe I could have foreseen what was going to happen. It was all my fault. I should've prevented it. I picked up my latest diary. My last diary. This year's diary.

This evening I did the one thing I swore I'd never do. I quarrelled with Nicole about the twins. And what's more, Judy and Julian were there, listening to every word. It all started over something so stupid. We sat down to a late dinner because Nicole came back home late from her office. She said she'd gone round to the pub for a quick drink with her colleagues. From the smell of her breath, I thought a quick half-dozen was closer to the mark. Then Julian asked me what I was getting them for Christmas.

'Can we have another pet, Nan?'

'A cat this time,' Judy piped up.

'You two aren't having any more pets. Not while I have anything to do with it.' Nicole leaped in before I had a chance to open my mouth.

'But you don't have to buy it for us, Mum. Nan could buy it for us,' Julian said.

'Oh no she couldn't. You're not having a pet and that's final,' Nicole said.

'Nicole, I don't mind—'

'I said no!' Nicole shouted.

'Don't take that tone with me. I'm not one of your children.' I frowned.

'Thank God! What would I do with three of you? Two children are two too many.'

'Nicole!'

'Don't "Nicole" me, Mum. You don't know the half of what I've been through. You think the twins are so sweet and innocent? Well, I could tell you a thing or two . . .'

'Nicole, you don't know what you're saying,' I said icily.

'Mum, please . . .' Judy began.

'Please what? Please don't tell your nan what you two are really like . . . ?'

Nicole's words were getting faster and more slurred now.

'Nicole, I think you should go and lie down.' I tried – and failed – to keep the censure out of my voice.

'Lie down? I don't need to lie down. I should have guessed you'd take their side. Nothing changes. They're always right and I'm always wrong.'

'That's not true. You're being ridiculous,' I said.

'Of course it's true. Well, I've got a little secret for you, Mum–'

'Mum, don't . . .' Julian was crying.

'No, Mum . . .' Judy ran to Nicole and tried to take her hand. Nicole pushed her away – hard.

'And the little secret is . . .' Nicole's laugh turned into a hic. 'Prepare yourself, Mum – the sun does not shine out of your grandchildren's backsides.'

'I'm not listening to any more of this.' I stood up, absolutely disgusted.

Nicole leaped to her feet so quickly her chair toppled over behind her. 'Mum, you must listen to me. Julian and Judith . . .' Even from where I stood, I could see that she was shaking. 'Those two . . . they're the devil's children . . .'

I'd had enough. I marched round the table and slapped Nicole hard. It was only the second time I'd ever laid a hand on her. The first time I didn't mean to. This time I did.

'You deserve to burn in hell for saying such wicked,

wicked things,' I told her. 'Julian, Judy, go to your room – now. And as for you, Nicole, I suggest you stay down here and sober up.'

I ushered my grandchildren out of the room.

I really don't know what got into Nicole tonight. Judith and Julian were almost hysterical. It took me ages to calm them down. I can't help feeling that in some way I'm responsible for Nicole's behaviour. She still sees me the way I used to be – not the way I am. She holds onto the past so tightly that I despair of ever getting her to see I've changed. I know my grandchildren aren't perfect – they have their moods just like everyone else. And I know I spoil them. But to call them the devil's children . . .

Nicole has just slammed out of the house.

I hope she realizes just what she said and makes amends to the twins. How could their own mother say something like that? I never thought of Nicole as the devil's child – not even when she was born – much less said it to her face. I can't understand why she would say something like that. I'm trying not to condemn her; after all, who am I to judge? I never exactly won any cups for being the world's greatest mother.

In a way I'm glad I'm driving to see Rebecca on Christmas Eve. I think both Nicole and I could use a break from each other. When I get back on Christmas Day, the dust should have settled. Things are always better on Christmas Day.

I laughed bitterly at the last sentence I'd written. I glanced down at my watch. Christmas Day was nearly over. There came a knock at the bedroom door.

290

'Nan, aren't you going to make us our hot chocolate?'

Julian and Judith stood just inside the bedroom. I smiled. They really did look like two angels. So calm, so serene.

'Of course I am, darlings. Back to bed and I'll bring it up for you,' I said as I got to my feet.

'We're glad you're our nan,' Julian said. 'Aren't we, Judy?'

Judith nodded enthusiastically.

'And I'm glad you're my grandchildren. Now back to bed, you rascals.' I forced a laugh.

God, I loved them so much. I'd do anything for them.

The twins ran back to their own room. I followed them, watching as they climbed into their bunk beds.

'Count to two hundred and I'll be here,' I told them, before closing their bedroom door. I heard their muffled counting through the door. After stopping off in the bathroom, I made my way downstairs. I had this year's diary in one hand, the bottle I'd retrieved from the bathroom in the other. I looked at my diary. I had to hold onto it. I'd never let it go again. I couldn't. The diary would have to be my strength, my courage.

In the kitchen I worked quickly until the hot chocolate was ready. Placing three steaming mugs on a tray, I carefully carried it upstairs.

'Here we are. Hot chocolates all round.' I smiled as I walked into the bedroom, tray in hand.

I handed one cup to Julian on the lower bunk, and

one cup up to Judith before taking the third cup for myself.

'Nan, this tastes a bit funny,' Judith complained at the first taste.

'That's because I wasn't watching the milk and it boiled. Milk should be warmed, not boiled, if you're making hot chocolate, otherwise it tastes bitter. That's why I put extra sugars in each cup.' I smiled and sipped at my hot chocolate. 'Come on, you two. Drink it down. It'll help you sleep.'

Without another word the twins drank to the bottom of their cups. Then I did the same.

'I'll tell you what. Would you two like to sleep in my bed tonight? I could hold you both and we could all fall asleep together.'

'That would be great.'

'Yippee!'

'Come on then.' I smiled.

The twins were out of bed and ahead of me within moments. I fingered the tablet bottle that was in my pocket.

'Forgive me,' I said to the empty room. Who was I speaking to? Alex? Nicole? God? Myself?

I followed the twins into my bedroom. They were already sitting up in the bed.

'What are all these books on the floor, Nan?' Judy asked.

'My diaries.'

'Can we read them?' said Julian.

'Maybe some time.'

292

I pulled off my dressing gown and got into the middle of the bed, where I sat between my grandchildren, my back against the headboard.

'Are you going to read us a story, Nan?' Judy yawned.

'Not tonight, precious. I've got something to finish. Snuggle down, you two, and go to sleep.'

The twins did as I asked.

'What are we . . . going to . . . do . . . tomorrow?' Julian's voice was getting fainter and fainter.

'Anything we want to do, my love,' I replied. 'Anything at all.'

A yawn from Judy, and the twins were asleep. I smiled down at them, then stroked their hair. Opening my diary, I began to write.

25 December

I got back from Oxford at about four o'clock in the morning and fell straight into bed. It seemed like I'd only just shut my eyes when the twins came bounding into the room, waking me up. Without warning Julian pulled back the curtains, nearly frying my eyeballs, it was so bright outside.

'Get up, Nan. It's Christmas Day!' they yelled, trying to pull me out of bed.

Where did they get their energy from?

I had a shower and got dressed before popping into Nicole's room. She wasn't there. I went downstairs. I called her several times but there was no answer. I went into the kitchen to make a cup of tea.

'Do you know where your mother is?' I asked the twins,

who were lying on the kitchen floor poring over a junior puzzle book. They got to their feet immediately. Judy giggled – an infectious giggle that soon had Julian smirking behind his hand.

'Where is she?' I asked, mildly curious.

'Nan, Nan, come on. We've got a surprise for you. We want to show you what we got you for Christmas. It's a special present,' Julian said.

'Yeah, very special. You will like it, won't you?' Judy asked anxiously.

At that moment I was more interested in where their mother was, and my morning cup of tea, but it was the twins' day and I didn't want to be a spoilsport. Besides, I wasn't going to get a thing out of them until the presents were opened. They took me by the hands and pulled me into the lounge. Nicole was sitting in the armchair with her back to me. She was facing the Christmas tree.

'Nicole, your children are kidnapping me!' I laughed.

Nicole didn't reply. She didn't even turn her head. She sat absolutely still. I sighed inwardly, guessing that she was still angry at me. Julian and Judy pulled me round the armchair. I looked at the tree, its green branches decorated with silver and gold and scarlet tinsel boas and fairy lights. It looked so beautiful. And underneath it were the presents, most of which had already been opened. I smiled at the sight, not at all surprised that the twins couldn't wait.

'Nan, look at your present,' Julian said proudly.

He and Judy spun me round. I smiled ruefully at Nicole. My smile froze and died on my lips. Bile stung the back of my throat. Both hands flew to my mouth. I had to clench my teeth and lips together to stifle the scream inside me.

Nicole's unseeing eyes were open and staring straight ahead. She didn't blink. She couldn't blink. A thin stream of dark blood ran from the corner of her mouth down her chin and onto her neck. I fell to my knees. My stomach was turning.

'Nan . . . Nan, don't you like it?' Judy asked, her lips quivering with disappointment.

I tightly closed my eyes at the sight. My whole body was shaking now. My face was so set I felt I'd never be able to open my mouth or my eyes again.

'You don't like it,' Julian said sadly.

'What have you done? What have you done?' I swallowed convulsively. I was going to be sick. I couldn't be sick. I opened my eyes to stare at my grandchildren. Out of the corner of my eye I was aware of Nicole. Nicole . . . sitting and staring . . .

'But, Nan, you said she should burn in Hell. You said she deserved to,' Judy said, bewildered.

'Only we couldn't burn her because you always told us not to play with matches and fire . . .' Julian said.

'So we did the next best thing,' Judy continued. 'We waited until she was sitting down, opening her presents. That's when we got her. We only did it for you, Nanny. We thought you'd be pleased.'

'Besides, she deserved it. She said all those nasty things about us,' Julian sniffed. 'And she didn't like what we did to the rabbit and the puppy.'

I stared at them. Such beautiful eyes. Such angelic, serene faces.

'Cloudy bit Julian's finger,' Judy said, frowning at the memory. 'We couldn't let her get away with that, could we?'

Julian started laughing. 'So I stood on her neck. It was so funny. Do you remember, Judy? Her neck went crunch. D'you remember?'

I covered my mouth with a trembling hand. Several seconds passed and I still couldn't trust myself to speak. Nicole . . .

Judy nodded and laughed with her brother. It was the laughter that did it. I was no longer shaking. I was very still.

'Then you got us Joey,' Julian said, his smile fading into anger.

'He widdled on me when I was holding him,' Judy said indignantly. 'It was disgusting.'

'So we—'

'Don't . . . oh, don't . . .' I raised my hand. My voice shocked me. It was so weak. I'd never felt so alone or afraid – not even when Alex died. This was much, much worse. Because I wasn't afraid for myself.

'Anyway, that was ages ago,' Julian said dismissively.

'Nan, don't you like your special present?' Judy asked.

I looked at her. My granddaughter – my precious Judith. I turned my head to look at Nicole. Nicole . . . sitting and staring . . .

I stood up slowly, feeling old. Very old.

'We're going to play with our presents now.' Judy smiled, first at me, then at her brother.

They skipped off into the kitchen. I closed my eyes and turned away from them. I sank down onto the floor as if I'd been struck. I tried to get up but I couldn't move. A long,

long time passed and still I couldn't move. At last I felt I had to stand up or I'd never stand again. My legs numb, I stumbled over to the windowsill. A photo of my daughter Nicole with the twins now took pride of place in the centre. Nicole was laughing, Julian and Judy proudly cradled to her.

Nicole . . .

I couldn't help it. I buried my head in my hands. If I clamped my teeth any harder together, they would crumble. If I separated them just a fraction I knew I would howl and scream and never, ever stop.

I don't really know what Julian and Judith did for the rest of the day. They played quietly and whispered to each other. I sat in the kitchen, drinking cup after cup of tea, trying to decide what I should do next.

This evening it came to me. The answer was quite simple really.

They won't separate Judith and Julian and me. I can't allow that. We only have each other now.

So we'll go to sleep.

And where we're going, no one will split us up.

Merry Christmas and a h

26

Resurfacing from Lily Channing's dream was like being deep down in a warm sea and slowly rising to the surface. My journey back to the train was so quiet and peaceful. A much slower journey back than from any of the other dreams. I'd been right. The way back to reality was getting harder; staying lost in the dreams I inhabited was getting easier.

I was back on the train and my heart wasn't even pounding. I squatted down beside Lily, taking her hand in both of mine. There was something I had to know. 'Lily, did you say you had two grandchildren?'

'That's right.' Her expression turned soft as melted butter. 'Judith and Julian. They're twins.'

'And you said you had a daughter called Nicole?'

Lily frowned. 'I can't remember saying that.'

'But you do have a daughter called Nicole?'

'That's right.'

'What did you get for Julian and Judith for Christmas last year?' I asked.

'Kyle, you mustn't,' Rachel said sternly. 'We haven't

got time for this. He's almost corporeal now, and once he takes his full shape you'll never get away. He'll take you with him. Is that what you want?'

Ignoring her, I repeated my question to Lily.

'I bought them . . . a puppy,' she said.

'And a rabbit the year before?'

'How did you know that?'

I shook my head. That didn't matter.

A rabbit and a puppy . . . And this Christmas her much-loved grandchildren would give her their very special present. Should I say something? Warn her? Tell her? What?

'Lily, don't get Julian and Judith any more pets. Don't even offer to get them another one.'

'Why not?'

'Kyle, no . . .' said Rachel.

'Lily, your grandchildren . . .'

'What about them?' She smiled at me. The mere thought of her grandchildren was enough to light up her entire face.

I couldn't do it. I opened my mouth but nothing came out. The dreams I'd inhabited were about possibles and probables, not certainties. If I tried to warn her, I might do more harm than good. Besides, it wasn't the dreams themselves that were important or even why I was suddenly able to jump into the dreams of those around me. Living through each dream, each experience with my friends and strangers alike had taught me something. Quite simply that I wasn't alone in being afraid. That sooner or later everyone had to face their own fears. Just like my dad had had to face his. Just like I had to face my fears now . . .

I realized that I wasn't just living though the nightmares of my friends. This feeling of being alone, of being helpless – this was my own nightmare. A nightmare that had been with me since the day my dad died.

'Listen to me, Kyle. It's not too late,' Rachel said eagerly. 'We can still get out together.'

'How?'

Rachel pointed up. 'Through there. I'll hoist you up. You go and get help and then we can all be rescued.'

I frowned. 'If I try to climb out, the train might tip. I don't think it's any safer for me to do it than it was for Lily.'

'It will be safer, because you're stronger, younger and faster. You can be up and out instead of scrambling around all over the outside of the train like she would have done.'

I looked up. Rachel had a point. Once I was hoisted up, I'd be in contact with the outside of the train for less than five seconds. I didn't even have to close my eyes to imagine how it would happen – straight up, then jump down onto the tracks. No mess, no fuss and no train plummeting to the ground. And by now they were bound to have turned off the electricity so there'd be no danger of stepping on the live rail. I could run up the track to the nearest station and get help for everyone. And running was something I could do. What could be simpler?

I turned to Rachel, doubtfully. 'I don't think you'd be able to take my weight.'

'Believe me, Kyle, I'm stronger than I look,' Rachel insisted.

'Why don't I help you to get out instead?' I suggested. 'That way there's even less chance of the train falling.'

Rachel shook her head. 'No, I need to stay. I have unfinished business here. Come on, we're wasting time. You need to get out whilst you still can.'

'Kyle, wait . . . Please wait for me . . .' The shadow's voice sounded strangely desperate. Or was the desperation mine?

I looked from Rachel to the shadow and back again. Rachel linked her hands together as she stood before me. Her hands made a perfect foothold. I could step into her hands and then boost myself up to the window above. I'd be out of here . . .

'Come on, Kyle. It's now or never.'

I looked up again. Patches of blue were struggling through the grey now, and I longed to be closer to it. Out there, outside I could *escape*. I wouldn't be part of all this any more. I'd be safe, I'd be free . . .

It was the hardest decision I'd ever had to make.

'Kyle . . .' Death began to move towards me, his footsteps silent and relentless.

'Kyle, let's go . . .' Rachel urged.

Running away . . . Running. I was so, so tired of running.

'I think . . . I'm going to stay here,' I said at last.

A strange resolve settled over me. I was going to stay with my friends. And if that meant meeting Death, then so be it. God knows, I didn't want to die. There were so many things I wanted to do, so many places to see and people to meet. Life was precious. Funny how it'd taken a train crash and facing the fears of my friends and strangers alike to make me realize that. Life was precious – and mine was running out. I guess it's true what they say: you can't really appreciate something until you're in danger of losing it or it's gone. So why wasn't I clambering out of the window above me? I really didn't have a clue. It was probably the worst decision of my life – but at least I wasn't running any more.

'Aren't you afraid?' Rachel asked me.

I turned to face her. 'Only an idiot wouldn't be terrified and I'm not an idiot.'

'Then go. The train could go over at any moment,' she urged.

'No. I'm staying here. We make it out together or we all go down together,' I said quietly.

Rachel's hands dropped to her side. She shook her head, her expression saying it all.

'I know.' I nodded in agreement. She was right. I was an idiot.

I could no longer ignore the footsteps crunching over the train debris as they came up behind me. He must be a solid entity now if I could hear his footfall. Death had finally caught up with me. But at least I could turn and face him. Even if I couldn't do anything else, I could do that.

One deep breath, then I turned round. A man stood less than a metre away, no longer shrouded in shadow. He was wearing trainers and jeans. I held my breath as I raised my head to look at Death's face. But before I could focus, a sudden pain sang in my head, like I'd just been punched in my temple. And it hurt like hell. It couldn't be another dream – I wasn't focusing on anyone. I wasn't trying to hide any more. But the pounding against my head didn't stop. I was on the verge of collapsing when the world became silent and still. And I was in the head of the very last person I'd expected. I was inside my dad's nightmare.

27

Tony's Nightmare

An accident is a strange thing. It's like, just for a split second, the whole world explodes in your head. And then comes that moment, that in-between moment. That split second which lasts for ever and resides somewhere between total calm and wild panic, between acceptance and rejection, sometimes between life and death itself. You can be born, live and die all within that one moment. You can see things more clearly in that fraction of a second than you ever have in your whole life before. At least, that's what happened to me. You see, my wife left me. It's that simple. She left me. And I didn't see it coming. I was busy with my travel business. Too busy. Yes, I travelled a lot, but very rarely with her. Yes, I didn't pay her as much attention as I should have done.

But I loved her and she left me.

'Fitz, I'm not happy.'

'Fitz, we need to go out more, just the two of us.'

'Fitz, you're not listening to me.'

All those comments were too subtle for me. Why

didn't Londie just come right out and say, 'Tony, I'm going to leave you if things don't change.'

I would have heard that. That would have got through.

She left me.

And even when I read her goodbye letter, I still didn't believe it.

It was all just a mistake, a misunderstanding. At least, that's what I told myself.

With each minute that passed, I expected to hear her key in the door, I expected to see her walk into our sitting room, her tail between her legs. And I had my greeting all prepared.

'What did you think you were playing at, Londie? I knew you'd be back. Like you could even find your way to the end of the road without me.'

Only I never got the chance to practise my well-rehearsed few lines. The intended audience never put in an appearance. And still I clung to the hope that Londie would come home. I rehearsed new lines.

'Londie, how could you put our son through this? D'you know what you've put *me* through? But I knew you'd be back. I never doubted it.'

She never heard those lines either. So after a few weeks they changed yet again. The hardest change of all.

'Londie, love, I'm sorry – OK. What d'you want me to say? I'm really sorry. I'll do better. I'll try harder, I promise. I didn't realize just how much I'd miss you. Please forgive me. Just give me one more chance, I promise you won't regret it.'

That was my last speech. It played to an empty house.

Kyle's birthday was the day when reality rose up and bit my heart clean out of my chest. Londie wasn't coming home. If not for Kyle, then certainly not for me. The next day I went to work on autopilot. I don't remember walking along the street to the station. The train journey was more vague than a blur. I blinked and I was at my desk. Another blink and an hour had passed and I was on the phone with no idea what I was saying or who I was talking to. By lunch time I'd had enough. I mumbled something to my boss about not feeling well and headed for the door before she had a chance to respond. I don't remember getting home, I just remember being home. I stood in my lonely bedroom looking at myself in the dressing-table mirror, *her* dressing-table mirror. Seeing myself as she must've seen me all these years. I don't remember what I thought then. Maybe because I don't want to remember. The whole day is a series of snapshots, fragments of moments frozen in my memory.

And then Kyle came home. I saw him looking at something I was holding. I looked down, mildly surprised to see the glass of whisky in my hand.

'What are you doing home so early, Dad?' Kyle asked.

I slurred out something about not feeling well.

I didn't get better.

I lost my job. I lost my confidence. I lost all hope.

Until one morning I'd had enough. It wasn't something I'd planned, it wasn't something I had to build up to. I just woke up one morning and wondered, What's the point?

Kyle was old enough to do without me. Londie sure as hell didn't need me any more. I'd lost everything. So what was the point? Funny how I remember that morning better than all the previous month of mornings combined. Kyle made me breakfast, but my head was ringing and my stomach churning and I just couldn't face it.

'Dad, you need to eat. Whisky isn't food!' Kyle shouted, his voice amplifying the rate at which my head was pounding.

I shook my head, wishing to God that he'd shut up.

'Dad, please eat. It's only porridge.'

'Kyle, will you piss off!' I pushed him away.

As I poured myself a glass of the sickness and the cure, Kyle said quietly from behind me, 'You're a selfish bastard, Dad. At least Mum went through the door to leave me. You couldn't even be bothered to do that. You just stayed put and left.'

I swung round, but Kyle was already out the door.

Tosser! I thought as I tossed back the hair of the dog.

And throughout the day I grew more and more angry. Three words played over and over in my head like some kind of tune I just couldn't get rid of – *What's the point?*

Kyle just didn't appreciate what I was going

through. Neither did Londie. Why didn't they get that? I . . . cared for them both. I was brought up to be the man, to take care of my family, to be in charge. All those times I sat on the sofa or at the dinner table with my family and I just wanted to hold out my arms to them, to tell them how much . . . how much they meant to me.

But I couldn't. It wasn't what I was supposed to do. All my life I've done what I was supposed to do. Different thoughts stampeded through my head, corralled by the drink I couldn't leave alone.

Hell! If Londie and Kyle needed proof of how much I loved them, then I'd give them proof. I glanced down at my watch: 3.50 p.m. Kyle would be home soon. Kyle . . . He wasn't the only one hurting. I'd show him just what I was going through.

I went into the bathroom and found Londie's bottle of sleeping pills in the cabinet. The bottle was three-quarters full. I took it and headed back downstairs. Sitting in Londie's favourite armchair, my whisky glass in one hand, the uncapped bottle of pills in the other, I checked the time on my watch again: 3.57 p.m. Kyle would be home in what? Twenty minutes? Thirty max. I tilted back my head and poured the whole bottle of pills down my throat. They were dry and bitter on my tongue. I washed them down with the whisky but that sour taste still sat in my mouth. Leaning back, I closed my eyes. I waited until I began to feel sleepy, but I didn't. I just felt hollow inside.

'I love you, Londie,' I whispered. 'I love you, Kyle.'

I'd never said those words out loud before. They were slurred, almost incomprehensible, but I'd said them. And then it hit me. The words weren't slurred with drink. They were slurred because my hold on life was slipping. What was I doing? I was being ridiculous, stupid.

What the hell was I doing?

Open your eyes, Tony. You need to be sick. Get this junk out of your system. Just open your eyes . . .

But I couldn't. Gravity had changed. Every part of me was being dragged downwards. I couldn't move, couldn't think. I was melting, merging into the chair.

For God's sake, Tony, open your eyes . . .

I didn't open my eyes again.

You see, Kyle didn't come straight home. He went to his friend Steve's house for a couple of hours. Why rush home to me? Why hurry home to clean up my alcohol-induced vomit and take off my dirty clothes and wash them and clean the house and do his homework and pretend to everyone outside that everything inside was just fine? Why run home to *lies*? So he stayed at his friend's house. And I didn't open my eyes again until it was too late . . . until it was over and I couldn't come back.

And that's when my nightmare truly began. Because hope was no longer something that was part of me. I'd relinquished that along with my life. It was only when it was too late to turn back that I realized what I'd done. I'd given up. I'd left my son Kyle behind.

How could I have forgotten about my son? The

blinkers covering my eyes had been snatched away by Death and I saw my true self for the first time. And my reflection was jagged and misshapen, like looking in a broken mirror. Only it wasn't the mirror that was broken, it was me. I could see it all now – the past and the present. The future was easy to see because I had none. Not any more.

If only I could turn back the hands of time, go back to yesterday, go back just a couple of hours to the moment when I opened the bathroom cabinet. If I could do it all again, I would close the cabinet door immediately, then go into my room and look at the photograph of Kyle, his mum and me in happier times. I'd cling to those happier times until they forced a smile from me. If I could only go back . . .

But life and death don't work that way. My deepest regret was my son. I should never have left my son. I have to find a way, somehow, some way of letting him know how much he means to me. Please, God, let me find a way.

I can't rest until I do.

I have one shot at this. One chance to get it right. I'll have to pick my moment so carefully. A point in time when Kyle will be able to see me, to hear what I have to say. If I try to go to him now, he won't hear me because he can't hear anything. He's too locked in his own grief to see anything outside himself. I wish I could show him that he's not alone. But how? *How?*

Kyle's thoughts have opened my eyes. His thoughts, like mine, now run along the lines, *What's the point?*

I can't let him think that. I won't. I'm going to show him how wrong he is to think that. But how? *How?* And how do I make my way back from this place? This . . . Hell?

What have I done?

28

I looked at the man before me. I could see his trainers, his faded blue jeans, his grubby blue T-shirt with a stain in the middle. He was just as I'd found him all those months ago. I took a step towards him, wondering if my senses were deceiving me yet again.

'Dad?'

The man raised his head to look straight at me. 'At last,' I heard him whisper. 'At last.'

'Dad!'

We were now less than a metre apart.

'Hello, Kyle.' Dad smiled at me, a smile like I'd never seen from him before. A smile that said so many things. Maybe I really was imagining things, because first and foremost the look on Dad's face seemed to say . . . No, I had to be dreaming.

'You're the one who's been calling me?' I asked, astounded.

Dad nodded.

It *was* him. But how could it be? I didn't understand.

'Have you come to ... take me with you?' I whispered.

'No, son.' Dad shook his head, his eyes the root of the sadness on his face. 'The last thing in the world I want is for you to end up in the same place as me. I needed to see you, to talk to you before it was too late.'

'Too late for what?' I asked.

Dad was standing in front of me. He was actually standing in front of me. I still couldn't wrap my head around that. I needed to know who he was, *what* he was. 'Are you ... are you Death?'

'No, I'm your dad.' The twinkle in his eye was so recognizable, as was the slightly ironic smile. This was much more like the dad I remembered – before Mum left.

'But you're d-dead ...'

Dad's smile instantly fell away from his face. 'That's what I wanted to talk to you about – and I don't have much time.'

What on earth could be so urgent that it'd bring my dad back from the grave?

And then Dad said the very last thing I'd expected. 'Kyle, you've got to stop blaming everyone except me for what I did.'

'What d'you mean?'

'Son, I died,' Dad said gently. 'It wasn't your mum's fault. It was my decision, Kyle. My stupid decision. I'm the one who literally threw my life away.'

'I know that.'

'Then when are you going to stop punishing your mother?'

'I'm not. It's just . . . it's just that . . .' Like fizzy drink from a shaken bottle, the words erupted. 'Mum didn't want either of us when you were alive . . . I mean, around. It shouldn't have taken your death to bring her back, not if she really wanted to be with me. But it doesn't matter 'cause I don't care. I don't need her or her guilty conscience.'

Dad sighed. 'The moment your mum heard what'd happened she came straight back. No one had to go out and find her, she came home. Doesn't that tell you something?'

I didn't answer.

'And Kyle, when are you going to stop blaming yourself?'

'Blaming myself?'

'For my death,' said Dad.

'I don't—'

'Kyle . . .' Dad spoke softly, shaking his head.

The lie died on my lips. I could feel tears stinging at my eyes.

'What happened to me wasn't your fault either,' Dad continued.

'If I'd come straight home from school instead of going round to Steve's . . .' I began, putting my secret thoughts into words for the very first time.

'Kyle, what happened was my misguided way of trying to get your mum back,' Dad said sombrely. 'Maybe it was a desperate cry for help. But it wasn't your mum's fault and it certainly wasn't yours. If you're going to blame anyone, blame me for getting lost in a sea of guilt and more than a little self-pity. You've got to stop blaming yourself – you're breaking my heart. And much worse than that, you're beginning to think that what I did was right.'

How did he even know that?

Dad regarded me, waiting for me to deny it. We both knew I couldn't. I was beginning to wonder more and more often, *What's the point?*

How could he know that unless . . . ?

'Have you . . . have you been watching me all this time?' I wasn't too keen on that idea. 'Have you been watching every little thing I've been doing?'

Dad did his best not to smile but failed miserably. 'It's not that I've been watching,' he said, his lips still twitching. There was a pause as his smile slowly faded. 'But I could sense you. I could sense how hurt you were inside – and how the feeling was beginning to swallow you up.'

'Sense it – how?'

'Kyle, when we die, we get to feel all the joy and all the pain we've brought to others. Except with you the feelings of pain didn't stop, they just got worse,' Dad said, his voice sorrowful. 'Your pain became mine.'

'So you did all this?' I waved my hand at the destruction all around us.

'Of course not, son. I don't have the power to affect things in that way. Just being here is taking all my concentration.'

'So no one caused this crash?'

'The dead don't have the power to affect events like this. It doesn't work that way.'

'So why appear here? Why now? Why not a month ago or six months ago?'

'It took this crash and your friends' nightmares and the very real presence of Death for you to accept me,' said Dad.

'Accept you?'

'I needed your belief in the possibility of me before I could appear. Without that, I'd never have been strong enough to reach you. I couldn't do it on my own.'

'I don't get it.' I frowned.

'If you don't believe in anything outside yourself, then how can those things really affect you, how can they touch you? If you don't believe in ghosts, one could be standing right in front of you and you'd never see it. To butcher a line from one of your mum's favourite films – if you don't have a dream, how will it ever come true?' But he'd barely finished speaking before he began to fade out, like a shifting hologram.

'Dad? *Dad!*' I shouted.

He was back and solid again, but I could see the effort was wearing him out. His shoulders were slumped, his skin ashen, his eyes, oh, so tired.

'Dad, are you all right?'

'No. But I will be if you'll believe me when I tell you that my death wasn't your fault,' said Dad.

Behind me Rachel began to slow-clap at my dad's

words. I turned in surprise. To be honest, I'd forgotten all about her.

'Very touching,' she told him.

'You need to stay away from my son,' Dad said quietly.

'But we both know I can't do that.' Rachel shrugged.

The two of them watched each other, their eyes holding a silent conversation from which I was totally excluded.

'Dad, this is Rachel. She's been helping me.'

'Kyle, helping you was the last thing she had on her mind.' Dad spoke to me but his eyes never left Rachel.

'You're wrong. She's the one who made it possible for me to hide inside my friends' dreams.'

I looked at Rachel. That slight smile I knew so well tugged at her mouth. I turned to Dad. He looked at me and shook his head, and then I knew I'd got it totally wrong.

I looked from Rachel to Dad. 'It's *you*, not Rachel, who's been helping me, isn't it?'

'It was the only thing I could think of until you could see me,' said Dad.

'But Rachel said we had to try and escape from you.'

'Yes . . . Rachel . . .' Something in the way Dad said her name sent a chill down my spine.

'D'you know her?' I asked.

'We've met. Just once before this. Just once. But it was enough,' Dad replied.

As I stared at Dad, it was like opening my eyes for the very first time. I finally realized what Dad was trying to tell me. Horrified, I stepped away from Rachel, backing up towards my dad. My eyes were drawn to her T-shirt again. The message on the shirt no longer seemed innocuous or intriguing. It had taken on a more sinister turn:

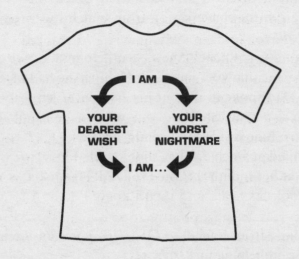

I didn't need to ask her to take off her jacket so I could see the back of her T-shirt. What would be there? One simple, monosyllabic word or a hooded skull or a skeletal hand clutching a scythe or just an image of her face? I didn't need to see the word or any of the images. I knew who she was now. Why hadn't I figured it out sooner? I turned to my dad. I needed to look at something real now. Something recognizable.

Feeling like I was emerging from fog, I picked my way through the words.

'So she . . .' I turned to face Rachel. 'You're on this train . . . collecting . . .' I couldn't say any more.

Rachel smiled. 'Of course. This crash is going to be called the miracle of the decade. A number of injuries but only one death. Imagine that. I only have one name on my list.'

Ice-cold pinpricks danced down my spine. I stared at her, horror-stricken. 'My name . . .' I realized.

'Your name,' Rachel confirmed.

I'd spent the last few months in a haze, wondering what was the point of carrying on? Now at last I had the answer. Life was the point. It was as simple and straightforward as that. But looking at Rachel, I began to recognize that maybe I'd learned that too late.

'I'm not dead. How can you take me if I'm not dead?'

'But you were supposed to die,' said Dad from beside me. 'I wanted you to hide out in your friends' dreams until I could get to you, but she got to you first.'

'Anthony, your attempts to stop me were so pathetic.' Rachel grinned. 'Hiding your son inside the dreams of others was a clever idea, I'll give you that – until I found a way to use it to my advantage. But did you really think I wouldn't find him?'

'It slowed you down though,' said Dad. 'At least until Kyle was ready to see me.'

'But you're the one who took ages to appear . . .'

What was Dad talking about? I was always ready to see him.

'Kyle, I've always been here but you only saw what you expected to see. It was only when you were ready to face me that you saw me for who and what I truly am,' said Dad.

'I don't understand.'

'That's the other reason I wanted you to live through the nightmares of some of your friends in this carriage, just for a little while . . .' Dad began.

I considered his words, having to rethink all my conclusions again.

'It was so that I could see I wasn't alone . . .' I realized slowly. 'That, for whatever reason, everyone has fears they have to face sooner or later.'

Dad nodded. 'Only it took longer than I anticipated and I had to let you jump into the nightmares of strangers. I just had to trust that you'd find your way out again.'

'But Rachel kept encouraging me to stay inside the dreams,' I said. 'She said it was the only way to escape from you.'

'Because if you made the decision not to come back, as long as each dream featured her in some way, then she'd still have you.'

'Have me how?'

'Your body would've still been on this train, but your mind . . . To all intents and purposes you would've been brain dead,' Dad replied. 'Rachel was more than willing to settle for that if she couldn't have all of you. To everyone else your mind would be in a vegetative state and that's the way you would've stayed until your heart finally ceased to beat.'

Horrified and shaking, I thought back. Apart from the first three dreams, which I'd inhabited before Rachel arrived in the carriage, the only two dreams where Rachel hadn't joined me were Naima's and Kendra's. I got it now. As far as Rachel was concerned there was no point in visiting either. Naima's dream didn't feature Death because Naima was dead already. And no one died in Kendra's dream because Mrs Guy was already a ghost. Rachel had obviously been able to sense whether or not her presence was required in each nightmare.

'Kyle, Rachel was counting on you not wanting to confront one of your biggest fears,' Dad told me.

'Seeing you again . . .' I understood now. 'I thought that if I somehow ever saw you again, you'd blame me for your death.'

My fear of ghosts and shadows was all tied up with seeing Dad again.

'You thought worse than that,' said Dad quietly.

Yes, I did. Dad was right. In my deepest, wildest dreams, when I dared to imagine seeing my dad again, I always thought he'd either blame me for his death – or, even worse, thank me for it. He loved my mum. After she left I was convinced he didn't love me. I felt like I ceased to exist for him. I'd never felt so alone in all my life.

'I made a mistake, son,' said Dad. 'The biggest

mistake of my life – because not only did it cost me my life, but it cost me you. I won't rest – I *can't* – until you believe that . . .'

'Dad, I—'

'This is all very moving but Kyle still has to come with me,' said Rachel.

'But I—'

'Shush,' Dad admonished. He turned to Rachel. 'My son isn't dead. You know the rules.'

'Don't quote the rules back at me. I know I don't get his soul until he's dead, but he would've been by now if you hadn't interfered,' Rachel hissed at him.

What did that mean?

'Dad . . . ?'

I followed Dad's gaze to look up at the broken window above us. The helicopter was still hovering beneath a sky that was now more blue than grey. The rain had finally moved on.

'I tried to escape out of there,' I told Dad.

Even now a part of me wondered if I hadn't made a mistake by not going for it. But even if I had made the wrong choice, I wasn't sorry. At least by staying, I'd seen my dad.

'D'you want to know what tomorrow's news story would've been if you had tried to leave this train?' asked Dad.

I wasn't sure I did, but I nodded at the intense look on his face. He held out his empty hand. As I watched, a folded newspaper materialized in it. He handed it to me. I opened it and was stunned to see my last school photograph covering at least a quarter of the front page. Beneath my photo, I read:

Kyle Fitzwilliam, aged fourteen, died while trying to escape from the second carriage of the upturned train in yesterday's train crash. Helicopter TV coverage dramatically caught the moment when the schoolboy clambered out onto the side of the train but, unable to keep his grip, slipped and fell to the pavement three storeys below. Kyle was killed instantly . . .

The newspaper print, then the newspaper itself, faded and disappeared from my hands. Shocked, I looked at Dad. He nodded.

My blood ran cold . . . I'd never really appreciated what that phrase meant before. But I knew now.

'Enough of this. Kyle, you're coming with me,' said Rachel.

'No, he's not,' Dad argued.

'Let's see about that, shall we?' She laughed.

Right before my eyes, Rachel became less real, more insubstantial. She was now the ghost and Dad was the real thing. They'd swapped places. And inexplicably, the more shadowy she became, the easier it was to believe in her.

'Dad, what's she . . . ?'

Dad was staring at Rachel, a puzzled look on his face. I don't think he even heard me. But suddenly he turned to me, his brown eyes dark and wide with dismay. He grabbed hold of one of my hands with both of his, pulling me round to face him and away from Rachel. It was the first time since he'd arrived that he'd touched me. His hands were surprisingly warm.

'Kyle, don't look at her. Whatever you do, don't look at her—'

Dad didn't get any further. There came a whooshing sound, like all the winds of the world were suddenly howling around the carriage. A dense, icy mist surrounded my head, suffocating me with the stench of the dead and dying. I couldn't get any air into my lungs and my heart was jack-hammering inside me. It felt like my whole head was burning up, but not from heat, from the intense cold. I tried to turn and look at Rachel. One of Dad's hands came out to turn my head back to him, but his hand passed straight through me. He couldn't stop me from turning round, but how I wished he had.

Death stood behind me and it was everything I'd ever imagined, every nightmare I'd ever had all rolled into one. This was a vision of Death worse than anything I'd ever imagined. A grey mist swirled around her . . . it, with a life of its own. I heard someone scream, a gut-wrenching sound of pure terror. It took a second or two to realize that it was me.

'I love you, Kyle. And I'll never leave you. Ever.' Dad's voice was light-years away. I couldn't turn my horror-stricken gaze away from Death.

'Kyle, I'll always be with you . . . No matter what she says or does, you mustn't . . .'

I heard nothing else. The icy-cold, swirling mist surrounding Death shot into my mouth and up my nose and through my eyes and into my ears. Screaming in agony, I scrunched my eyes shut and, pulling my hand away from Dad's, tried to cover my ears. My whole head was being crushed in a vice and I've never felt pain like it.

'Let's take a look at your worst nightmare . . .' Rachel's voice echoed in my head.

I fell to my knees, knowing I was a fraction of a moment away from dying.

29

The very next moment all the noise and the cold and the pain stopped. My heart howled in my chest. The memories of what I'd just been through echoed within me, but strangely that's all it was, an echo. I opened my eyes slowly.

What on earth . . . ?

I was back in my house, in my bedroom, lying on my bed. I sat up slowly, still disorientated. What was I doing back here? And how did I get here? Where was Dad? What was that mist which invaded my body and burned my insides like poisonous gas? Why was I back home? Swinging my legs off the bed, I stood up. Even though I recognized my bedroom at once, it still took more than a few seconds to get a handle on what was happening. I was definitely back home, that much was obvious. Back home and back in my room. That could only mean one thing. Dad must've battled Rachel for me. And he'd won. I was safe.

Safe.

. . . safe?

'Mum?' I left my room and headed for Mum and Dad's ... for Mum's bedroom. She wasn't there. I paused in the doorway. I hadn't been in this room since Dad died. Not once. But for some inexplicable reason I wanted to go in now. One slow step followed another until I was in the centre of the room. I looked at the bed, which was neatly made with hardly a wrinkle in the duvet. After Mum left and while Dad was ... around, it was never made, unless I did it. I turned towards the dressing table. It was covered with Mum's skin-rejuvenating lotions and anti-wrinkle potions. The room smelled faintly of her floral perfume. There was nothing left of Dad. No aftershave, no men's deodorant, not even his comb. I couldn't see him in this room at all any more.

But I could see Mum.

It was strange but at that moment, standing in Mum's bedroom, I could see Mum more clearly than I had for the past year. I realized that I'd stopped seeing her from the moment I stopped looking for her, on my birthday. I shook my head as I remembered Dad's eager face, asking to see the card, the message, the *anything* I'd received from Mum. I'd hated myself for disappointing him – but I'd hated her more. The day of my birthday changed so many things. When Mum walked out, buried deep down inside me was the hope against hope that she'd come back by my birthday, maybe even come back *for* my birthday. I have to admit that, like Dad, I thought she'd be back, even if it was just for my sake. Every morning when I woke up and every afternoon when I came home from school, I looked for her.

The day after my birthday I stopped looking.

When Dad died, Steve's mum and dad let me stay with them. I would've been happy to stay with them for good but Mum came home three days later. I hated her for that. If Dad meant nothing to her alive, why should his death bring her running back?

But I understood a lot more now.

'Mum?' I called out again, louder than before.

I checked through the whole house. She wasn't there. The house was empty.

I stood still and listened, just to make sure. No pipes gurgling, no tumble dryer vibrating, no dishwasher running – nothing. It was so quiet. A sudden thought occurred to me. I turned to the hall clock. The second hand moved with silent deliberation. I know this will sound silly but it was kind of a relief to see it. Time was moving as normal. I was back home and out of harm's way, out of Death's way. She'd just been messing with my head, that's all. Patting my jacket pocket to make sure I had my front-door keys, I headed out of the house. The neighbours' cars sat outside their houses. The road, like the air, was still. There wasn't even a breeze.

Suddenly ravenous, I decided to take a trip up to the local deli rather than search through our fridge for something to cook. The day was warm and bright. I strolled to the top of my road, enjoying the peace. I walked past the roundabout, along the street, then over the usually busy junction to the high street. I say 'usually busy' because today it wasn't. In fact, I didn't even have to push the button and wait for the lights to change before I could cross. There were no cars on the street. Not one.

There were no people around either.

By the time I made it to the deli, which was the first in the local parade of shops, I was getting twitchy. Surely this couldn't be right? There was absolutely no one around. Frowning, I entered the deli. The smells of assorted cheeses and sausages and fried onions hit me immediately, making me hungrier. I looked around. The place was empty. Why on earth would the owners leave the shop empty without locking the door? I was getting distinctly nervous about being by myself in an empty shop. I didn't want the owners coming back and wondering if I'd nicked something. Crisps and snacks from the newsagent's would have to do. Three shops later I was more than twitchy. I was freaking out. Where was everyone? The newsagent's was open, but there was no one in there either. What had happened to drive everyone out of their shops? If something had happened, like a suspected gas leak or something, that still didn't explain where everyone had gone.

I headed out of the newsagent's and went into every shop along the street. They were all open for business. They were all empty. And the street was deserted. No cars. No dogs. No birds or planes in the sky. No people. What the hell . . . ?

Thoughts can creep up on you, or they can hit harder than a wrecking ball.

Dad didn't win after all . . .

I walked faster, away from my house, away from the local shops. Picking up my pace, I started to trot. Before long I was at a full-out run. My feet seemed to know where to go before my head did. Forty minutes later, bathed in sweat, I was at the shopping centre. Our local shopping centre was vast, with stores which were known nationwide. They were all open, even the jewellers, with light pouring from every display window and out of every open door. Muzak chimed relentlessly around me.

But no people. Not one.

'*Hello* . . .' I shouted at the top of my lungs. '*Hello. Is anyone here?*'

Was it my imagination or did the muzak get fractionally louder? Or maybe it was my heartbeat. I went into every shop and shouted, desperate for someone, anyone, to hear me. There was no doubt about it. The realization crept through me as well as hitting me all at once. The shopping centre was completely empty.

But hang on . . . That tinny, pipey music had to be coming from somewhere. I wandered from shop to shop and from floor to floor. I even tried the doors marked PRIVATE and STAFF ONLY. I found the security room, with its bank of monitors showing CCTV footage from all over the centre and even the two huge car parks outside. I scanned the monitors, eagerly searching each one for a face. Just one face would do. But there was no movement of any kind.

Panic, bitter as vomit, began to churn and rise within me, but I fought it back down. This was silly. There had to be a perfectly logical explanation for all this. I sat in front of the monitors for one hour . . . two . . . three. Nothing changed. Each time I tried to leave the room, every time I turned my back on the monitors, I whipped round to watch them again. It was like a game of Grandma's footsteps. Part of me was convinced that whenever I turned away, everyone in the shopping centre was standing in front of the CCTV cameras dancing and having a party, and whenever I turned back, they ducked out of sight. And no matter how many times I told myself off for being stupid, I still found it hard to tear myself away from the monitors. But after three hours I had to face facts. There was no one in the shopping centre, no one in the car parks.

No one.

I went down to the electrical discount store on the first floor. It was one of those shops where TVs blasted your retinas with bright lights and fast-moving images. The huge TV at the front of the store was showing a well-known and very funny CGI film, but every other screen in the place was filled with white dancing lines of static.

I set off for home. At that moment I needed to be at home very, very badly.

Still no cars. No traffic. No noise. I rang the

doorbells and knocked on the doors of every house – and I mean every house – within ten streets of my home. In some the lights were on; in most they were off. But no one answered the door.

This was all wrong. I couldn't be the only one . . . How could that be? It didn't make any sense. Was I the last one, the only one . . . ? What had happened? Something terrible must've happened. But then, why not to me . . . ?

'Get a grip, Kyle,' I ordered myself.

I mean, not only was that just plain daft, it was also impossible. There was no way in the world that I could be the only one left in my neighbourhood.

Please, God, don't let me be the only one left. I don't want to be by myself . . .

I finally set foot inside my own house.

'*Mum?*' I called, my voice croaky and hoarse from all the shouting I'd done that day.

No reply. Not that I'd been expecting one. But that didn't stop me shouting for her. After searching through the entire house again, I switched on my TV, hoping to see someone, anyone. Hell! I'd even settle for one of those boring house make-over programmes. There was nothing. The screen was dark. I checked to make sure it was working by grabbing the nearest DVD to hand and putting it in the DVD player. The film started without a hitch. I turned off the player and tried flicking from channel to channel. The screen was still dark. I gave up on that and tried the radio. Sounds like crisp packets being scrunched up filled the airwaves from every station. I gave up on that too. I ran upstairs and flung myself down on my bed, trainers and all. Had something happened to keep everyone indoors or had everyone gathered in one central location because of some threat? Pulling my mobile out of my pocket, I wondered who I could phone for information. Even though I'd probably get a rollicking, I decided to phone the emergency services. I'd forgotten my phone was dead so I went into mum's room to use the land line extension. The number rang and rang and no one picked up. What could've happened to stop the emergency services from answering the phone? And if there were some huge emergency, surely there would still be people on the street – the police or even the army? Where was everyone? Why had everyone disappeared? Where had everyone disappeared to? What the hell was going on? And where was my mum? I tried the emergency number on and off for the next hour but still no one replied. All my questions sprinted round my mind until, exhausted, mentally as well as physically, I fell asleep.

The next day found me back at the shopping centre, as did the day after that and the day after that. I spent my days eagerly scanning the banks of monitors, searching each one for a face. Just one face would do. But there was no movement of any kind. I sat in front of the monitors for hours. Nothing changed – not even the muzak, which was on a continuous two-hour loop. If I could've found that muzak CD, I would've smashed it to smithereens. Where was my mum? My friends? The rest of the country?

After three whole days of solitude, I decided it was time to move on. The silence around me was driving me out of the house and out of the neighbourhood and out of my mind. There was no way I was the only one left in the area. (The country? The planet?) That would've been too ridiculous. But I'd have to move further out to find others who were isolated like me, who maybe even thought that they were all alone too. I packed up a large rucksack with some clean clothes, plenty of water, fruit and crisps and headed out. I wasn't particularly worried about finding food – every supermarket and grocery shop I passed was open and well stocked.

'Strange to close my front door, knowing this is the last time I'm going to be here for a while.

'Bye, house. Bye, Mum . . . wherever you are.'

I'd taken to voicing most of my thoughts out loud, just to hear the sound of my own voice; to hear something apart from my own breathing and my heart thumping. I set off down the road, turning back once or twice just in case I was walking away from other people instead of towards them.

On the second day I reached the motorway. There was nothing on it. Nothing. It was stupid, I know, but I walked in the central lane of the motorway as I headed south. I was so desperate to see someone else that I was prepared to risk getting run over to do it.

'You'll hear a car coming a mile away,' I told myself.

And though I listened hard, I heard nothing but my own footsteps on the tarmac. After a couple of days of walking along the motorway, I got off and made my way via normal roads. The motorway was hard on my feet and harder on my sanity. It was eerily quiet walking along with nothing moving in either direction; it only served to emphasize my loneliness. At least on the ordinary roads I could hope to meet someone else around each new corner. Every so often I'd knock at a succession of doors, ring a few front doorbells, enter a shop or two and shout '*Hello?*'

But there was nothing.

I was nowhere.

Had I died in the train crash, after all? Was that it? Had I died and gone to Hell? If this was Hell, it'd been selected by someone who knew me better than I knew myself. Real Hell for me wouldn't be a fiery pit inhabited by the Devil and his demons. What I was going through now, living through now, dying through now . . . this was Hell. Hell was spending the rest of eternity totally, completely, utterly alone. Loneliness was silence and solitude and isolation. But mostly silence.

Just under a fortnight later I was back at home. I'd travelled as far south as I could before realizing that it didn't matter how far I went or how fast, I'd never meet up with anyone else. Death's words kept haunting me.

'*Let's take a look at your worst nightmare . . .*'

Well, now we both knew. When I finally made it back home, I immediately went up to Mum and Dad's room and sat on their bed. I couldn't even smell Mum in the room any more. I went into the bathroom, stripped off and had the world's longest shower. For all I knew, the world's only shower. I listened intently to the sound of the water playing over my skin and running down the plughole. For the first time since I was a little child, I gave in to what I was feeling and let out the tears that had often threatened. Unfamiliar tears burned my eyes and spilled down my cheeks to get lost in the shower water running over my face. I tried to choke back the accompanying sobs, but my body wouldn't let me. The next thing I knew, I was crying like a baby. Sobbing and heaving like someone who'd forgotten how to cry and was having to learn all over again. Furious with myself, I punched the shower wall, then again, and again, until I didn't even have the energy to stand. I sat down on the shower floor, drawing up my legs as the water cascaded all over my body. Only when the water ran stone cold did I attempt to move. Slowly turning it off, I stepped out and grabbed the largest towel off the towel rail. Trying to scrub some warmth back into my icy skin, I became lost in my own thoughts.

I had plenty of food and drink so there was no danger of starving. But what I yearned for was something far more unexpected.

I wanted someone to touch me. Just touch me. To feel someone's hand on my hand, my face, my arm, and have them tell me that everything would be OK, that I wasn't alone. I wasn't prepared to spend the rest of my life like this. There was only one thing left to do. I put on clean jeans and a gleaming white T-shirt. I was ready.

I walked out of my house and carefully shut the door behind me. Standing in the middle of the empty road, I stretched out my arms.

'Where are you, Rachel?' I called out. 'I know you're close. Are you watching me and having a good laugh? Well, come and get me then. I'm ready now.'

The words slipped away from me like ripples moving out from the centre of a pond. I spun round. The road was still empty.

'*Come on! What're you waiting for?*'

I knew she was near by. I could sense her, stalking me like a predator. She was watching, waiting to see what I'd do next. I sat down in the middle of the road, cross-legged. I wasn't going anywhere. I had nowhere to go. So I'd sit for as long as was necessary and wait for Rachel. I closed my eyes – I didn't need to watch her approach.

My thoughts took flight and flew off in all directions. I didn't try to catch them, I just followed as best I could. Despair pecked away at me from the inside out. I thought of the train and my friends' nightmares – and Dad. Where was he? He'd deserted me, just like everyone else. Like Mum and all my friends and . . . and . . .

'*Kyle, I love you. And I'll never leave you. Ever. I'll always be with you . . .*'

That's what Dad had said. But he'd lied. Where was he then? Where was he . . . ?

'*I'll always be with you . . .*'

I still remembered the way he'd said that, the earnest, honest expression on his face as he spoke. Maybe he'd had no choice but to abandon me.

Or maybe he hadn't abandoned me at all . . . My eyes flew open. Dad . . .

Oh my . . . I'd been wrong. All this time I'd got it so wrong. I wasn't alone. Dad was with me. He'd always been with me. I'd just been looking for him in the wrong place, that's all. He wasn't somewhere outside of me, some place I might never find. He was inside my head and inside my heart. And now that I was seeking him in the right place, I could feel him there. I could feel him. Mum was there too, and all my friends and all the people from the train carriage. Everyone I'd ever met, they were all with me if I wanted them to be. And I did.

So how could I ever be alone? It was just impossible.

I smiled, the first sincere, genuine smile I'd managed since I found myself off the train and in this place.

'Come and get me, Rachel,' I whispered, the smile still on my face.

It was time to stop running.

'You've lost, Rachel . . .' I said. Now I wanted to see her coming. She didn't scare me any more. 'Even if you swoop down and take me with you, you've still lost.'

I stood up, no longer afraid. Dad had taught me that. I closed my eyes and inhaled deeply, to breathe in the fresh air, to breathe in life and love and hope. No matter what Rachel said or did now, I knew I would never be alone again.

When I opened my eyes I was back on the train. I blinked like a stunned owl, turning my head this way and that. I still remembered the train, but time had blurred all the little details. I had to take them in again.

The helicopter was still hovering above us. The sound of banging and metal hitting metal came from somewhere outside. I looked up and down the carriage. I was still the only one on my feet, but I was back – as if I'd never been away. I'd been gone for weeks and it'd all lasted how long? A second? A minute? Maybe two? A thumping noise started up from inside the train, not in our carriage but close. I started towards it. Lily rose unsteadily to her feet as I approached.

'Someone's knocking,' she said.

'I heard it too.'

'What is it? I'm scared.'

'I'm not,' I replied. I was in no rush to meet Death again, but I was no longer afraid of her. And it was the truth. Here and now, at this precise moment, I was as far from being scared as I could get. I'd seen my dad and he loved me. Mum had come back home when Dad died because she loved me too. Funny, I'd never thought of it that way before. I'd put her return down to guilt or having no choice – but she did have a choice and she had chosen to come back and be with me. My relationship with Mum wasn't perfect, not even close, but it'd be better now if . . . when I got off the train.

'I think . . . I think someone's trying to get into this carriage,' I said to Lily.

Both she and I made our way to the end of the carriage. The door between the carriages was now horizontal instead of vertical and there was an upturned seat partially blocking the way. The banging came again.

'Hello?' I called out uncertainly.

'Hello in there. Thank goodness!' a man's voice called out. 'We're from the fire service. We've got paramedics with us but we can't get through. There's something barring the way.'

Relief like angel's wings lifted me up and danced me around. The fire service and paramedics had reached our carriage. Well, almost!

'Just a minute,' I called back.

'I'll help,' said Lily.

'I don't think that's a good—'

'I can help,' she insisted, interrupting me.

I decided not to argue.

Lily and I grabbed hold of the seat and tried to heave it out of the way. It took a couple of minutes to shift it sufficiently to clear the door, but we did it. The gap wasn't very big but surely it was big enough for someone to get through and help us make it wider. Quiet discussions were going on in the other carriage. I heard a woman's voice, soft but emphatic. I bent down for a better listen, but just then a woman's face appeared in the gap between the carriages. She started to crawl though the narrow space. She wore an orange paramedic's uniform, which snagged once or twice on bits of twisted metal or jagged glass as she crawled though the horizontal space in the door where the window used to be.

Once she got to her feet, the woman smiled at me, placing a reassuring hand on my shoulder. 'I'm Sarah. I'll be here until everyone's out of this carriage. But first let's try to clear some more space.'

Between us, me, Lily and Sarah managed to move more of the debris away from the carriage door.

'Try now,' Sarah called out.

A fire-fighter tried to crawl through the same space as her but, being bigger, was finding it tougher going. I squatted down to help him.

Sarah turned to Lily. 'Are you OK?'

Lily nodded, perspiration clinging to her forehead and under her lip. The fire-fighter finally managed to squeeze through with me pulling on his arms.

'Thanks,' he said, rubbing at his hip. 'I'll work on getting the door open from this side.'

'I'll go and see who needs me,' said Sarah, already heading down the carriage.

'Don't worry.' The fire-fighter smiled. 'There are cranes being attached to this carriage and the one ahead as we speak.'

That explained the noises outside.

'Are we . . . am I dreaming this?' I couldn't help asking.

Cranes and paramedics and the emergency services. Were we really going to be rescued? Was it really over?

'What's your name?' the man asked.

'Kyle.'

'Well, Kyle, this is real. You'll soon be out of here. It must've been a nightmare when the train was hit but you're safe. The nightmare is over.'

His words made me start. Was the nightmare really over? It was for me, but what about everyone else? What about all the things I'd seen? Were they real? Should I warn my friends? Should I warn Lily? I was going to try. Even if none of them believed me, I had to try. And if I told them and they wouldn't – or couldn't – believe me, then I'd write it all down. Every action, every word. I'd write it down so I'd have a permanent record.

'How bad are the injuries in this carriage?' the firefighter asked. 'D'you know?'

'Some people are badly injured, some are still unconscious – but we all survived,' I replied.

And we had survived.

We were all going to make it.

Lily turned to me and smiled. 'Today is a good day, don't you think?'

But I didn't have to think; I knew.

Today was the best day ever, because it was the start of the rest of my life.

'I don't suppose you've got a mobile on you?' I asked the firefighter. 'I want to phone my mum.'

Author's Note

The vast majority of the thirteen nightmares described in this novel were inspired by real nightmares I've had over the years. Looking back I can now see what real-life events created or 'inspired' my bad dreams. Some of those events were less than pleasant and the nightmares they produced were always terrifying to me, but writing down my nightmares has always been my way of trying to deal with them and take control of them. A few of the nightmares featured in this book have been previously published as short stories in anthologies but all of them have been completely rewritten to work within the context of this novel.

Malorie Blackman

ABOUT THE AUTHOR

'Few writers can sustain a plot as well as Malorie Blackman' *Sunday Telegraph*

MALORIE BLACKMAN is acknowledged as one of today's most imaginative and convincing writers for young readers. *Noughts & Crosses*, her first book in an award-winning sequence set in an alternate society, won several awards, including the Children's Book Award, and she has also won numerous awards for her other books for the Random House list. Both *Hacker* and *Thief!* won the Young Telegraph/Gimme 5 Award – Malorie is the only author to have won this award twice – while *Hacker* also won the WH Smith Mind-Boggling Books Award in 1994. Her work has also appeared on screen, with *Pig-Heart Boy*, which was shortlisted for the Carnegie Medal, being adapted into a BAFTA-award-winning TV serial. Malorie has also written a number of titles for younger readers.

In 2005, Malorie was honoured with the Eleanor Farjeon Award in recognition of her distinguished contribution to the world of children's books. She lives with her husband and daughter in Kent, along with a large collection of books – over 15,000 at the last count!

MALORIE BLACKMAN
The NOUGHTS & CROSSES sequence

'Intelligent, emotional and imaginatively wicked'
Benjamin Zephaniah

'A conceptual masterpiece' *The Times*

Sephy is a Cross – the daughter of
one of the most powerful men in the
country. Callum is a nought – a second-class
citizen in a world run by the Crosses. In their
world, noughts and Crosses simply don't mix.
Against a background of hostility and violence,
can Callum and Sephy find a way to be
together? They are determined to try.

And then the bomb explodes . . .

So begins this riveting sequence of novels set
in an alternate reality where black and
white are right and wrong.

NOUGHTS & CROSSES 978 0 552 55570 8

'Flawlessly paced' *The Times*

KNIFE EDGE 978 0 552 54892 2

'Relentless in its pace and power' *Guardian*

CHECKMATE 978 0 552 55194 6

'Another emotional hard-hitter' *Sunday Times*

Not suitable for younger readers

MALORIE BLACKMAN

DOUBLE CROSS

*Just this once . . . Please let
me get away with it just this once . . .*

Tobey is a nought – a nought boy at an exclusive
school. But he can't keep clinging to some kind
of no-man's land while the streets around him
are carved up by rival gangs. Offered the
chance through a mate to earn some ready money –
just for making a few 'deliveries' – Tobey knows
he faces a crossroads in his life. He doesn't want
a part of that world. But – just once – would it
hurt to say 'yes' . . . ?

His girlfriend Callie has her own demons to
face. Her fears of the past have left her afraid of
the future.

As Toby makes his decision, he little realizes how
easily he can bring the violence down on both
himself and Callie . . .

Explosively page-turning, dramatic and full of
relevance for our world today, *Double Cross* is
Malorie Blackman's fourth novel in the award-
winning *Noughts & Crosses* sequence.

Not suitable for younger readers

978 0 385 61551 8